Books by Niki Livingston

Theia's Moons Series

Eyes Wide Shut

Enyo's Warrior

Protectors of the Stars

Guardian

The Chaos Awakened Saga

Marked Chaos

Expanded Chaos

Transformed Chaos

Novels

Be My Leprechaun

Novellas

Wrong Side of the Mirror

Novelettes

A Web Through Time

Wicked Heart

Wicked Soul

Jolly Old Monster

Unable to Wake

THEIA'S MOONS

Eyes Wide Shut

NIKI LIVINGSTON

Eyes Wide Shut

Publisher: Unbound Wonders Press

Editor: Novel Nurse Editing

Cover art © Niki Ellis Designs

nikiellisdesigns.com

ISBN-13: 978-0-9976644-0-9

To connect: www.NikiLivingston.com

To my family — thank you for the undying support.

Prologue

MALKIA'S HEART THUNDERED against her ribs. "Raul, what are you doing?" she screamed at her husband as he ran toward her parents.

He reached Malkia's mom and wrapped his arm around her waist. As Raul and Malkia's dad lifted her mother to her feet, her ankle twisted, and she stumbled forward, pulling her husband down with her. Her shrieks of pain sent chills prickling down Malkia's spine.

Her fingers curled tightly around Mataya's shoulder.

A blast of light snapped her attention toward the window, and terror gripped her like a vise. She choked in a breath and pressed Mataya and Esta behind her. The flames rose higher than the roof peaks of the neighboring homes, engulfing the one directly across from them. People's wails filled the smoky air.

The safety of the basement was about ten feet away, but felt miles from her reach. Another explosion ripped through the air, filling it with a thick haze of smoke, and Malkia's whole body shook as the quakes neared their house. Even if they made it to the sublevel shelter, she feared there was no escaping.

Malkia's attention flashed to the door that led to the downstairs and then anxiously she whirled to look at her family. Glimpsing out the window again, her gaze landed on a dark object plummeting from the skies seconds before it exploded on the settlement across the river. The tremble rumbled toward their house, throwing Malkia, Esta and Mataya onto the floor as the entire building trembled around them.

The smoke assaulted Malkia's senses, and she rolled to her side, coughing against the wood floor. Her eyes burned, and she blinked to clear them. She groaned as she twisted to her other side, squelching back a gasp of alarm at Esta's little face a few feet away. A deep gash lined her tiny cheek and tears streamed endlessly through the dripping blood.

Leaping back onto her feet, Malkia scooped up her baby girl, hushing her wails of terror that were preventing her from inhaling a good breath. Malkia shifted Esta around to check for other injuries, while glancing frantically back at Raul.

The four others lay sprawled across the ground and the wall that had once stood next to them nearly covered them in pieces.

Raul climbed to his feet and wiped the dust and smoke from his eyes. His gaze met Malkia's for a split second before turning to his father-in-law. Malkia gritted her teeth, watching as Raul's face turned beet red while he heaved a sizeable chunk of wall off her dad's leg. Malkia's brother tugged at her mom to help her stand, but blood oozed from the top of her head and her eyes rolled into the back of her head as she became dead weight.

A deafening silence surrounded Malkia as she handed Esta to Mataya and stepped toward her family. A moving object caught her eye and her gaze flashed to the sky. She froze. Someone directly aimed a fighter vessel toward their house. Her chin quivered as she met Raul's terrified stare. He glanced at what Malkia had been looking at and then focused back on his wife.

"Malkia, RUN!" Raul yelled.

Malkia scrambled toward her sister and baby girl, clutching Mataya's arm and dragging her and Esta toward the downstairs door. Seconds later, the explosion of the bomb ripped through the air and blackness engulfed her.

When she woke, there were strangers standing over her. A woman with a slash down her a face and neck, helped her to her feet and smoothed down her hair. Malkia blinked several times in confusion, then twisted around to find Mataya lying wide-eyed and frightened on the broken floor. Esta was nowhere to be seen.

"Where's my baby?" she screamed, her eyes flashing around at the people.

She collapsed next to Mataya and grabbed her arms. "Where is Esta? What did you do with her?"

Mataya's chin quivered, and a flood of tears washed down her cheeks, leaving trails of soot in their wake. Malkia's gaze swept across the room. The pit of her stomach fell. Her parents' home was demolished beyond recognition. The only portion standing was the downstairs door and the wall to the side of it. She again scanned the spot where Malkia and Mataya had been lying and realized it was the only area not covered with broken ceiling pieces.

In that moment, it dawned on her, Esta and Raul, along with her parents and brother, were buried under the rubble of this house.

ONE

A Broken Promise

THE WAR ENDED soon after the death of Malkia's family, and although she survived, a piece of her soul had perished with them that day. Those distant memories surfaced at the most inconvenient times.

A hawk swooped down low and landed on her friend Jayde's shoulder just as her eyelids batted open. Malkia's attention refocused, pushing the recollections of her past to the back of her mind.

Jayde's facial muscles twitched from her sight, returning from the hawk's view, and then she turned toward Malkia. "He's riding in at a gallop." Her fingers trailed down the feathers of the bird. "And he looked terrified. I still think we should stop him on the outskirts of town and find out what he knows."

Malkia drew in a deep breath and nodded. "I will follow you. Let's go meet this wanderer." Before the battle in the sky, she would have not thought twice of this man, but her people depended on her intuitive discretion to protect them.

Jayde whispered to the hawk, and it spread its wings and leaped into flight.

Malkia gripped Parowan's mane and threw her leg over the back of the beast, watching Jayde do the same with her pegasus. They rose into the air with a flap of the beasts' wings. As they flew over town, Malkia beckoned at Dario and then Curtis, letting them know to follow her. Moments later, they all landed in the meadow beyond the town's boundary.

"What's the rush?" Dario asked, jumping off the back of his ebony-haired winged horse.

"The man who circled around town a few days back is returning. He should round the corner of that hill soon," Jayde said, pointing toward the north. She patted her winged horse on the nose before following Dario toward Malkia and Curtis.

"Did the hawks notice anything else unusual?" Curtis asked, crossing his arms over his chest.

Jayde settled her hand on her hips. "No. But I can check again once we speak to this man."

Malkia's ears perked up at the beat of hooves pounding furiously against the soil. The four of them whirled around and stepped onto the path, waving their hands as the stranger came into view. He slowed to a trot as he neared, then halted completely a few yards away.

"Good day." Malkia raised her hand. She smiled warmly as she strolled toward him. "Are you in trouble? After you avoided us, we didn't think we would see you again."

"You noticed me?" His brows raised in question, pulling the reins and forcing his horse to step backward a few feet.

She paused, holding her ground, her hand hovering next to the dagger slipped in its sheath against her hip. "We keep watch of anyone or anything that comes near our home."

He nodded, his gaze darting around at the four of them. "Then I hope you're ready for what's coming. I encountered a horde of ruthless barbarians traveling your way." He gritted his teeth and glanced back the way he'd come, as if he were expecting others to be waiting. "I nearly walked into their camp but spotted one of their people and could conceal myself. Later, I snuck in and found imprisoned women and children, along with beheaded men. Your town is in their direct path, so my reason for returning is only to warn you to leave." He focused on Malkia. "These people are savages, and they will do anything to control the towns and individuals they encounter. If I were the leader of this group, I would run, and I would run fast."

Dario shrugged his shoulders and rolled his eyes at Curtis. "How do you know we are on their direct path?" he asked, shielding his eyes from the suns as he peered up at the man.

"There's a ravine to the east and no inhabited towns to the west, at least not as close as you. They are traveling south, and you will be their next stop." The man fidgeted with the pack slung on his back, adjusting it higher. "I'm only here to warn you. Don't believe me, if you choose. But it will be a grave mistake." He maneuvered his horse around the four of them.

"Are you leaving?" Malkia shot Dario an icy look for his behavior.

The man nodded. "I'm placing as much distance as I can between this group and myself, and I suggest you do the same." He tipped his hat toward them, clicking his tongue and pressing his spurs into the horse's sides. The beast flinched and shook his head before he trotted down the road. Seconds later, they were galloping out of sight, leaving the four of them to chew on his words.

"Do you really believe what he said?" Dario asked, wrapping his arm around Malkia's shoulders.

Jayde kicked at the soil as her gaze rose to the skies. "We would be foolish to not check. I'm sending the hawks as we speak."

"And we will send the scouts out as well," Malkia replied. "Jayde is right. We can't take our chances." Dario's jaw clenched, and Malkia tilted her head to see him better. "Is everything okay?"

He let go of her shoulders and nodded, glancing away. "Yes. We should return to town to arrange the scouts and inform the rest of our people."

Malkia raised her brow at his receding back and trailed after Curtis toward their pegasi. Peering at Dario, she nibbled on her bottom lip, unsure of Dario's vibe. He had never treated strangers like he had today, unless he knew their intentions were to hurt them. Shaking her head, she flung her leg over Parowan's back and patted the beast's neck, then followed the others back to town.

Malkia sprinted over the rocky trail, racing toward her childhood home, when she noticed a woman and child whispering frantically to one another. Malkia skidded to a halt. The river behind her parent's home sounded like thunder against the boulders and her curiosity to hear the two overcame her.

She tiptoed closer. They seemed oblivious to her presence. Her heart thrashed inside her chest when she inched closer, then stood still and quietly watched in awe as the familiar woman embraced the young child. The woman's hair cascaded over her shoulders, brushing against the child's cheeks, and the girl smiled as she snuggled closer. Their muffled voices pressed at Malkia's ears and she leaned in closer, but for some reason, her feet would not budge.

Despite being immobile, they piqued her curiosity. A sadness yanked at her heart from the sight of the woman. She believed she knew her, recognizing her exhausted eyes, but Malkia's memory failed to give her more than that.

The lady spoke again to the child, her tone quiet and shaking with urgency. "Malkia, we'll be back to retrieve you as soon as we can. Please, please forgive us."

Malkia's heart leapt into her throat. That's right, the child was her. How did she forget?

The lady's eyelids brimmed with tears, and Malkia watched as they tumbled down her cheeks. Tugging the child close, the woman held her with trembling hands. A man walked into view and stood next to them, then wrapped his hand over the woman's shoulder. He waited patiently, his expression devoid of emotion.

Malkia's gaze turned to the child, whose sobs rocked her small frame. Her grief filled the space and bit at Malkia's heart. These people meant something to her, and it was frustrating to not remember why.

"Malkia." The woman's voice quivered as she gazed down at the child. "I wish we could allow you to remember us. It's just not safe. You'll be in my heart always, and as soon as we can, we will return."

Malkia jolted upright and gasped in a breath of air.

Every time she had this dream, she woke in a frenzy. The familiar woman said those words and Malkia would scream, thrash, or wake breathless, and be completely out of touch with reality. This time was no different. She clenched her fists together and cursed the unease and grief swirling like a tornado in her mind.

Her arms shook as she propped herself up on her elbows and glanced around her room. Shadows of the outside life danced along the walls and gave the room an eerie sensation. Sometimes they appeared as shadows of people, but tonight, they appeared even more so. She slid out of her bed and tip-toed to the large window to remind herself that her mind was playing tricks on her.

It was quiet outside, aside from a slight breeze. The trees swayed with the wind, and Malkia watched the beautiful scene before her, enjoying the peace it brought to her heart. Theia's beauty hung in the sky above, reminding her she was safe.

The large planet was said to be the mother of their moon, Esaki, and the other moons around her. With the guidance of the Alethieans, the light beings who guarded Theia and her moons, and the Mother planet lighting her way, Malkia had always believed she was protected. Even after all she had witnessed and survived, she chose her connection with the Divine rather than falling into doubt and despair.

She blinked away the urge to return to the memories she had tried desperately to bury away in the recesses of her mind, but Raul's obsidian eyes filled her thoughts. He knew the end was near. The terror in his expression had spoken volumes, but even in that moment, he had tried to save her family.

Her breath caught in her throat, and she stared at the quiet world outside, forcing her mind back to the present situation. Her people, Mataya... everyone depended on her to remain level-headed. She choked back the tears and gritted her teeth. The thought of abandoning her home broke her heart, but she feared a repeat of the sky people's slaughter if they remained.

The voice of the wanderer came back to her thoughts. *"These people are savages, and they will do anything to control the people they encounter. If I were the leader of this town, I would run, and I would run fast."*

She knew their small town was defenseless against those heathens. She wanted to stay and protect the one place she had ever called home, but she knew it would end in death. There had been so much loss back when the war had erupted, and she could not face another day like that, which was why they were leaving today.

She would not make the same mistake twice.

Eight peaceful years had given her plenty of time to rehash her poor decisions and know when running is the best option. There was one town to the east that she felt they would be the safest, while waiting for the threat to move on. Jasper, their leader, had been hospitable and welcoming when she visited a year earlier. At the very least, he was a person who would assist with options and guidance to keep her people safe.

It was a long trek on foot, but Dominique and Nedra would take their pegasi and ensure Jasper had the room and ability to provide them with protection.

She glided across the floor and found the matches and candles that sat on the table next to her bed. Lighting the candles, she crammed her few belongings into her knapsack, with the edges of her mind yanking her back to the sky people's war and the day she lost everyone in her family, except Mataya. Her husband, her daughter, her parents and her brother were all gone, in one fell swoop.

To this day, she did not understand how she had survived, but Mataya was alive because Malkia had sheltered her with her own body. Malkia's back showed the scars of that day, but those were her only physical reminder. They had never recovered Esta's body.

It was the last day anyone had heard the explosions and the flying crafts overhead. It had taken nearly a year for people to believe it had ended, and another to rebuild their large city, into a much smaller town, to accommodate their vastly reduced group.

Throughout the years, many wanderers, scavengers, and intruders came through town. Some had stayed and become a part of their family. Others had visited and continued on their way, while many attempted or succeeded at swindling or stealing livestock, crops, their water supply and anything of value. They had learned to be accepting, but cautious and to protect their own.

However, after that last stranger came through the day before last, warning them of the large assemblage heading their way — and the scouts and hawks confirmed his story — she knew it was time to leave. The scouts returned with appalling stories of women and children tied up or locked in cages, along with men being strung up and pulled behind their horses. Malkia had contemplated fighting, but with their trifling numbers, her people had no chance of survival unless they surrendered.

The first sun washed its light across the valley as Malkia finished packing the rest of her belongings. It was time to prepare and face the beginning of their new lives. She had to go speak to Jayde, needing to know the whereabouts of the savages, based on her sight through the hawks.

Malkia scrubbed and washed her hair and body in the washbasin. Knowing it was probably the last time she would get a proper cleaning before they arrived in Domesca, she made the most out of her cleanse. While she slipped on her clothes, she viewed her image in the broken mirror and examined her scars. Her long blonde hair hit the small of her back, reminding her of the lady in her dream.

She took a startled step toward the mirror, touching her cheek with the tips of her fingers. The lady's eyes were a brilliant green, just like hers. They were nearly identical. Malkia gulped down her trepidation as her gaze slid down the slight curves of her body. The woman's tall and slender stature was similar to hers as well. The resemblance was uncanny.

Malkia's mind jolted back to reality when she heard a knock at her front door. She yanked her shirt on and pulled her hair into a low ponytail. When she opened the door, Dominique and Nedra were standing there, with their pegasi behind them.

"We are leaving," Dominique said. He furrowed his brows. "How far away are the brutes?"

Malkia stepped into the sunlight, shielding her eyes from the glare with her hand. "Last night, they were almost three days' ride north of us. They could be closer if they traveled through the night. As soon as we have confirmation, and the people pack their belongings, we will be right behind you."

"It's going to be a brutal ride for the group," Dominique said, shaking his head. "I wish we could find a way for those kids to arrive in Domesca quicker."

"I know. Me too, but this is not for you to worry about. We will make it. Now scoot." A soft smile surfaced on Malkia's lips. "You two have all the fun."

"Oh, honey. We *are* the fun." Nedra winked before embracing Malkia. "See you soon."

"See you soon," Malkia replied. She hugged Dominique as well and watched as they mounted their pegasi and flew away.

TWO

The Journey Begins

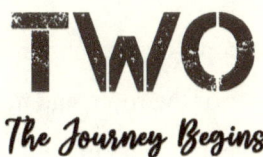

AFTER DOMINIQUE AND Nedra were out of sight, Malkia shuffled back inside her small home and returned to her room to grab her saddlebags. As she passed Mataya's room, she peeked inside and noticed her sister's brunette hair sticking out from beneath the blanket. She placed her bags by the front door and returned to Mataya's room.

"Mataya. Rise and shine," Malkia said as she ran her hand through her sister's hair.

Mataya's eyes slowly opened, and Malkia noticed the extreme difference in them. They were more wide set and fringed with long lashes, revealing a beautiful hazel color. Malkia pressed her lips together, examining her sister's heart-shaped face. Malkia's was oval and long, with cat-like eyes that were set closer together. A cold sweat broke behind her neck and swept down her spine. The differences were vast, and it was making Malkia question her entire existence.

"It's too early," Mataya whined and dove farther into the blankets.

Malkia stood and pushed away her apprehension. "Mataya, it's time to leave. We have to be out of town by mid-meal. If you want to go without your belongings, keep sleeping."

Mataya lay under the blankets for a minute before she slowly squirmed to free herself. When she poked her head out, Malkia noticed the crimson lines spread across the whites of Mataya's eyes as she narrowed them with irritation. She slowly unraveled herself and rose from her bed.

"I really hate these people," she muttered quietly, grabbing her saddlebags from the corner of the room and to pack her belongings.

"Me too," Malkia whispered, walking out of the room.

She stepped outside and whistled loudly. Parowan, her winged horse, landed softly next to her. She guided Parowan toward Jayde's house and landed near the front, where she was brushing her pegasus. Jayde waved at Malkia as she approached her.

"Any news?" Malkia asked.

"Nothing more pressing than what we already know." Jayde raked her hand through her hair and wiped the sweat from her brow. "Their group moved all night, but they were slow, and I haven't checked for a few hours. I stayed up late, watching them, and overslept. Once I finish packing, I will check again. Unless you need me to do it now?"

Malkia shook her head. "Pack your things, and I'll meet you in the pastures. If their progress worries you, then you know where to find me. I just wanted to stop by and make sure you got some sleep and checked on their movements." She tossed Jayde a weary smile.

"Don't stress too much. We will be okay. We're a solid group, with a vigorous leader." She winked at Malkia. "I trust you."

"Thanks." Malkia's smile stretched across her face. "I needed to hear that. I'll see you soon."

After returning home, Malkia finished packing her bags and did one last walk through to ensure she missed nothing. She stopped outside

Mataya's doorway and watched her heave her bags over her shoulders.

Mataya turned toward the door and smirked. "Are we still leaving?" A spark of hope glistened in her eyes.

"Nothing has changed. Let's eat and go meet everyone in the east pastures." She stepped into the room, her jaw tightening at the thought of what was ahead. "I need to meet with the trackers and Jayde as well. Once the rest of the town shows up, we will have a quick meeting and then head out."

Mataya's chin quivered, and tears flooded her eyes.

Malkia curled her arms around her sister and hugged her close. "I know this feels like a dream, but we've got this. Another adventure that will lead us to a better life," Malkia whispered into Mataya's ear.

"Thanks. I'm not sure I would make it without you." Mataya pulled away with a sigh.

Malkia chuckled half-heartedly, squeezing her sister's arm. "Sure, you would. We are made from the same star dust and have the Aletheian's light to guide us. I love you, baby girl."

"Love you, too." Mataya scooped up her backpack and saddlebags and followed Malkia outside to finish packing their pegasi.

It was going to be a long trek, and the pressure weighed heavily on Malkia's shoulders.

In silence, the sisters strolled toward the east pastures. Malkia's thoughts turned to her life before the sky people and their wars. She had been young, but she could remember the joy she had felt back then. Life had been serene. People, animals, and nature lived in harmony with one another.

Then the technology from the skies had been introduced, and it had been a drug to the Esaki people. Within a few years, all the mystical creatures had withdrawn into nature, and no one seemed to miss them. Malkia was as much to blame as anyone else. The heavens had literally opened and gifted them a whole new world.

Not long into their new lives, the fighting erupted, and death spread like wildfire across the Esakian moon. It took twelve years from the point of receiving all those amazing gifts to turn them around and destroy one another with them.

When Malkia had awakened from that last bomb, she pleaded for death. Her baby girl and the love of her life were gone. To this day, her heart ached from the memories. For a time, she barely held herself together, but then there was Mataya. She had to survive for her.

As they neared the pastures, Curtis's erratic waving forced her back to the present.

"Justin just returned from the north." He leaned over and inhaled a deep breath. "The group is closer than we thought. He barely escaped and is afraid they might have sent trackers after him. He told me he did everything he could to throw them off his trail, but he couldn't wait any longer to return. Their group will reach our town as early as tomorrow morning."

Malkia cursed under her breath. "Where are Justin and Kendrick? Kendrick should have been back from the east before Justin."

Curtis ran his hand over his nearly bald head. "Kendrick returned about an hour ago. He ran into Skye, and she sent him home to help prepare his family for the journey. According to him, everything is clear to the southeast. Now the trick is to depart before one of their trackers arrives and sees which direction we go."

Malkia nodded in agreement, biting her lower lip. "Let's round everyone up for a quick update and then leave."

"I will let Skye and Dario know and then meet you at the far end of the pasture with everyone."

"Thank you, Curtis," Malkia replied as he hurried toward the masses.

It didn't take long for the rest of the townspeople to arrive. Within the hour, they gathered around Malkia and Parowan. She licked her dry lips and drew in a long breath. Even to this day, her feelings of inadequacy were taking center-stage in her mind.

The group hushed when she raised her bow in the air. "This is what I know. The trackers are progressing quickly toward our town. Maybe a half a day away. However, their group is only a day behind them. We'll need to depart once instructions are given. For those at the end, I task you with covering our tracks." Her gaze landed on a large gathering, several of them waving their hands, and she nodded at them. "Thank you for volunteering."

"How long until we reach Domesca?" a woman asked, her black as night horse pawing impatiently at the dirt.

"Nearly a week."

Several people groaned, but the woman nodded her head with somber acceptance.

Malkia's free hand gripped Parowan's mane. "We will travel until late tonight, going south. There's a small, abandoned town where we can rest and sleep for the night. In the morning, most of the group will veer east, while a couple dozen of us will head south, diverting their trackers from your trail." She paused, placing her bow behind her back.

"Do I need to answer questions?"

"I have a question," a female voice called from the crowd.

Malkia glanced toward the sound of the voice, seeing her tall neighbor standing next to her horse, eyeing Malkia with her usual disdain. She didn't trust anyone, and Malkia often wondered why the woman stayed in their town.

"Yes, Amandine?"

"Why are we heading south? Why can't the larger group head east now? This plan makes no sense to me when we can all head east now and the smaller group can head south."

Malkia's brows furrowed. Amandine had lived her long enough to know the area. "By heading south as a group, the chances of them suspecting our group splitting up decreases. The pegasi can fly most of the way, giving the appearance of a meager group. As you know, if we head east from here, it will land us on the wrong end of a massive ravine. Best course of action for the group is to travel south. If you have a better idea, please let us know now. We are all ears."

Amandine stared at Malkia for a moment, then shook her head and mounted her horse.

Malkia glanced around the crowd again. "Any other questions or suggestions?"

Murmurs of nos and shaking of heads were her response as everyone mounted their horses and pegasi. Malkia glanced at her team leads: Skye, Curtis, and Dario. Justin and Kendrick, along with Mataya, were standing with them. She steered Parowan toward them.

"Let's move forward. Stay with your groups as much as possible. I will send messengers your way if there is a change in our circumstances." She ran her hand down the side of Parowan's head, connecting to the beast's energy to help sustain her confidence. "However, we will need to use some of our traveling time to come up with a plan for when we separate."

The leads nodded and turned toward their groups. As they pressed forward, leaving their town behind, Malkia noticed Justin and Mataya speaking in hushed tones. She had noticed them spending more time with one another, but whenever Malkia asked her about it, Mataya claimed they were just friends. However, Malkia could see there was more, and why her sister was attracted to him.

Justin's tall and robust stature towered over Mataya, and it comforted Malkia that he was protective of her sister. His dark, chestnut eyes were engaging, and his black hair was full, which showed off his tattooed, copper skin. Top it off with a quick wit, a great sense of humor, and compassion that reached to the ends of the lands. He was a keeper. It would thrill Malkia to see those two together.

Malkia thought again how stunning Mataya was, with her long, dark hair and large hazel eyes. The complete opposite, Malkia had light-blonde hair and her eyes did not keep the mesmerizing affect Mataya's had on everyone she met. Mataya had inherited their mom's beauty, while Malkia's features did not fit in with either parent. Mataya was shorter, with a curvy slender body, while Malkia was tall, thin, and only slight curves.

Skye shifted her pegasus closer and then reached out and tapped Malkia on the shoulder. "How are you holding up? I know the pressure has been heavy on your heart, and I wish I could ease your troubles."

Malkia smiled sheepishly. "It's the burden they voted me to bear."

Her gaze drifted to her friend. "You help by leading your group. I really appreciate all you do for our people."

Skye leaned toward Malkia as she whispered, "You know, you really should give Dario a chance. He would do anything for you."

"Skye, this is definitely not the time for romance." Malkia's eyes darted behind her, making sure they were alone. "Plus, I'm not positive I could ever love anyone the way I loved Raul. He was my world."

Skye chuckled, her black irises dancing with the reflection of the sun. "Silly girl, Raul loved you more than life itself, and he wouldn't want you to be without love in this world. I think I knew my brother well enough to know he would never want to see you lonely. Just think about it."

Malkia set her gaze toward the ground, wanting to escape the conversation. "Thanks. I will."

"After we split, what is the plan?" Skye asked, taking the hint.

"This is what I have worked out in my head." Malkia pulled her hair back after it had fallen out of its ponytail and eased it into a low bun. She swept the loose ends behind her ears. "You and Curtis will take your groups and half of Dario's and divert to the east. Justin has discovered a spot about two days northeast, where you will stop and wait for us. If we don't meet you there within a day, you are to continue east for one more day and then deter to the north. You may encounter a few small towns. If you do, make sure you warn their inhabitants of the savages and allow them to join you if they want." She quieted and stared off at the horizon. This plan had to work. Her chest burned from her tense nerves.

Skye matched her pegasi's steps to Parowan's. "Anything else?"

Malkia tapped the edges of Parowan's saddle. "Traveling north to the castle will take about four or five days. Like we discussed yesterday, Justin knows the way and will lead you there." She looked back at Justin, and he nodded in agreement. "Continue to have trackers sent out. Have them backtrack and make sure no one has followed you. If this group catches your trail and follows your tracks, you must devise a new plan, and send a messenger back our way with the update." She clasped her hands together and blew out a long breath. "Of course, this is all if we don't catch up to you. If all goes well, we will have successfully diverted the savages. As soon as we know they are far off your trail, we will head toward the meeting point."

"I'm going with you, right?" Mataya asked from the other side of Malkia.

"Absolutely not," Malkia and Justin replied in unison.

Mataya's brow furrowed as she grumbled, "Why not? I'm not a child anymore, and I'm not leaving you. You'll have to tie me up and force me away."

Justin's eyes narrowed to crinkled slits, and Malkia sighed. "Mataya, what do you want me to do? I have to worry about everyone else. Are you telling me, if I do not listen to your tantrums, you're willing to endanger our entire group?" She leaned forward on Parowan and squeezed Mataya's arm. "You'll be safer with Justin and the larger group. You are not a child, but you lack experience, which could make the situation more dangerous for the rest of us."

Mataya's mouth formed into a pout as she huffed and glanced away.

"Any other questions?" Malkia asked, straightening back up and glancing around at the few in proximity.

"Have you picked who will accompany you and Dario?" Skye jabbed her thumb over her shoulder toward the townspeople.

Malkia turned to look at Dario, who was tending to his group, before answering. "We haven't chosen everyone we need, but we have decided on a few. Jayde, for her ability to see through the hawks' sight. Porter, for his tracking skills, and we'll need Jacob for his ability to call upon the pixies."

"Malkia, have you tried using your telepathy abilities?" Mataya asked, waving her hand toward Malkia. "You used to use it all the time before Mom and Dad died. Why can't you anymore?"

Ever since the explosion destroyed her home, her telepathy with others who possessed the same gift had been severed. At one point, not too long ago, she had heard the cries of someone young and frightened in her mind, but the connection disappeared just as quickly as it had come and there had been nothing since.

She shook her head. "It's long gone. I'm not sure I will ever have that ability again." She turned toward Skye. "Will you speak with your group and let Curtis and Dario know our tentative plans?"

Skye nodded, her black curly hair bouncing as she turned her pegasus around and trotted toward the other leads.

"Everything is going to be fine," Mataya said, having her pegasus match Parowan's stride. "I bet feeling like you have the whole town's fate in your hands is overwhelming, but we all love you, and *I* always feel safe when I know you're in charge. I am sorry I was pushy earlier. The thought of not having you with me is petrifying and I'm not dealing with it very well." Her fingers twirled in her pegasus's mane. "But I will be brave for you and for everyone else."

Malkia's lips twitched up into a tight smile, and she nodded. "Now if only some of your courage will rub off on me."

THREE
Unexpected Visitors

THE DAY FLEW by, and the group progressed quickly toward their resting point. Malkia continued to send trackers ahead and back the way they came, even if only to ease the pressure on Jayde to monitor their journey.

The abandoned towns and cities crept up on them one at a time, displaying their pasts through their unkempt appearances. The broken buildings and homes were scattered throughout all of them, each having a story none of her group would ever know.

Many of her town's people had never ventured so far out of their little village, and their gasps filled the air when the hovering structures of a larger city came into view. They kept their distance, in case there were wild animals roaming in the buildings, but it was fascinating to watch the expressions on the faces around her as they viewed the difference in how others had once lived.

Even with the threat looming behind them, it was easy to admire their awe-striking moon. If there was one thing Esaki did not lack, it was the vegetation — the massive trees, with their purple and red leaves, the stunning bright green, auburn and purple flowers, as well as the birds who seemed to have stories to tell with their pleasant songs.

The most captivating sight was of Theia, with her magnificence hovering above them through it all.

The old cities, with their shattered homes and broken roads, added a bit of charm to the healing moon. With far less of a population, Esaki's greenery had overtaken and rewritten what people had left behind. A bittersweet view, but Malkia's gratitude for a life she once did not want poured freely from her heart.

The day faded as they neared the small, abandoned town they would rest at for the night. Malkia calculated their arrival to be within a few hours after sundown, and she was looking forward to taking a break and sitting down with the trackers for an update.

As if Jayde had read her mind, her pegasus galloped beside Malkia. "They made it to our town." Her golden eyes were wide with worry.

Malkia exhaled slowly, trying to cage her anxiety. "Justin was right. They made it there just as he predicted. Is it the entire group, or just their trackers?"

"Just the trackers." Jayde's teeth grazed her bottom lip, a nervous habit from her childhood.

Malkia nodded. "The town is not far. Just up there." She pointed forward and to her left. "As soon as settle for the night, let's take a moment and update all the leads."

"Sounds good. I'm going to check on my mom and help her settle in. I'll meet you at the main campfire." Jayde pulled back on the rope attached to her pegasus and eased her way through the crowd.

When they were all settled in their camp, and most of the townspeople were asleep in their tents, Malkia followed Skye to the center fire. Dario, Curtis, Mataya, and Jayde were waiting with the trackers. Malkia nodded toward Jayde.

Jayde rose and bounced on the balls of her feet. "It was really difficult to see. Their trackers are sly devils." Her lips twitched with a smile, but it quickly faded. "But the hawks finally found three. One of them had just come through the woods and was observing our town. And, my Theia, his features were frightening." She shivered and closed her eyes, taking in a deep breath. "I've never seen a human appear that massive and burly before, which makes me wonder where these people really came from." She looked around the group with expectant eyes.

Malkia raised her brows and nodded for Jayde to continue when no one spoke up with an answer to her unasked question.

Jayde rubbed her hands down her hips. The tension shook in her flexed fingers. "Anyway, I'm not sure if he noticed our absence, but he turned back into the woods and whistled. That's when I spotted the two other trackers sprinting in his direction. They have gathered just inside the woods on the north end of town and have ventured no closer. I'm thinking they must be waiting for others. As for the group, they are only a few hours... *Oh wait*." Jayde sagged against the boulder behind her, falling into a forced trance. Her ebony hair slid in front of her face.

It seemed like the entire group held their breath, waiting for news. This was the point they had feared the most, their disappearance being discovered. They were too large of a group for these savages to ignore, and it was silently clear that it was only a matter of time before the tyrants were tracking them.

Jayde's arms twitched. She swept her hair out of her face and focused on Malkia. "There is one more tracker. The hawks missed this one. He must have high-tailed it back to the large group once he heard the whistle. He was speaking to another man, who was shouting and pointing toward our town. Now, they are all moving toward us, and somehow their large group is speeding up." Her voice cracked with emotion, and she wiped at her eyes. "They saw the hawks, and I think they shot one with an arrow!" Jayde cradled her face in her hands.

Malkia settled next to her friend and curled her arm around Jayde's thin shoulders. She knew how much the hawks meant to her.

"There's a possibility these savages will catch up to us." Malkia eyed her leads, placing her hand on Jayde's shoulder. "I'm not sure how the trackers will respond when they discover our absence, but chances are, they might head out after us immediately. We won't have much time here, so we all have to come together with our ideas and have a simple plan on what each group will be doing." She twisted to stare at Curtis and Skye. "The larger group has a long journey ahead of them without Dario, me, and a few others. We are depending on you two to keep everyone safe."

Skye and Curtis nodded and turned toward one another.

Malkia rose to her feet and rubbed her hands together. "I need to ask a favor from a few of you. Kelsey, Janesa, Kendrick, and Damion, we need you four to accompany Dario and me south, while the rest of the group heads east. We have a handful of others we will ask as well, but we need your abilities to help distract those savages from the bigger group. Would you all be willing to come with us?"

The four of them nodded in unison. "A terrifying adventure for only the brave," Damion said with a smirk, sticking his tongue out at Curtis.

"And that's why she chose you to accompany her on the easy road," Curtis replied, without missing a beat.

Kendrick chuckled and shoved Damion back into his seat when he lunged at Curtis.

Malkia grinned at the exchange before pulling Jayde aside. "Are you okay?"

"I'll be fine," Jayde said, clenching her jaw to stop it from quivering. "I can handle this, Malkia. It's painful to have one of my hawks hurt or killed, but we all have a part in this plan. I will be fine."

"I know you will. I just don't want to push you too hard. You're not unbreakable." A wary smile surfaced on Malkia's lips. "Please tell me if it becomes too much. Your health and endurance are far too important to our group."

Jayde quickly nodded, tears brimming in her eyes. "Don't worry. I've got this."

Jayde walked away from Malkia and sank to the dirt next to Curtis. Malkia sighed and closed her eyes for a moment before strolling to the group and sitting next to Mataya. Her mother had told her stories of those who had the power to communicate with Esaki's creatures. These chosen people had a connection far stronger with the Aletheian's than anyone else. Jayde's gift was divine, but it came at a cost.

Over the next couple of hours, they kept busy giving out ideas and thinking through unique plans. Progress was slow, but Malkia was grateful for the support they were choosing to give one another.

Her own thoughts took her mind away from the others as she absentmindedly scanned over them as they talked. Her gaze landed on Jayde just as she fell into another trance. Jayde's face grimaced several times.

"Hey," Malkia called. Her finger came to her lips, hushing the group, then she pointed at Jayde. Curtis glanced her way and quickly cradled his arm around her for support.

A moment later, Jayde returned from her reverie and gaped sadly at the group. "Apparently, the fourth tracker has closed in enough to communicate with the other trackers. The three of them are sneaking into our town right now. As of a few minutes ago, they had not reached it, but they were close. I'm not sure what their plan is, but I'm assuming they are smart enough to know they cannot take on the whole town with just the three of them."

"We all hope you're right," Malkia murmured, her lips set in a grim line. "We will continue to monitor the group through the sight of the hawks. Jacob, we need you to begin your work with the pixies. Jayde, please rest, but ask your hawks to keep us updated on anything those savages do. We all need to rest, so each of you should take—" Malkia's voice quieted as she noticed Jayde fall into another trance.

The hawks obviously forced the spells, which they only did if they had vital information. Malkia was afraid they were going to put too much pressure on Jayde's body, making her inoperable for the rest of their journey.

She was only out for a moment before her wide eyes focused back on the group. "They have discovered we are gone. They peeked in the windows, then braved to venture indoors. Now they are running through town, checking every dwelling. They were shouting, and the fourth tracker is now returning to their large group. We might not be able to stay here all night. Their group will arrive in our town before sunrise."

Panic roiled through Malkia's stomach. She had hoped they would have taken more time to check on their homes. It would be only a matter of time before they were tracking the group. Even with nearly a day's head start, Malkia feared it would cut it too close.

Dario's arm snaked around her shoulders. "You need to lie down and rest. The next few days are going to be rough. We all need some sleep before we take on this group."

"No, I can't," Malkia snapped as she paced the small space between a boulder and her people. "My mind is racing, and there is so much to do before we separate. I do not feel confident enough to handle this pressure. I am terrified our plan will not work, and the group won't be safe. They need to leave soon, so we can cover up their tracks." She halted, her eyes wide as she looked at Dario. "I don't think my anxiety will allow me to sleep. You go rest and tell the others to do so as well. I will wake everybody when it is time to depart."

Dario shook his head and Malkia watched as he walked away, wishing he would stay with her. She could use his mind to throw around ideas with, and it would be nice to have someone keep her company, but she didn't have the heart to ask him to stay. She found a rock to sit on and went over some ideas rolling around in her head.

"Malkia?"

She jumped from the sound of the deep voice and whirled around. Dario was standing a few feet away, his jaw clenched, and his arms crossed over his chest.

Malkia rose from her rock and rushed toward him, then wrapped her arms around his tall frame. It was so much easier to sort through her mind if she had someone to help her. She pulled away and gazed up at him and smiled. "Thank you for returning. I really can't do this alone."

He grinned back at her, and for a moment, they stared at one another. Then Dario cupped her chin to pull her face toward his and pressed his lips to hers.

It lasted only a moment, but when Malkia drew away, her brain was in a fog. She stumbled backward and glanced at Dario. For an instant, she noticed pain in his eyes, but as quick as it was there, it was gone.

He shook his head and walked to the rock where Malkia had been sitting. "Let's finish this, so we can move out," he said, looking down at the rock as he patted it for Malkia to sit again.

Malkia walked back to the rock and put her hand on Dario's shoulder. His expression was blank as he peered up at her. She shook her head and sank to the rock, holding back her tears.

"We have about two hours before we should start waking the others who would like to join us going south." Dario spoke quickly, his eyes glazing over. "We will need to speak with Jacob and find out what the pixies have decided. Then the large group will require preparations for their journey east." He paused, his deadpan expression remaining in place, as if he were under a spell. "Once the others have left, we will do all we can to cover their tracks and make it appear as if we all continued south. We will hightail in that direction as quickly as we can, and we'll set up points along the way to keep them confused and distracted from the east."

It was as if he were reading her thoughts.

He knew her too well. She peered up at Dario, the lines around her eyes deepening. "Dario, I care about you, and if we weren't running for our lives, I could probably think more clearly about you and me. I don't believe this is the time or place to jump into something we both know could have sparked from the high emotions of the situation."

Dario shook his head again, his face turning a deep crimson. "Are you blind, Malkia? Do you really think my feelings ignited from all this?" His arm swept out at the sleeping townspeople. "Maybe your reaction is from the emotional rollercoaster we are facing, but my feelings toward you have been strong long before this whole situation began." He clenched his fists and turned away from Malkia and stepped toward the others. After a few feet, he stopped and turned back toward her. "What do you want me to do first? Is there something to prepare before we wake everyone? Should we find Jacob?"

"Yes, Jacob first." Malkia slid off the boulder, then quickly pressed her lips together to stop the quiver and followed Dario.

They picked their way through the masses of people asleep on the ground. Malkia could see Jacob near the edge of the group, talking with Kendrick and Skye. She led Dario toward them.

Jacob's face lit up with a smile when he saw the two of them approaching. "Good, you are here. I was just on my way to find you when I ran into these two. The pixies trust you, Malkia. You might not realize this, but they have monitored you, and are aware of your empathetic and fierce leadership."

Malkia half-smiled, glancing at Dario. His expression had softened, but he avoided her stare. She wasn't positive why they had hesitated before now to contact the pixies. If she had known they had been watching her, she would have built this relationship long ago. "Thank you, Jacob." She beamed at the group, her nerves easing for the moment. "I appreciate you connecting with them. Will they be willing to speak with me personally, or do they prefer to only speak through you?"

"They said they will speak mostly to me, but when it is necessary, they will request your presence," he replied, stuffing his hands in the pockets of his trousers. "They have already sent some of their assemblage to observe the savages and will report back to me within the next hour. I know Jayde is sleeping, so this will make it easier for her as well. Seeing through the hawks' eyes is draining, and I don't want her giving up before we even start this."

"We are happy for their help." Malkia turned to face everyone else. "This would be a good time for all of you to get some shuteye."

"I'm running on adrenaline, and I don't think I could lie down even if I tried." Skye smirked, wringing her hands together as her gaze darted around at the others.

"Same," replied Kendrick and Jacob in unison.

Perspiration beaded just inside Malkia's hairline. She nodded in agreement, wiping her hand across her forehead. "I'm feeling the same way, but I worry if we all don't rest, then we will be useless when it matters most."

They all stared back at her with raised brows and defiant looks.

She sighed and waved her hand. "Fine. If you really cannot sleep, then put together some ideas to cover the tracks of the larger group."

They split in separate directions, and Dario hurried away from her, making it obvious he didn't want to speak. It upset Malkia to see him troubled and angry, but she could not focus on his affection for her.

She strolled to where Mataya was sleeping and settled in next to her. As she softly played with her sister's wavy hair, her thoughts turned to the past, when she was happily married and still had her beautiful baby girl, Esta.

It had overjoyed Mataya to have a niece to play with, and their family was ecstatic about the baby. It had been a wonderful part of Malkia's life, and once again she yearned to return to that time.

Mataya was nine years younger than her and had always been her little baby sister. She wanted to protect her from every danger, and now that they were facing it again, Malkia's emotions were on the surface for this girl. She just wished she could go back and protect her baby girl and husband as well. The sadness of that day overwhelmed her.

She leaned her head back against the tree behind her, taking in the sight of the stars above. Her mind was finally quieting down, but the moment her eyes closed, quiet footsteps snapped her back to reality. Jacob raced up to her and whispered into her ear.

He had heard from the pixies. They slipped away, and she followed Jacob to the edge of the campsite.

"The pixies have news." His breath came in short, and his eyes widened even more than they already were. "The trackers didn't leave immediately. They waited until their leader arrived at the edge of the forest. Once he saw the size of our town, he gave them the orders to find us. He believes we are large enough to do damage to his plans and does not want us to escape. Fortunately, the trackers are still a half day behind us. This will give us time to move the larger group out of the area, cover their tracks, and head south. Do you want everyone to wake up now, or should we wait?" He finally drew in a deep breath and raised his brows as he waited for her to answer.

"They could use a little more rest," Malkia replied, peering over the campfires. "Let's find Dario, Skye, and Curtis and meet back at the center fire. Once we are all on the same page, we can wake up the rest of the group. If you see them before I do, let them know to meet there."

Jacob nodded. "Sounds good. Is there anything you would like me to tell the pixies?"

"Yes, tell them thank you. If they are able, have them return to watch the trackers and their group. And I would love an update before we leave."

"I will inform them," Jacob said, turning away from Malkia. "I'll meet you at the center fire as soon as I am done speaking with them." His voice trailed off as he jogged away.

Malkia hurried out to find her team leads. She ran into Skye after a few minutes, but Curtis and Dario seemed to have disappeared. She was worried something had happened. It was not like either of them to disappear saying nothing.

She and Skye separated to search for them, and they agreed to meet at the center fire in fifteen minutes. Malkia walked into the forest, hoping to find Curtis and Dario there. She wandered around for several minutes until she could no longer see the lights from the campfires.

When she turned back around, she smacked into a warm body. "*Ouch!*" she exclaimed. She rubbed her nose and glanced up. The older bearded man before her was a stranger.

He stifled her scream with his hand and put his finger to his mouth. His eyes were wide and intense as he glared over her shoulder. "Get behind me," he hissed in a hushed tone. The fear in his eyes convinced Malkia to follow his orders.

She slid behind him and peeked around his shoulder. A massive beast was lumbering through a clearing. Malkia's breath caught in her throat, and she cringed at the thought of running into that fiend instead of this wild man. She hoped the latter was the better of the two.

As it neared them, a pain radiated in her head, and a sudden peculiar but familiar noise vibrated inside her skull. Her temples pulsated from the confusion, and she blinked several times, struggling to focus on the scene in front of her.

The man yanked out a large knife and waved it erratically at the beast. His other hand reached back and pushed her away from him. She tripped over her own feet but rolled to a crouched position, trying to keep both eyes on the beast. In all her travels, Malkia had never seen an animal as big as this one. It had to be at least four or five times larger than Parowan, and it appeared as if it had two heads.

Without warning, its large wings spread and its spiky heads reared backward, whipping its necks around to stare straight at her. Malkia scrambled backward and stifled a scream with her fist, finally realizing what beast was hovering above her.

FOUR

Divide and Conquer

MALKIA WHIRLED AROUND, searching for a place to escape the dragon. The strange man glanced back at her, just as her foot snagged on the root of a tree and she stumbled to the side.

The dragon's beady red eyes stared at her through the darkness and one of its heads twisted as if it were examining her. She froze in place, petrified to move from her position. The man yelled as he raced toward the beast. The dragon's heads whipped back to face the man, giving her the opportunity to run.

Malkia leapt to her feet, searching desperately for a tree large enough to shelter her from the breath of the beast. When she turned, enormous arms wrapped around her waist, then dragged her down a path and behind a tree. A hand stifled her screams. She wrenched her head to one side and when her assailant held her tighter; she bit down on the edge of a finger.

The man cursed under his breath and loosened his grip. Dario.

She whirled around and threw her arms around his neck. He grunted but squeezed her tight before leaning back and pressing his finger to his mouth. His other hand slid down her thigh as he snuck past her and crouched by the edge of the tree. A shaky breath left his lips before he leaned forward to peer around the trunk.

He gripped the base of the tree and shot her a terrified look. *It's coming*, he mouthed to her.

A man bellowed, and the dragon growled. Malkia pressed her back against the tree trunk, terror gripping every inch of her body. Groans filled the stale air, followed by a gurgled yelp, before the forest became silent again.

Malkia and Dario peeked around the tree. A two-headed dragon laid dead a few feet away. The strange man stood next to it, holding a large blade. Green liquid oozed from a slit in the dragon's neck, covering the front of the man from head to toe.

Malkia squeezed her hands into fists and stepped out of the shadows. "Where did that come from?" she asked, pointing at the dragon.

The man's brows twitched, and a smirk rose on his lips. "From up north. You are lucky I was already tracking this beast. These are one of the most vicious dragons. Dumb as a rock, but will rip a human to shreds without a passing thought." He wiped his blade with a cloth he pulled from a pouch strapped to his leg.

"I did not know these creatures existed," Malkia muttered, stepping closer. "I mean—" She paused, catching her breath. "There were stories about them, but in all my travels, I have never encountered one, nor have I ever met someone who has seen one. I'm sorry I walked in on your little show, but if I had any idea there was a dragon nearby, I would have stayed as far away as I could from this area."

"Actually, it was a surprise to me this one flew so far. If I did not have my pegasus, I would not have been able to track it. I have been tailing him for days, way up north, when he shot up into the air and began his flight down this way. I stayed behind him for almost a day before he landed." He shook his head. "I thought I could start tracking him again, but not much later, he shot back into the sky. We landed here and within a few moments you walked into our fight."

Malkia released her held breath.

"Who are you?" Dario asked, his brows knitting together.

The man moved around the beast, wiping the remnants from his knife on the side of his pants and looking at the two heads lying on the ground. A smile lifted the edges of his lips when he turned to look at them. "I'm one of the few dragon slayers left in this world. After the sky people arrived, the dragons disappeared more than they already had, and when the wars began, I did not see again them. It was as if they no longer existed. I was out of a job. It hasn't been until the last few years when they ventured out of their caves." He slid his knife into its sheath strapped to his side. "I was a dragon slayer before all the madness, so I returned to my occupation. And now I'm here saving all of you."

"And you do not know why it flew this far? Are there dragons that live down this way?" Malkia asked, still stunned.

"Honestly, I don't know that answer. I have never seen a dragon this far south, but that doesn't mean they don't live here. But flying that long, I've never known that to happen. Sometimes they act out of character and do bizarre things."

As he finished speaking, Skye sprinted toward the three of them, with Curtis a few feet behind her. Worry etched lines in their faces, and when they saw the dead dragon, they skidded to an abrupt stop behind

Malkia and Dario. Their gazes darted between the dead dragon and the stranger.

"Who is this, what is that and what is going on?" Curtis asked loudly, his jaw clenched.

"This man saved my life," Malkia replied. She pointed at the man and beast. "Dragon slayer, dragon... and dragon slayed."

Curtis looked around the dark forest. "Seriously? I miss all the fun." He teased, but the humor didn't reach his eyes. A wary smile surfaced on his lips as he patted Malkia's shoulder.

"Well, dragon slayer, what are your plans now that your dragon is slayed? Will you be returning to the north, or are you sticking around this area?" Malkia asked.

"Going home," he replied, settling his hands on his hips.

"Us too," Malkia said. "We are traveling as a group to a new home. What is your name?"

The dragon slayer stepped forward, running his arm over his forehead. "Tatum. I haven't been home for nearly a year, and I am looking forward to seeing my family again."

"Where is your home?" Dario asked, stepping around Malkia and running his fingers down the scales of the dragon.

Tatum pursed his lips, eyeing Dario with a guarded expression. "I'm from Domesca, a town northeast from here. Beautiful city, surrounding a massive castle. Since the wars ended, it has been a sanctuary for many."

Malkia's eyes widened when she heard him say Domesca.

Tatum noticed her expression change. "What's wrong?" he asked, turning his suspicious gaze to her.

Inhaling sharply, she replied, "Really? Domesca is your home? Our group is heading to your town once they wake."

"Why?" he asked, his eyes narrowing to crinkled slits.

Malkia rubbed her hands together. "We are on the run. There are a large group of savages on our tails and the only safe place I could think of was Domesca," she said a bit too quickly. "The group asleep just outside the forest are my people. When I came across Domesca during my travels last year, Jasper treated me like family, and now I need him to do the same for the people who count on me to keep them safe. Will you help them? Several of us," — she waved her hand at Dario — "will continue south to divert the brutes, while our people sneak off to your home."

Tatum remained quiet, his gaze never leaving Malkia's eyes. After several breaths, he turned away and walked a few feet deeper into the forest. Malkia wiped her sweaty palms down the sides of her trousers, trying to not let the worry invade her thoughts. This man had to be on their side.

Tatum turned back to face the four of them and nodded. "I will do it. I would hope you would be there if the roles were reversed. I will show your group the way to Domesca, and I will speak with Jasper on your behalf."

Malkia walked toward Tatum and held out her hand to him. He grasped her wrist, and she reciprocated, then she threw her arms around his large body and embraced him tightly. "Thank you. You're our angel. You don't know how much I have prayed for someone like you to come along."

Tatum stepped away from the embrace and shook his head. "Thank the dragon. If he hadn't led me here, I would have never met you. But." He paused, his gaze wandering across the group. "I can definitely see the Aletheian's hand in this. To land right here in the place where you are walking, it has to be their intentions." He scooped up his pack and slung it over his shoulder. "I know a shortcut back to Domesca. It will shave off one day. We will have to head east for almost two days, but there is a passage that can be taken afterward which will cut through the forest and onto the path toward my hometown. Do you need us to send someone back to guide you?"

"No, I know it." Malkia shook her head. "We will all be on our pegasi, anyway. Skye, Curtis, we will no longer plan on meeting you at the stopping point to the east. Keep going until you arrive in Domesca. We will catch up with you either on the road or after you have reached his town." She turned back to face Tatum. "Thank you again. Let's wake everyone and prepare for departure."

As they neared the center fire, Malkia noticed Jayde sitting near the fire in a trance with a clenched jaw. Malkia raced toward her friend.

Jacob approached her as Malkia sank next to Jayde. "The pixies should return soon, but it looks like Jayde might have details beforehand. By the way, where were you? The entire group of you disappeared." He ran his hands through his hair when he looked at the others and noticed Tatum.

Malkia rubbed her temples, trying to knead away an incoming headache. "We ran into this man in the forest." She pointed at Tatum. "He's a dragon slayer and from Domesca. Tatum will lead everyone to his home. He has also agreed to speak with Jasper and convince him to shelter and protect them while they wait for us. Tatum, this is Jacob.

He will travel with me to the south."

Jacob leaned forward to shake Tatum's wrist. "Nice to meet you. You say you are a dragon slayer. Is that a joke?"

Tatum chuckled. "Not at all. Go look for yourself. I killed a dragon just inside the forest. He was about to eat your fearless leader before I arrived."

Malkia was not paying attention. Her eyes were on Jayde's face as she came out of her trance and gasped. She looked at Malkia with startled eyes. "Malkia, they are moving so quickly, faster than I thought possible. It's like they are super humans. They will catch up to us, if they continue at the speed they are going."

Malkia jumped to her feet. "Wake them up. They have to leave now."

"Dario and Skye, are your groups ready to leave?" Malkia asked, racing toward them.

"My group is all ready and waiting," answered Dario.

"My group is as well," replied Skye, her gaze darting from one end of the group to the other.

Malkia's lips set in a grim line. "Good. I just spoke to Curtis, and his team was at the forefront, ready to move forward. Please pull your groups together and explain to them what to expect. They need to follow Tatum's instructions to the letter in order to make it to Domesca. Dario, have you prepared the families who will separate?"

Dario nodded. "They have teamed together to make sure everyone stays safe."

"One more time." Malkia pivoted to look at Skye. "You will travel east for nearly two days, instead of three, and then you will divert northeast. Anyone on a pegasus must fly out, but tell them to stay as low as possible. The fewer tracks visible, the less we have to cover up." She turned back to face Dario, rolling her shoulders to ease the rising tension. "Once they leave, we will lead the tracks to the dragon and make it appear as if we ran in several directions but, in the end, we moved south. The dead dragon should create some confusion and hopefully distract them from the larger group entirely."

Dario and Skye nodded, and they steered their pegasi away, leaving Malkia and Mataya to say their goodbyes. Mataya was busy packing her pegasus and didn't look up at Malkia.

Malkia walked toward her and pulled her into her arms. "I love you, girl. You mean so much to me, and I will do everything in my power to return to you. Please, please stay with Justin and let him protect you." Her fingers combed through Mataya's hair as Malkia leaned back to look her sister in the eyes. "Help with the families. Please be a beacon to these people we love so much. Show them what you are made of. Be a light to them, and I can guarantee it will make you feel better, as well."

Tears streamed down Mataya's cheeks. She hiccupped and threw her arms around Malkia. They embraced in silence, too terrified to talk about the what ifs.

She finally pulled away from Mataya and gripped both of her shoulders. "Be strong, sister. We are made from the same energy. You can do this."

Mataya smiled through her tears. "I will make you proud and I *know* I'll see you soon."

Malkia kissed both of Mataya's cheeks and squeezed her tight one last time.

FIVE

Impending Danger

THE SUNS' RAYS beat down on Malkia and even with a wide-brimmed hat protecting her face, it felt like it was burning. The first sun had dipped lower along the horizon, but the heat remained unrelenting even with the second sun being the cooler of the two.

Malkia wiped the sweat from her eyes and mouth and ignored the stench wafting from beneath her arms.

Jayde and the pixies had confirmed the trackers had fallen for the bait to continue south, even though they spent about two hours at the campsite, sniffing around the dragon. They had checked the tracks, and at one point considered heading east. However, all four continued south, and the relief washed through everyone.

The pixies had gone farther north and were checking on the group of savages. Waiting for answers was excruciatingly painful.

Jayde raced up next to Malkia with a scowl scrunching her brow. "I took a glimpse at all four trackers. They're still gaining on us but have thankfully slowed. Maybe this plan of yours will work after all." She winked and the edges of her lips twitched with a small smile.

"So far, so good." Malkia licked her lips and looked away from her friend. She did not have the heart to mention her growing doubts.

"Malkia," Dario said as he pulled his pegasus beside her. "Have you seen Porter recently? He left over an hour ago to check the paths to the west, and he should have returned long before now."

"He went alone?" Malkia asked, swiveling her upper body in her seat to search the group for Porter.

"We had no choice but to send him alone. We have used our resources up." Dario's muscles in his jaw twitched. "We have to keep enough people here to keep up with the appearance that our entire group rode this way. The ones we can spare, we've had to send them out alone."

Malkia's heart sank. An awful feeling swirled in the pit of her stomach. Porter's disappearance was not good.

They rode in silence for a few minutes while Malkia sorted through her thoughts. What if someone was setting a trap for them?

Malkia tilted her hat up and peered at Dario. "What do you think we should do?"

"Finding him has to be a priority. I've had Kelsey take some sleeping herbs, so she is resting in the wagon." Dario waved his hand toward the wagon. "She had just fallen asleep when I heard the news about Porter. We can let her sleep for a short time, and hopefully with her sight she will give us an idea of what we might expect. We send two of our best to look for him on the outskirts of the forest and when the pixies return, we ask for their help as well. Maybe even you can look, Jayde," he said, shooting her a cautious look with trepidation washing down his expression.

Jayde nodded with a yawn. Between little sleep and spending most of her waking life in the trance of the hawks, she was really doing a number on her mind and body.

With a glance at the wagon that Kelsey slept in, Malkia's spirits plummeted. Kelsey received visions through sleep. It had been a useful gift to their town occasionally, but it was not always reliable. Although grateful for whatever help they received, Malkia knew Kelsey wouldn't be able to guarantee them any guidance.

Realization of how terrible this evade and escape idea was bubbled to the surface of Malkia's mind. What had she done?

They desperately needed sleep, and if they didn't rest soon, there would be no escaping the trackers if they started closing in. These trackers were superhuman. The chase had been going on for nearly two days and them slowing for a moment here and there had been the most reprieve she and her group had received.

It was pointless and impossible. The reality struck Malkia like ice-cold water.

"Dario, pick your two most alert and capable riders and give them instructions needed to search for Porter. The rest of us will stop here." Malkia pointed up ahead, toward a thick area of trees. "We are all taking a brief nap. This should give you enough time to prepare your guards, find Porter and hopefully return."

Irritation clouded Dario's features. "Malkia, the trackers are too close. We don't have the time to waste."

"We have the time. Not much, but some," Jayde said with a wave of her hand. "Let them sleep for a spell. Then we ride fast."

Dario glanced around at the weary group, and then back at Jayde. "Are you sure?"

Jayde nodded.

"Okay, go," he said. His fingers turned white as he clutched the reins harder and pulled back. "I will arrange the search party and meet you over there."

Malkia watched him go and exhaled slowly. There was deep admiration and love for that man. She wanted him. Yearned for him, even, but the time could not be worse for these feelings to arise. She forced them to the back of her mind and turned Parowan toward the covering of the tree's umbrella.

Jayde and Malkia found a shady spot with some tall grass. They pushed the grass down and covered with their blankets. Most of the group was already sleeping. They were all exhausted.

She should have stopped earlier.

Her gaze drifted toward Dario. As if sensing her, he glanced up and smiled at her. There were three men and two women surrounding him as he spoke, and she knew he would take care of the situation while she slept. She returned his smile, easing herself to the ground. The blackness filled her mind almost immediately, and she slipped away into a deep sleep.

"Malkia, wake up," someone hissed in her ear.

Her mind swam with confusion, but somehow, she pried her eyes open. "What's wrong?" she murmured, pushing herself into a seated position. "Is everything okay?"

"Yes and no," Dario replied. His fingers curled over her shoulders. "We need to wake Jayde, but she won't budge. I just woke Kelsey, and she told me the trackers will catch up to us before the second sun sets and will capture you. We need the sight of the hawks right now."

Malkia rolled to her knees and crawled closer to Jayde, shaking her arm. "Jayde, time to wake up." Jayde stirred but did not wake. Poking at her again, Malkia called out her name several times.

Finally, one of Jayde's eyes opened. "Wh-what?" she asked, stuttering across the word. She gulped and squeezed her eyes shut.

"I'm so sorry, Jayde. We have a problem. The trackers are close, and Kelsey has seen them take me away. We need to find the trackers." Malkia's voice rose an octave as she glanced behind her, expecting the trackers to already be there.

Jayde coughed, and Malkia's gaze shot back to her friend to see her eyes were open.

"I. I. I can't think." Jayde shook her head and her brows lifted slightly before her eyes rolled back into her head. She slapped away Malkia's hands, and on shaky legs, rose to her feet. One ankle twisted, andMalkia she swayed to one side, then stumbled face first against a tree.

Malkia leapt after Jayde, cradling her friend in her lap and wiping the blood from her forehead. "Don't move. Your body needs more rest. We shouldn't have woken you."

Jayde squinted at Malkia, before turning to the side and throwing up.

Malkia glanced at Dario in desperation. He scooped Jayde into his arms and sprinted toward Damion. "Damion, we need your help!" he shouted as he grew closer. "Jayde's body has shut down. We need her sight right now, or else we won't be able to see how far the trackers are from us. Can you use your healing ability?"

"Wait, Dario," Jacob said from the shade of a tree. "Let me see if the pixies have returned. If they're here, maybe they can give us an answer and Jayde can keep resting. I will be right back."

Jacob raced toward the thick part of the trees and disappeared before anyone had the chance to object. Dario laid Jayde on a blanket and motioned for Damion to begin his healing process.

Malkia stepped closer to Dario and curled her hand around his arm. He didn't look right away, but after a few quiet moments, his gaze drifted to meet hers. There were tears glistening in his eyes.

He abruptly glanced away, moving toward the other two guards. "I'll be back in a minute. Damion, don't stop working on her, unless healing her becomes too much for her system. Whistle when either she regains consciousness or when Jacob returns."

Malkia scrunched up her nose as he walked away. He was keeping something from her.

Kelsey's back was toward her as she helped one of the other guards ready the pegasi. There was more to this story and Malkia was going to find out what it was.

"Hey, Kelsey!" Malkia shouted, waving her hand to get the other woman's attention. "Can we talk?"

Kelsey turned toward Malkia. "What's up?"

Malkia stopped a few feet away from the redheaded woman. "What did you tell Dario about the trackers? Why is he so upset?"

"I told him they will capture you, and their leader will not want to give you up." Kelsey's forehead puckered and she licked her chapped lips. "I also told him this will all happen before final sundown."

Malkia was dumbfounded, and she nibbled on her bottom lip as she stared at Dario. *Was he just upset because they would capture me? Why does he think we could not stop them?*

"Thanks, Kelsey." Malkia rolled her shoulders back and sighed. "It just seems like there is more." She turned away, but Kelsey grabbed her shoulder.

"Wait," Kelsey whispered. "He told me not to tell you."

Malkia whirled back around.

"These men will execute Dario. That is why he is so upset. He knows unless we leave and change our plans, he won't be able to stop them from taking you away."

SIX

Surprise Dealings

MALKIA'S MIND WENT blank for just a split moment before adrenaline kicked in. Her gaze flashed to Dario again. His pointed stare was glued to her. Glancing at Jayde and Damion, Malkia inhaled sharply at the lack of progress in healing Jayde. She whirled around and raced toward the umbrella of trees where Jacob was hopefully speaking with the pixies.

Dario shouted after her, and Kelsey joined in, both demanding that she stopped. Malkia ignored them. She needed answers. Dario was her rock, and there was no way those savages were succeeding under her watch.

As if he knew she was coming, Jacob stepped into the light and pressed the branches back for her to enter. She raced by him and into the shadows but jolted to a halt when she came face to face with dozens of pixies.

They were breathtaking and entrancing. Their beauty was nearly overwhelming, and their light, warm and inviting. A deep sense of peace settled over her as she gazed around. They were only a foot high, with silky wings and a pulsating aura that beamed light from their bodies. All possessed long, satin hair, with a diversity of color. No one was identical, and their divinity radiated to the depths of Malkia's soul.

They were all watching Malkia as she took in the splendor of this moment. One of them flew forward and placed her hand on Malkia's cheek. A warm sensation spread through her body, and her worry disappeared.

"Malkia," the pixie murmured with a soft smile. "Everything is in its perfect order."

Malkia gawked at the creature, unable to find her voice for several breaths. Finally, she croaked out her questions. "What about Dario? Will he survive?"

"We do not know, but we can tell you the world is already a better place because of you. As for the people tracking you, they are near— less than an hour away and closing in. Their group is only a few hours behind them, and they are determined to capture you and your people as their desire to control consumes them." The pixie's smile melted into a frown and her gaze flitted briefly toward another pixie who appeared out of thin air. She refocused on Malkia. "You must divert to the west immediately. Porter is there. Your men have found him and are returning. If you leave now, you will meet on the path and increase your chances of escape."

Malkia nodded, but could not move.

The pixie inched even closer. "You are meant for extraordinary events," she whispered in a tone that shook Malkia's nervous system. "Now go. Do not delay your escape any longer."

The pixie flew back toward the others, and together, they disappeared into the shadows. Malkia stood frozen for several moments before she could pull herself from the pixie's lingering essence.

Jacob curled his fingers over her shoulder, forcing her back to reality. Now she knew why it required someone with his special ability to speak with the pixies. Their divinity was overpowering and exhausting.

Malkia turned and faced the edge of the trees, where her people were probably waiting for her. She stepped out from underneath the canopy, and Dario, Kelsey, and a few others greeted her.

Dario grabbed her hands and peered into her eyes. "Malkia, don't worry about me. I won't let anyone take you away, and I'll save you no matter what it takes. Please, let's go now. Jacob told us we have to head west, according to the pixies. Is that what they told you?"

"Yes, they also told me Porter and the other two men are returning right now, and we will find them as we head west. If everyone is ready, let's leave." She paused, brushing away the tears in her eyes. "I won't take any chances of losing you, Dario. Yes, I will worry about you. You are my rock, and I cannot lose you. Ever."

Malkia whistled, and Parowan trotted toward her. She mounted the beast and raced toward the rest of her small group. The others followed her on their pegasi.

She moved into the middle of the meager crowd. "The pixies have told me Porter, Alex and Levi are safe and returning to us as we speak. They also informed me the trackers are less than an hour behind us and are closing in, with their group only a couple of hours behind them." Her fingers wrapped around Parowan's mane while she did her best to ignore the terror swirling inside her gut. "They said the best way to evade the trackers is to divert to the west, toward Porter and the others, and pick them up as we escape. Leave the trailers here, but grab what food and water you can carry."

Malkia rode toward the trailers. She pulled open her saddlebags and shoved as many essentials as she could into them. The others followed suit once she eased Parowan toward the west. They were well on their way, with Jayde sleeping against Damion's chest.

It worried Malkia to think how far they had pushed Jayde. She had only been a teenager when the sky people's wars ended and had not understood her ability, let alone how much usage her body could tolerate. The mistakes Malkia had made these past few days were piling up.

They rode silently through the forest and only spoke if it was necessary. Worry clouded Malkia's mind. The trail they were forging was obvious, and the pegasi were not exactly quiet, with their large bodies pushing through the vegetation.

It wasn't long before they heard rustling through the thick vegetation. A few moments later, Alex and his pegasus walked around some trees and bushes, followed by Levi and Porter.

Porter's leg dangled with raw flesh hanging from his kneecap and teeth marks overran his face and neck with deep lacerations. Malkia leaped off Parowan and ran toward Porter.

"What happened?" she asked Levi and Alex.

"Ask him. He has been out of it most of the way back. We stopped asking him and let him rest," replied a frustrated Levi as he slid Porter off the pegasus and into Dario's arms.

Dario eased Porter onto the ground, and Malkia grabbed his face to look at the teeth marks. They weren't as deep as they appeared at first glance, but they were enough to cause too much blood loss, along with his torn-up leg. Damion handed Jayde to Kendrick and approached to see what he could do to heal his friend's body.

Porter looked at Malkia and smiled. "The pixies saved me," he mumbled, gripping her forearm. "A ritter attacked me. The pixies intervened before he ate me for dinner. The beast was ready to tear me apart."

"A ritter?" Malkia's gaze flashed to the surrounding brush, envisioning the massive rodent eyeing them from the shadows of the tree's umbrella. "We already have enough problems. The river is our best bet. I hear ritters stay away from fast-moving water, and the trackers will lose our scent as soon as we enter the river."

"Do you think the trackers can smell us?" Kelsey asked. She briefly glanced Dario's way, then pinched the bridge of her nose and closed her eyes.

Malkia puffed out her cheeks and blew out a quick breath. "I don't know. I know they have gained on us faster than we expected, and we masked the other group's smell. Deductive reasoning makes me believe one or all of them has a dog's ability to sniff out their prey. Not to mention their super speed. I have seen nothing like it before now."

Damion was working quickly on Porter's leg. His healing was slow. Malkia motioned for Kendrick to mount with Jayde and everyone else to find their rides. She waited a few more moments and then tapped on Damion's shoulder.

"We have to leave. Will he be okay long enough for us to make it to the river?"

"How long will the journey take?" Damion asked.

"We should make it before the last sundown," she replied, tilting her head to search the sky.

"Yes, I think he will be fine. Let's go." Damion climbed to his feet and mounted his pegasus, holding Porter in front of him.

They picked their way through the brush and eventually found a path wide enough for the pegasi to travel faster.

As they neared the river, Malkia felt an uncanny sensation spread in her stomach. She whipped around to look over her shoulder, fearing they were being watched. Several gazes met hers, but all of them belonged to her people. Her heart thudded against her ribs and panic bit at her throat. She swallowed hard, ignoring the dread clawing at her chest. Something was not right.

Dario noticed her fidgeting and rode up next to her.

"What's wrong?" he asked.

"I think we are being watched," Malkia whispered back to him.

Dario glanced around as well. "Why do you think that?"

"I can feel their eyes on us, but I don't know where they are hidden." She gulped again and wrapped her hand in Parowan's mane. "Dario, if they are the trackers, there will be no way for all of us to escape. I'll distract them, while you guide everyone else to the river."

Dario's eyes narrowed, regarding her with a scowl. "That's not happening. You are not getting away from me that easily. Let's send the group ahead of us. A few of us can stay back and keep a lookout. If they move, we will intervene."

A flood of tears threatened to spill from Malkia's eyes. She quickly wiped them away. If Dario stayed, he would die. She needed him to go with everyone else, but how would she convince him if he had no intentions to leave her side?

They did not have time to argue.

"Fine. We will do it your way," she muttered to Dario.

He moved his pegasus back toward Alex and Levi and asked them quietly to follow him to the back of the group.

Malkia rode toward Kendrick. "Kendrick, I need you to take the group quickly and quietly toward the river. Fly in the air as soon as I'm out of sight, and don't stop, no matter what happens. Find a safe place to hide away. Us four will follow shortly."

Kendrick's brows furrowed into a scowl, and Malkia thought he would object, but then he shook his head and, without a word, rode to the front of the group.

Malkia made her way back toward Dario, Alex, and Levi. This plan had major flaws, and she despised every step that brought her closer to its beginning. Even if they distracted one tracker, what would stop the other three from following the group? How would she protect Dario if he's fighting to rescue her and save the group at the same time?

"Help me," a child cried, interrupting her thoughts.

Malkia jumped, nearly tumbling off Parowan. She shifted around in her seat, looking for the child. There was no one, except for her group moving away and the three men riding toward her.

Had the voice been in her mind?

She froze and focused on her thoughts. *Who are you?* She asked in her mind.

Misty, the child replied.

Where are you, Misty?

I don't know. Some bad people took me and now they give me gross goo to stop the mind reading, but today they forgot. I hate it here.

How can I rescue you from these people?

Misty was quiet for several breaths and sweat trickled down Malkia's spine.

They're so mean, and they scare me. We're chasing some people. That's all I know. The leader wants them desperately, and he is frightening. They have some of their wolf-men chasing after them, and from what I heard, we almost caught up with them. Do you know who they are?

Malkia glanced at Dario as he approached. His forehead creased, and he waved his hand as if he was trying to talk to her. She shook her head and focused back on the scared child. *My group is the one they are after. You say there are wolf-men after us? What are wolf-men?*

Ugly, that's what they are. And fast. They can smell you. They look almost like normal people, except they are super tall and their teeth are sharp. And sometimes they snarl, just like a dog. One of them killed my dad and took me and my mom. They're horrible and if—

Misty's thoughts broke off.

Malkia glanced around hastily and realized their dire circumstances. Her decision placed the four of them, and possibly the smaller group, in danger. She heard snarling in the vegetation in front of them. As all four of them whipped around from the noise, another snarl from their left side brought their attention there.

"Fly," Malkia quietly ordered, staring relentlessly at the three men in front of her.

Malkia slapped Parowan's side, and the three men did the same to their pegasi. Feet beating against the terrain filled the air. Malkia's stomach knotted, and she leaned closer to Parowan. She was nearly clear of the tall vegetation when one creature who was chasing them collided into Malkia. Panic assailed her, and she shrieked and clamored for the edge of her saddle, but only found empty air. She tumbled backward and struck the hard dirt ground with a thud. She gasped for air before another creature rammed into her, flinging her into a nearby tree.

Blood trickled down her face, streaming into her mouth, and she gagged from the coppery taste. Her breath came in short, while she blinked feverishly, trying to restore her sight.

She heard Dario yell her name and her entire body locked up with fright.

They will kill him.

She rose slowly, but her head swam, and she toppled down to the ground and scratched her face against the brush. Her eye stung, but her sight returned as she could finally inhale deeply and catch her breath.

"Run, Dario, run!" Malkia shrieked as loud as she could holler. Her voice was cracked and shallow.

She searched the vegetation, trying to gain her bearings, and focused on the nearest tree. Trying to rise again, she stumbled forward and caught herself against that tree. A flash to her right caught her attention, and she twisted enough to watch Dario sprint toward her. She heard the whistle of an arrow before she saw Dario fall.

Shock washed across his features, and he struck the ground so hard, he slid several feet before smashing into the base of a tree.

"*No,*" she screamed, sprinting toward him.

Before she reached Dario, someone, with a forceful grip, snatched her up and yanked her away from him. She cried out and beat her fist against the man's shoulder. He squeezed tighter, and a hand eased against her mouth, shoving what tasted like lakseed onto her tongue. She tried to spit, but he pressed his hand tighter against her lips, crushing her gums into her teeth. They forced the herb down her throat.

When he removed his hand, she bit down on his shoulder. He grunted and slapped her face away, then twisted her around to face away from him. The vegetation whirled past her, small branches slapping her in the face and chest, bruising and cutting her more.

Blackness inched across her sight, and she whimpered as she slipped into an unwelcomed slumber.

SEVEN

Captivity

MALKIA'S HEAD FURIOUSLY pulsated as she drifted toward consciousness.

Her body ached everywhere, and the dried blood tugged at the tender skin beneath her eyes. Her instincts kept her calm and her eyes shut, grateful for the mindfulness training she received over the years. Loud, angry voices surrounded her, and she did not want them to know she was awake.

"Always the fools. How did they *all* outsmart you?" A man's deep voice rumbled from a short distance from Malkia. "I need the men. Every one of them. We will use her as bait. Return to the forest and find them."

"The group escaped by the river," another man's deep, but much quieter voice replied. "We searched up and down it for miles, but they must all be on pegasi as well, because there is absolutely no sign of them. I really think—"

"I don't ask you to think!" the angry man shouted. "I ask for results. You could not even catch this woman's pegasus. Why didn't you take it down the same time you dismounted her?"

"But she's the leader, I know it. I thought you said to catch the leader. Our focus was to capture her and then go after the—"

A crack of bones reverberated in the space around Malkia, followed by a thunderous thud near her body. She stiffened slightly.

"Stop thinking," the angry man hissed. "This woman is not the leader. Who is senseless enough to give a woman control? Do your job the way I instruct you to do it. I want the rest of the group, and I want the man you shot. How did his body just disappear?"

Silence greeted his question.

He huffed, then whispered, "You brainless fools better bring those men to me, or you will find yourself in the cages with the dogs."

She heard someone approach her and internally grimaced at the wretched smell of their breath. Keeping her breathing deep, she forced herself to remain still.

"Take her to the cages and order the women to clean her. I want her washed and brought to me as soon as she wakes."

Cold hands dragged her forward and threw her over their shoulder. She peeked through her lashes to gain her bearings, but the man carrying her was sprinting, and his jolts prevented her from seeing clearly. After a few moments, she heard something creak open. She stiffened as he dropped her, and her left shoulder slammed into the hard ground.

"Clean her up," the man snapped.

The door slammed shut, followed by silence. Someone's small hands wrapped around her shoulders and heaved her a couple of feet. They placed a wet towel on her head, and someone attempted to wash her hair. It had to be caked with blood and dirt.

She slowly opened her eyes and scanned her surroundings. There were women and children all around her. Some were eyeing her. Others were off in the corners, sheltering their children from the hands of the savages. Most were whispering to each other.

"You're awake," the woman who was cleaning her hair said.

"Where am I?" Malkia asked.

"You're in hell," the woman replied. "Welcome to the worst nightmare of your life."

"No, I've already been through that. This is definitely not my worst nightmare." Losing her family would always claim that spot.

The woman gawked at her with a puzzled look but shook her head and continued to pour water onto Malkia's hair. She scrubbed at her scalp, and Malkia felt blood flow again and pour down the side of her face.

She yanked away from the woman and held her head where her wound was. "*Careful*," Malkia stammered, glaring at the woman.

"Sorry, I didn't realize this was your blood! I thought it was someone else's," the woman blurted, and her lips set into a straight line.

"Don't worry about it. I can clean myself up." Malkia grabbed the water jug and rag from the woman. "What is this place, and why are you all in this cage? Isn't this a little cramped for all these women and children?"

The woman nodded. "There are four other cages like this. They are full of women and children. We're basically slaves to the men of this group. Some of them are even husbands, sons, brothers, and fathers to these women and children. They have all chosen to follow The Leader, either by choice or by force, and it's pitiful. We do what we can to survive. A tent covers the cage, but if you could see the massiveness of this group, it would terrify you. There are hundreds of these men, and all they are after is more of them. They want to take over this entire land." The woman shuddered, closing her eyes. "You should hear them talk. It's frightening."

"I have heard them talk, but only a little. Do they give you enough free time outside these cages to eavesdrop on their conversations?"

The woman laughed and sat back on her heels. "I'm married to the heathen in charge of this group. I have the pleasure of going to his tent every few days so he can have his way with me. I'm usually allowed to spend that day sleeping in a comfortable bed and eating the best food, so trust me, I take what I can get to escape this dark hole."

Malkia frowned at the woman. She was allowing herself to be used, just so she could find a few precious moments of peace and comfort.

The woman continued. "That's why they brought you to me. In fact, to us." She nodded at the other women. "There are five of us in total. I am Astrid." She patted her chest. "We are all his wives. He trusts us to clean you up and bring you to him the way he desires. He doesn't like filth, and he won't allow you to meet with him until you are washed and presentable."

"Let's finish, so I can end this charade," Malkia replied, her eyes narrowing with disgust.

The woman helped Malkia scrub her hair and bandage her wound. Astrid had joined the heathens over a year earlier and had worked her way to being one of The Leader's wives for nearly five months. She used her few moments of freedom to find out about her brothers and mother. She had discovered one of her brothers had escaped, and the other was also alive but had submitted to the army of the savages. Her mother was not in a cage but was forced to marry one of the other men and kept tied in his trailer. She told Malkia she would give anything to free her mother from the torture she was enduring.

"Maybe someday you will have your chance," Malkia murmured, staring hard at Astrid.

Astrid glanced at Malkia with another puzzled look, but then shook her head and uttered, "I doubt it. You haven't seen what these people can do. They're horrid. Even the women who were originally with the group are as callous or they're too frightened to object. The leader's first wife is one of the worst. She's just as nasty and violent as him."

After Malkia finished washing, and Astrid had smoothed a shawl over Malkia's hair and torn shirt, Astrid eased toward the door and blew into a blow horn. After a few minutes, a massively large, hairy man yanked open the door and peered inside.

Malkia took a step back. The hair on his arms and hands was as long as wolf's fur, and he could crush her with his bulging biceps. They were wider than her thighs. She could never overpower him on her own.

"Bring her to me," he demanded, signaling her to move forward with his pointer finger.

Astrid grabbed Malkia's arm and hauled her toward the brute. He yanked Malkia out of the cage, his fingers digging into her upper arm, and dragged her toward a row of tents, where she saw men drinking and jesting. As they approached, she heard whistling and crude taunting from the men. Keeping her face straight forward, she focused her eyes on the direction he was towing her.

As they neared the largest of the tents, he slowed and towered over her. He was massive and every muscle in her body screamed for her to run, but she held her ground and glared up at him.

"Bow when you enter, or you might not live to see tomorrow. It would be a dreadful waste." He snickered as his gaze slid down her body.

Malkia wrinkled her nose with disgust, her eyes burning with hatred. He laughed harder as he shoved her toward the door. She glanced back at him, and he motioned for her to enter the tent. Anxiously eyeing the tent doors, she eased inside and noticed the dance of candle flames. She also noted a woman standing in the shadows. Malkia stepped forward and dropped to her knees, tilting her head into a bow.

The woman in the shadows chuckled. Malkia watched as she sauntered out, moving toward her. As she neared, Malkia realized this woman had to be the first wife. She was taller than Malkia, with a heavyset body frame. Her face had a dark beauty, but her angry scowl and shadowy eyes gave her an intimidating appearance.

Is she the actual leader? Malkia thought.

The woman strolled around Malkia, examining her. Her hand flew forward and grabbed a handful of Malkia's hair. She yanked her upward, forcing her into a standing position. Malkia winced. The woman studied her up and down, smiled wickedly, and let go of her hair as she walked away. Malkia fell back to her knees, grimacing when her left kneecap shifted against the ground and sent a shooting pain up to her thigh.

"My husband hasn't returned. You may sit where you are and remain immobile until he arrives," the woman commanded as she continued to walk back into the shadows and shifted behind a curtain.

Malkia glanced around, hoping she was alone, but as she peered to the side, she noticed a burly man staring at her. He motioned for her to sit and then looked away. She sank to the floor slowly, eyeing everything she could see.

She took in all her surroundings and searched for ways to escape. She hadn't been sitting long when she heard the loud laughter of a man seeping through the curtain the woman had walked behind. Malkia knew he was going to be entering soon, but did not know what to expect. She prepared her mind and heart for the worst.

The tall man walked through the curtain and abruptly halted, scrutinizing Malkia from the shadows. Malkia could not see his facial expressions, but she could sense his contempt. Once again, he walked toward her, and when he stepped out of the shadows, Malkia inhaled sharply.

What she saw was unexpected. He was extremely striking, with devilishly handsome features. The candlelight flickered at the right moment, catching the smoky gray in his irises and a guarded look that sent chills down her spine. His black hair fell in short waves around his face, framing a hardened expression. As he walked closer, the muscles in his arms and chest caught her eye and she gulped at the thought of how easily he could end her life. Attractiveness aside, he was a cold-stone killer.

But most of all, there was a familiar spark between them, and that terrified her the most.

A smile suddenly danced across his expression, and his dark eyes twinkled as he sat on the floor a few feet in front of her. "What's your name?"

She clenched her fists together in her lap and pushed away the uneasy feeling they had met before. "Malkia."

"Are you from the town two days north of us?"

"No," she lied.

"Are you sure you want that to be your answer?" he asked, a frown forming on his face.

Malkia looked him square in the eyes and said, "Yes."

"Fine, where did you come from, and where is the rest of your group heading?"

"We came from the east. Our town was raided a few weeks ago, and we're the only ones left." She broke eye contact and glanced at the floor, wringing her hands together. "We were heading southwest, looking for a new place to call home. I'm not sure where my group escaped to after we figured out you were following us, but even if I knew, I wouldn't tell you. If you're looking for a group from up north, we ran into them a few hours back. They were headed south."

He stood as she finished, and in a flash, he yanked her off the ground by her shirt and put her nose to nose with himself. "You lie, woman," he hissed, spit forming on the edges of his lips. "There were no other groups. There's only one, and you're the one from the north. We aren't imprudent. My wolf-men have been sniffing you out since we discovered your town, and you reek of the scent. Do not lie to me again, or I will have you hung by your neck, here and now." His gruff voice grew hoarse as he spoke.

Malkia knew she would be dead if she didn't stop lying. Refusing to divulge the entire truth, Malkia stared relentlessly back into his eyes. "Fine, we are that group. However, the raided part is true. We have been picking up the pieces and burying our dead for the past couple of weeks and then we departed. We were afraid the group that had raided us would return."

The leader dropped Malkia and walked away from her. He said nothing for a few minutes as he paced the floor. His eyes crinkled with thought, and she prayed he would accept her story and that the Light Beings would spare her friends and family and provide them a safe passage away from this savage and his wolf-men. She knew they would be done for if they found them before they reached the safety of Domesca's fortress.

After a few minutes, he returned to Malkia and seized her hand to help her rise. After she was standing, he motioned for her to follow him to the table in the center of the room. He pulled a chair out for her. "Sit down," he demanded.

She settled onto the chair while continuing to keep her eyes on him and the surroundings she could now see. The leader strolled to the other side of the table, sat in a chair, and folded his arms on the table as he studied her with doubt in his eyes.

"I don't remember seeing any fresh graves when we passed through. Where are these graves?"

"We didn't bury them. That would be a dishonor to their names. They each received a proper ceremony and were returned to the heavens by fire. I will never tell you where this occurred, as it is sacred to me and my people."

"We will see," he replied.

He continued to stare at her, trying to weigh her down with his glare and untrusting eyes. Malkia glowered back, not letting her lack of confidence show. They remained there for a few minutes, eyeing each other before he finally shifted away.

He walked to her chair and leaned over her, so he was close to her face again. He was intimidating, but Malkia held her ground and glared back. "Where are the men who were with you? Which one is the leader of your group? Do they have any abilities that will help them fight us?" He asked all three questions quickly.

Malkia didn't hesitate with an answer. "They executed the leader of our group in the raid, back in our town. We have been on our own since we fled, and we never appointed a new leader. There were a few of us who took charge, but we have no official leader. As for where the men are, I'm assuming they either caught up with the rest of the group, or they are still in the forest waiting for a chance to rescue me." She stiffened, realizing she didn't want him thinking anyone would come back for her. "However, they have families to consider, so I'm sure they left me to fend for myself. What abilities would help them fight you? We don't have any secret abilities."

He scowled at her with his jaw clenched tightly, slamming his fist onto the table. "Liar! A group that significant would have to possess someone with an ability. Disclose the information I desire, or I'll send you out to the wolf-men, and they can decide what to do with you!"

Malkia quivered. She was doing everything she could to appear confident and unshaken, but his large stature and brash voice made him frightening. She continued to stare at him, and after a minute of glaring at one another, he regained his composure and walked back to his chair.

Malkia drew in a shaky breath. "Fine, I will tell you the abilities they have, but it is nothing compared to what your men possess. I'm not sure how any of my people could escape yours." She closed her eyes briefly, praying she would be rescued soon. "Two of the men I was with have heightened strength, and the other has extra speed, but nothing matches to your wolf-men. In fact, it completely threw us off when we realized your wolf-men were on our tails and gaining on us at astounding speeds. None of us even realized these men existed on this moon."

She paused, watching the leader's deadpan expression. There was no chance she would disclose Jayde's or the other's abilities. This was the best she could give him. "I'm telling you the truth. There is nothing to fear from the men in my group, and there is no reason to search for them."

He clenched his jaw, and his gaze wandered the room as his eyes glazed over. "We will find who we want to. There is always room in my army for more men, and if they have any useful abilities, they are even more welcome. However, I already have several other men and women who have these abilities you speak of, so your men aren't my top priority. What I want information about is this group that raided your town. What abilities did they have that caught you off guard and enabled them to kill so many of your people? Because I know there aren't many groups close by that can even come close to what I have here."

Malkia had known he would eventually come back to her lie about the raid to her town, but she had hoped it would have waited for another day. However, she knew her family's and friends' lives depended on her ability to lie through her teeth and convince this savage they weren't a threat or any use to him.

She closed her eyes, breathing steadily to calm her nerves. "They came during the night, which is what caught us off guard." Malkia opened her eyes, nibbling on her bottom lip. His gaze fell to her mouth and for a moment his guarded expression disappeared. "Of course, we always posted guards around town during the night, but these people were discreet. They seemed to know the town well enough, which means they'd probably been surveying us for some time." She raked her hands through her hair.

"Sounds like your leader was naïve and foolish. Good riddance to him." His tone had a hint of humor in it that grated on Malkia's nerves.

Ignoring his rude comment, she continued. "There was one man who could disappear and reappear in different places. I met him personally, since he was the one, along with others, who broke into my house and slaughtered my family. I am not sure why he spared me, but he disappeared a few times and then reappear around our house. Before I knew it, they were gone, taking our livestock, gold, water supply, and anything else they could carry. They left half our town dead, and almost everyone else injured."

His expression softened once more, and he leaned forward to rest his arms on the table. "Then what did you do?"

"The people who came to my house didn't even touch me. They laughed at me and told me they were going to kill me, but after they raided my house, they left. I didn't leave my house for hours, in fear of them returning. I hid in a closet until daybreak, and when I ventured out, I found my family dead and many of my friends lifeless on the streets. It was the most horrid moment of my life." She thought back to the actual day her family died, and the emotions rose easily. Tears brimmed in her eyes, and she quickly wiped them away. "As for their abilities, the only one I saw who had anything remarkable was the one man. I heard from others there were people who had super-fast speeds, and one neighbor said there must be one who could speak to dogs, because not one of our animals defended us. Not even a bark to warn us."

The man listened quietly to her story, and as she described the various abilities, his eyes widened, and a smile twitched on the edges of his lips. Little did he know she had seen none of these abilities before, except in stories from her parents.

Once again, he rose from his chair and paced the floor of the tent. After a few minutes, he returned to his seat and smiled at her. "I like you," he cheerfully said. "You're full of useful information, not to mention you are exquisite and not easily intimidated. I could use someone like you to be a leader to these women. There are too many of them who cry, and moan, and cause me all kinds of headaches. Plus, you are easy on the eyes and that will make many men happy."

She curled her lips with icy contempt. She didn't want to be used as a trophy, to parade around in front of others. He laughed when he noticed her obvious dislike of his suggestion. She knew he was not asking her, but telling her. At first, she thought she would rather remain in a cage all day, but after a moment, she realized if she played the game, she could probably gain more freedom and eventually break away from these savages and return to her group.

She nodded in agreement. "Whatever you want."

The man laughed, his eyes scanning over her body and face. "Now you need to return to your cage and sleep well. I have much for you to attend to tomorrow, including keeping me company."

He whistled. The wolf-man who had brought her here poked his head inside the tent and motioned for her to follow him. She hurried toward the door without looking back at the savages' leader. She didn't want him to think she was vulnerable, afraid, or moldable. He could have her for the time being, but when the moment arose, she would be long gone, and he would never see her again.

The wolf-man curled his hand around the tender flesh of her arm and jogged toward her cage with her in tow.

"Why are you in such a hurry? I can barely keep up with you, and you're hurting my arm," she daringly said.

He roared with laughter, then sneered down at her as he grasped her arm firmer. "Wouldn't you like to know? I'll tell you this: if I find your friends, I'll rip them to shreds. Too bad you aren't out there to warn them. Instead, you will sit in your little cage, like a good little woman, and think about what I might do to them."

She wished she hadn't asked. She knew if Dario had survived, he would wait for a chance to free her. Not to mention, Alex and Levi would never leave her or Dario. If Dario perished, she knew Alex and Levi were out there waiting to rescue her. The thought made her cringe, realizing she needed to escape before they captured anyone else.

As they moved closer to the cage, Malkia examined the surrounding area. Other tents surrounded it, and the forest was at least fifty yards away. Theia loomed above the forest, her presence creating a feeling of home that made Malkia's desire to end this imprisonment even more imperative.

When they reached the cage, the wolf-man opened the door and shoved her in. The door slammed behind her, and the lock clicked. She glanced around and noticed everyone was lying down, either sleeping or staring at her.

Astrid stood and motioned to Malkia. She eased her way through the bodies of sleeping women and children toward Astrid. Astrid had made a makeshift bed of worn-out blankets and pillows, and Malkia was thankful to see some place for her to rest her head and maybe sleep away her troubles. She chuckled bitterly at the thought and ignored Astrid's confused look as she nuzzled into her pillow.

She was about to fall asleep when Astrid whispered in her ear. "I was afraid I wouldn't see you again. I guess it went well enough for you to remain alive. When you have a chance tomorrow, I would like to hear about it."

Malkia nodded, but before she had a moment to think about talking to Astrid about her night, she slipped into a deep sleep.

EIGHT

Visionary

"WAKE UP, MALKIA," Astrid said, shaking Malkia. "Time to get ready for the day."

Malkia opened her eyes slowly and peered around her prison. The women were bustling around, organizing themselves and their children for their day. They seemed fine with their circumstances and used to the fact they were living in a cage with very little to have for themselves. It made Malkia sick to think how horrible these people were.

She rose from the ground and brushed her hands through her hair, accidentally pulling on her head wound. Wincing from the pain, she felt the bruises more today than yesterday, and her body ached from sleeping on a hard surface.

Astrid curled her hand over Malkia's shoulder. "You look worse for wear. You should really let me examine the rest of you and ensure there isn't anything else that requires medical help." She eyed Malkia up and down, frowning at the enormous bruise running along her arm.

Malkia shook her head, her fingers trailing over the bandage. "I'll be fine. I'm pretty sure the only blood spilt was from my head, and that's cleaned up. Maybe tonight you can put a fresh bandage on it and make sure it is not getting infected."

"Actually, I should probably do that now," Astrid replied. She pulled Malkia toward the bandages in the cage's corner. "The leader will want you in prime condition when he sees you today. We should run a comb through your tangled hair as well."

Brushing her hair reminded Malkia about her backpack. Had it fallen off in the forest? Did the savages have it? Malkia's pulse quickened, as her most precious possessions were in the pack. Pictures of her husband and baby girl were stored in there, and she had refused to give them to Mataya, but now she wished she had. A sob rose in her throat, and she struggled to push it back down. How could she be so careless? Now they could know her most private secret, and he would use that to hurt her.

Malkia let Astrid clean her wound and replace the bandage. She brushed her hair and helped Malkia clean her face and exposed body. She felt better once she washed off, but her body still ached.

"You have some nasty bruises on your back and legs. It's going to be a rough day for you. They will push you, and the best thing for you is to fight through the pain and survive the day. I know how it feels. I've been there several times, and I don't wish this kind of pain on anyone. Please be tough and make it through the day," Astrid pleaded, her eyes swimming with pity.

Malkia didn't understand why Astrid cared so much. She was skeptical about the woman's intentions, but played along anyway. She suspected Astrid was to make sure Malkia did what she was supposed to and didn't mess with anything.

"When do they let us out?" Malkia asked.

"They should be here soon. We'll go eat breakfast as a group, as we usually stick together and do things as a team. We aren't really allowed to interact with the other women, unless The Leader specifically requests us to help. Keep your head down and don't look at the men or women who roam free. If you act tough, they'll taunt you, and seeing the bruises you already have, I wouldn't risk more. After breakfast, they will have a lot of work for us to do."

"Breakfast, work, keep my head down—got it," Malkia mumbled to suffice her.

It was only a few moments later when Malkia heard footsteps and voices outside, and then the cage door rattled before it opened. The women and children rose and walked out of the cage quietly and in an orderly fashion. She joined them, keeping her head bowed as she returned to the beauty of the outside.

She wanted to look around and find her bearings, but she did not want to upset Astrid, or anyone else, for that matter. Instead, she stole glances to her sides, keeping her head slightly down.

There were several men walking around, and she spotted the tents from the night before. The forest was on the righthand side of her. Now, she could tell the forest was southwest of the cage and about sixty to seventy yards away. She made these mental notes and then focused on as many details as she could without catching anyone's attention.

They entered a part of the campsite where she heard laughter and bolstering, and the smell of food swept into her nostrils. She was starving and realized she hadn't eaten in at least a day. She followed the other women toward the noise and the sweet scent, hoping the savages would ignore her.

"Where's the new girl? I hear she is something to look at!" A man's voice rose above the others, striking Malkia straight in the heart.

She suspected she was going to be in for a fight today, until she heard the next man say, "I wouldn't be messing with her. I hear The Leader has taken a liking to her, and we all know the trouble that brings to the rest of us."

Laughter shot through the air, and Malkia tried to relax. At least having The Leader's attention made her somewhat safe from the heckling and fighting. They finally reached the food, and she was able to dish herself some sludge. They tossed a couple of pieces of meat on top, and it took all her willpower not to shove them in her mouth.

She walked quietly with Astrid to their table and sat next to her. Eating her porridge, she tried to ignore the tasteless sludge. After a few bites, she couldn't handle it anymore and pushed the salty meat piece by piece into her mouth, enjoying their savory taste.

She peered around at the other women, but nobody seemed to notice her sudden change of delicacies. She chewed slowly and returned to eating the sludge.

As soon as the women finished their breakfast, they took their dishes to the cleaning area. They had soap, dishrags, and large kettles full of water. A few women began cleaning, while others waited on the men and women at the other tables. Astrid pulled Malkia toward the clang of dishes.

"We are on dish duty. You can dry the dishes while I clean them. Rumor has it The Leader will come around soon to fetch you. Best if you were doing something useful when he shows his face. He doesn't like anyone who stands around and twiddle their thumbs."

Malkia clutched a dry rag, pulling it from the pile lying on the table. Astrid handed her a wet bowl, and they worked in silence.

"Where's the woman from last night?" The Leader's voice caught Malkia's attention.

"She's doing dishes with Astrid. Did you not catch her name?"

"Does it matter?" The Leader growled.

"I guess not," muttered the other man.

Malkia continued her chore, ignoring the rude comment by The Leader. She didn't care if anyone knew her name. In fact, she wished they would just forget about her, so it would be easier for her to slip away.

In the corner of her eye, she glimpsed The Leader watching her from a few feet away. She pretended to not see him and continued drying the dishes Astrid stacked for her.

"Come with me," The Leader demanded.

Malkia turned slightly. He stood like a statue with his arms folded and his jaw clenched. She set down the dish and rag, glancing at Astrid. Astrid shot her a sideways look but continued washing dishes. Malkia walked toward the leader, and when she was nearly there, he pivoted on his heel and strolled into the thick of the campsite. She quickly walked behind him, wondering why he was in such a hurry and where they were going.

They passed several tents with men and women cleaning their weapons or wiping down their horses. Not once did she see a pegasus, which was why they didn't chase her group in the sky. The clang of metal on metal brought her attention to the children and women shining armor. The Leader was forming an army, but for what reason?

Then there was Misty. Why hadn't she been able to contact her again? Malkia's gaze swept from one end of the campsite to the other, but none of the children looked her way. It would take a miracle to find Misty without more freedom.

After walking for several minutes in silence, the leader halted in his tracks and turned to face her. He gave her a once-over and grinned. She grimaced at the look on his face.

"I need a new wife," he boasted, smiling wickedly at her.

"Good for you," Malkia replied venomously.

He tilted his head back and laughed, then stared at her for a moment. He smiled again and walked toward a small tent off by itself. Malkia froze.

Does he think he is going to have his way with me? Malkia thought. *Does he think I will marry him or that I'm imprudent enough to follow him into that tent after the way he gawked at me?*

As if he heard her thoughts, he turned back toward her with the same wicked smile on his face. He motioned for her to come toward him and pushed the entryway flap of the tent to the side. He looked back at her again.

"What are you worried about? I plan on being a perfect gentleman," he said, his smile softening and her heart melted more than she would have liked. "Unless you don't want me to be."

Malkia edged toward him as if she could not help herself. Where had she met him before? And why did he feel safe and a threat at the same time? It was confusing.

When she passed The Leader, he touched her shoulder, and his smile sent chills shooting down her spine. She forced a guarded smile, then awkwardly shifted into the tent. Inside, a woman sat cross-legged on the floor with parchment and paints lying around her.

The woman glanced up at Malkia and grinned. "You must be Malkia."

NINE

Playing the Game

"THAT'S ME," MALKIA replied, looking around at the small space. It was filled with paintings of people. "What's going on?"

The Leader cradled his arm around Malkia's shoulders, leaning down toward her face. Her heart fluttered anxiously. "Alexa will have you describe the man who executed your family. She's going to draw him for me. This way, I can help you avenge your family, all the while gaining myself a great fresh addition to my army." He turned toward Alexa. "You know the drill."

Malkia tensed and spoke before Alexa could respond. "I don't want you to avenge my family, and I definitely don't want to see that man again. Why would I give you any details that would help strengthen your army?"

He smirked. "Malkia, you're one of us now. Help where you can, and you'll find your accommodations far more comfortable."

He bent down and pressed his lips against her forehead before turning around and leaving the tent. Malkia stood there for a moment, not knowing how to respond to his actions and request. She did not appreciate him kissing her, and she didn't want to describe a man whose existence was a lie. If he ever discovered she had fibbed about that man, he would probably murder her himself. She needed to escape soon. Before she told too many more lies, she had to remember.

Her attention turned to Alexa after several breaths. "I guess it's just you and me. When do you think he'll return?"

"I have no idea, but I know we are being watched and guarded." Alexa gathered her paints and scooted closer to the parchment next to her. "If you think this is a good time to run, rethink your decision. I've tried to escape before and quickly realized how many people were watching me. It's not worth the wrath of that man."

Malkia sank to the ground next to Alexa. She blew out a long breath as Alexa picked up her paintbrush and raised her brows expectantly at Malkia.

"Fine," Malkia muttered.

Her description of the made-up man was bits and pieces of people in her past life—her dad's facial structure, her mom's dark hair, Raul's wide shoulders and muscular chest. It would be enough to suffice The Leader's curiosity and hopefully give her some clout to gain some freedom.

Alexa seemed pleasant, but Malkia was skeptical about where her loyalties rested. The women seemed satisfied with their roles as slaves in this army. Either that, or they all were so frightened by what they've seen, they have given up. Malkia couldn't understand the happy and content way Alexa worked. After she completed painting her pretend disappearing man, Malkia asked her why she was here.

"You mean why I'm happy to stay with this group?" Alexa asked, propping herself back with her hands.

Malkia nodded, her brows furrowing. "Well, yes. But I also want to know where you came from and how you became a part of this group."

"First off, I just make the best out of a very horrible situation." Alexa frowned, biting her lip. "The Leader allows me to paint and draw and he leaves me alone, as long as I do these minor tasks. When I paint a person with an ability, my painting will inform me where they are located. He's thrilled to have my power in his control, so he treats me well and no one bothers me."

Malkia gulped when Alexa explained her ability. No wonder he had been so confident. What would happen when he realized the man on the parchment didn't exist? Would he not believe her, or would he think the man was dead? This made-up man's ability was too significant, and Malkia did not believe the leader would retire the idea easily.

Alexa studied Malkia's face, misinterpreting her shocked expression. "I know you probably think I'm a horrid person, allowing such a power-hungry man to use my ability to find more immoral people, but I had to do whatever I could to keep me and my family safe. My kids remain safe, and the leader gave me this tent to paint in, along with a tent for me and my kids to sleep in. We're comfortable, and they taught the kids how to fight along with school things, like language and reading. I find their future is far more important than anything else."

"Alexa, you don't owe me an explanation. If they treat you well and you feel good about what you are doing, then explain nothing to me." Malkia paused, eyeing the opening of the tent. "Where did you come from, and how long have you been with this group?"

"Since nearly the beginning. It has been about three years. I found them when I was running from my children's father. He was a confused and sick man." Alexa shook her head and closed her eyes. "We lived in the woods up north, away from any real civilization. I always wonder if that made him go mad." She opened her eyes, drawing in a deep breath. "He began slaughtering our livestock and telling me he was going to destroy us all. Day after day, he would go out and exterminate another animal, and each time he returned, he said the day was growing closer to when he would put us all out of our misery."

Malkia reached over and squeezed Alexa's hand. "That's awful. How did you escape?"

"One night, I drugged him at dinnertime, and I gathered my kids in my arms and ran. I had packed a backpack earlier that day with clothes and food, but that was all we had. I took the last horse we had living and fled. My kids were only three and six. They didn't understand what was happening, but I couldn't let him take their lives. So, when I met this group, they were far better for my family than my husband. I was thankful for the protection and the new home. The only reason I ever wanted to escape was when I witnessed the wolf-men murder a family right in front of me."

Malkia inhaled sharply, and Alexa stopped talking. A sad smile surfaced on her lips as she gazed at the painting of the man she had described.

"Those wolf-men are easily set off. I still cannot believe they slaughtered that family with no remorse. I have no idea where their ability came from, but it's destructive. The Leader controls them and thinks they are his greatest weapons." Alexa shook her head, sighing. "He wasn't as power hungry when I first joined the group. He only had one wife, and he was mostly just creating a large group to ensure everyone's safety. I'm not sure when the group turned ruthless, but I think it had something to do with the death of his children."

Malkia sat up straight. "He had children?"

Alexa nodded. "He had three children with his first wife. I know someone invaded their town and exterminated many people. From the rumors, his children were—"

"I think that will do," the leader said from the entryway. "I'm not sure you should speak about other people's business."

Alexa jumped up and handed the painting of the disappearing man to him. Malkia slowly rose, eyeing the leader as he scanned the painting. She wasn't sure what he was searching for, but disappointment melted down his expression.

"Have you received a location?" he asked Alexa.

"No, I haven't received a vision from this painting." She closed her eyes. "I've never had an issue before, except if the person is deceased. If their spirit is not here, I cannot even find their body." She opened her eyes and blinked several times. "The only other explanation I can think of is if Malkia didn't provide an accurate description."

They both turned Malkia's way. She shrugged her shoulders. Of course, it wasn't accurate. The man didn't exist. "What did you expect? It was a chaotic night, and there were other people in my house as well. I hid my face from them as much as possible because I was afraid and my eyes were blurry from tears. I don't know why it surprises you that this description is not entirely accurate. Experiment with his looks, and maybe you will stumble upon the correct description."

The leader's brows bumped together in a scowl, but he regained his composure quickly and smiled at Malkia. She guessed he had a soft spot for her, but after his "new wife" comment, she was afraid of being an object of his affection.

He walked to Malkia and grabbed her hand. "Thank you, Alexa. Please do what Malkia suggested and play around with his painting until you receive his whereabouts. I'm counting on you to come up with some kind of idea on where he is at."

He pulled Malkia out of the tent and strolled toward the center of camp, continuing to hold her hand. She didn't like where this was going. He was being far too nice. Her pulse quickened with anticipation.

"I feel awful that I made you sleep on the hard ground last night, especially with your bruises from that senseless wolf of mine. He can be a little too quick on his feet and doesn't understand his own strength. I'm really sorry about the pain you might be feeling today." He drew her hand up to his lips and kissed it. "How would you like to sleep in a bed tonight?"

"No, I'm fine," Malkia replied abruptly. She didn't want him to think for even a moment that she would consider sleeping with him.

He laughed. "I don't mean in my bed, even though I wouldn't mind. I mean, in your own tent, with your own bed. A washbasin will be brought in for you so you can soak your sore muscles and then have a great night's sleep on a proper bed, with pillows and blankets."

Malkia stared at him, not quite knowing how to respond. He had an agenda. His other wives all slept in a cage together. "What about your wives? Why would you give me my own tent when you give them the floor almost every single night?"

His fingers curled around her upper arm, and he slowly backed her against a tree. He leaned closer, never taking his eyes off hers. "I don't know. You intrigue me. You make me feel happy, just by seeing you. I don't want to feel weak like this, but at the same time, I am loving every moment. I could not stop thinking about you last night, and today, just being in your presence makes me weak in the knees."

Malkia could not hide the shock. That wasn't the answer she was expecting. "What about your first wife, the mother of your children?"

His smile disappeared. "My first wife and I haven't been happy since my kids were murdered. She's filled with an insurmountable rage toward me. If she could leave this group and run far away, she would. I won't let her, but I might change my mind. I would let them all go if you chose to be with me."

"You would let everyone go free? You would stop this madness and stop fighting and killing others?"

He twitched when she said killing, but then he looked at her with a small amount of regret in his eyes. "Yes."

"You would really give this entire charade up? You've only known me for one day. Do you really believe you're thinking with your mind at this moment?" She couldn't believe she was trying to talk him out of it. She had his heart in her hands, and she was pushing it back at him.

He stepped back and walked away with his hands balled into fists. Malkia remained next to the tree, afraid of what might happen. She recognized kindness in him, and wondered if he really wanted to return there, before all this madness had started.

Frustration crinkled his eyes when he finally turned back around. He strode back toward her and grabbed her hand again. "Do you want the tent or not?"

"I-I don't know," she said, stammering. "Can I bring Astrid with me? Can the children all have beds too?"

"Yes, you can bring Astrid. No, the children cannot have beds tonight. But maybe another night. Maybe things can change around here. Will you let me spend some time with you tonight in your tent, before Astrid joins you?"

Malkia took a step backward and tried to pull away from him, but he held on tight. "Um—I guess. I'm not sure what you want from me. You can't just leave your wife. You should work things out with her."

He dropped her hands and threw his arms in the air, shaking his head. "Malkia, please stop right there. You don't know what you're talking about. She doesn't want to work anything out. She despises me and wishes she had died with our kids. We thrive off each other's hate for one other and for everyone else."

He yanked her forward. They strolled toward the middle of the campsite until they neared his tent. To one side, they had set another tent up, and he motioned for her to go inside.

A large bed on the far end of the tent was the first thing that caught her eye. On the other side, a water basin stood and Malkia could see the steam rising from the hot water. There were clothes hanging near the bed and a towel laid out by the basin, with a rug leading from the basin to the bed.

The Leader placed his hand on her shoulder. "Would you like to have lunch brought to you, or would you rather eat with Astrid and the other women?"

"If I ate with Astrid, do I have to stay and do chores, or can I come back to the tent?"

"I told everyone you are not to do any chores until your wounds have healed, including your bruising. I want you to rest. If you choose to eat with the women, please let me know when you finish, and I'll escort you back here."

Malkia stepped closer to the basin and closed her eyes as the steam glided across her cheeks. "Can Astrid come here and eat with me?"

He nodded. "Absolutely, I will go fetch her myself and bring your lunch as well."

He was almost at the tent door when the words burst from her lips. "I don't even know your name."

He glanced back at her. "Only my first wife and the few of us left from our town know my name. I'm 'The Leader,' and that's it."

He started to leave, but stopped. He looked back at her again and smiled. "You're enchanting, Malkia. I could stay with you forever. Since I've met you, there's a calm in my soul that I have not felt for years. If you really want to know my name, I'll tell you. If you really want to know the real me, I will show you."

Malkia nodded and smiled shyly at him, playing his game. "I want to know your name, and I would love to know the real you." A part of her was not lying. Having him near her was intoxicating.

He was by her side before she had a moment to breathe, and he tugged her into his arms. As she bit down on her bottom lip, he dipped his head closer and sealed his mouth over hers. She did not resist, and a wave of electricity jolted through her veins, melting her effortlessly into his body. His tongue parted her lips, and his kiss demanded more. She drank in his scent and bathed in the euphoria of his touch, forgetting the world and all the chaos that surrounded her.

When she finally broke away, she felt his smile against her cheek, and it warmed every inch of her body.

He whispered into her ear, "Damon. My name is Damon."

TEN

A Love Triangle

DAMON HAD NOT been gone long when Malkia heard Misty's soft cry in her head. The word "help" reverberated through her skull, along with Misty's sobbing.

Misty, I hear you, Malkia replied in her head.

Help me! Misty cried in return. *They want to take me away from my mom. They want to use me to find others like ourselves, and they are threatening my mom's life to get me to do it.*

Who's they? Malkia's clenched the edge of the water basin, wanting nothing more than to climb inside.

The bad people I told you about. The wolf-men have been threatening my mom all morning, and they just left. They forgot to drug me again, but they will be back soon. They always come back.

Malkia sighed and wrung her hands together as she paced the floor, turning her back on the steamy hot water that would soothe her aching muscles. *Listen to me. I'll find a way out of here. Go along with what they ask, but lie for as long as you dare. I'm the only one near enough to be heard, so as long as you don't tell them about me, you won't have to lie about anything else. I'll break out of here as soon as I can and then I'll come for you. Do you hear me?*

Misty's sobs grew louder, even in her thoughts. Malkia was afraid they would hear her and come back and drug her before Malkia found out where she was located. *Misty, you must calm down. I will find you. Please listen to me.*

I am, Misty replied, her sobs quieting.

Okay, now I need you to tell me where you are.

I'm in a cage.

Malkia had only seen the cages nearby her own that were filled with women and children. *Are you alone in the cage?*

No, my mom is here, but that's it. They won't allow me near anyone else.

Have you noticed any objects that stick out around your cage? Trees, tents, other cages… anything that will help me find you?

No, they rarely let me out, and we just arrived. I can't—wait! Misty paused for a moment. *There was a tree stump a few feet away from our cage. I saw it when they brought us lunch today. It's really close to the cage. One guard had his foot on top of it while he was sharpening his knife.*

That's great, Misty. I'll start searching for you. I don't know when I'll be outside next, but that will give me something to look for. Pretend to work with them for as long as you can. I promise I'll find you.

Okay, I will do—Oh no! They're back. Please no—

Her words cut off into silence. An overwhelming swell of grief filled Malkia's chest. These people were barbarians. She could not understand why they would use and hurt a child to gain power over other people. Her heart ached as she thought of Misty being alone and terrified, and Malkia tilted her head to the ceiling to plead to the Alethiean's for help.

"She is just a child," Malkia whispered to the Light Beings. "Save her, please."

She sank onto the bed and was just about to recline onto the pillows when Damon waltzed back inside. He noticed her on the bed and a grin broke out across his face. Astrid walked in behind him and threw her a puzzled look. Malkia shrugged and glanced back at Damon, who was setting her lunch on the small table in the corner.

"Eat well, Malkia. I need you to heal quickly," Damon said, his eyes swimming with admiration.

Malkia felt a similar pull. She clenched her fist and shoved away the ridiculous feelings for this barbaric man. What in Theia was happening to her? "I will. When will you be back?"

"After lunch is over. I have to attend to a few chores, but when I return, I'll need to speak with you about some issues. Astrid, make sure you take care of the dishes and then come find me. I'll be over near the cage on the south end of the camp."

He didn't wait for a response from Astrid, throwing one last look at Malkia and then ducking out of the tent.

Malkia focused on Astrid as soon as he left, and she smiled. "Well, we might as well take advantage of this. Who knows how long he will give us a tent?"

Astrid's lips puckered. "Let's eat. And then I want to hear details." She pulled out her chair and sat without taking her eyes off Malkia.

Malkia sighed as she eased herself off the bed, knowing this entire meal was going to be an interrogation. *I might as well get it over with*, Malkia thought as she plopped onto the other chair. She smiled half-heartedly at Astrid and ate as she waited for the never-ending questions coming her way.

Malkia jolted awake. It was still dark outside, but daylight had to be near. A dull light was outside her tent, but she didn't know if it was the early signs of dawn or one of the lit torches.

She missed Dario so much, her heart ached. Every moment they were apart, a tiny part of her heart shattered. But then there was Damon. He had taken her breath away the night before, and just the thought of his touch made her pulse quicken.

Why was this horrible man causing her to tremble with desire? Why was she even considering doing what he wanted? He had told her last night that he would discontinue his pursuit and leave all his wives if Malkia agreed to stay with him. They had talked about his life before his children died and then about life before the wars. He had hated the sky people from the beginning and knew they were only bringing greed and hatred to their moon.

His last kiss had confused her and left her in disarray until she fell asleep.

She hadn't spoken to Astrid about it, but the woman knew something was amiss. She continued to press for answers, especially for the reason Malkia had received a tent when Astrid slept on the floor in a cage. Malkia had told Astrid the tent was for her as well, and since Malkia had been helpful to the leader that day, she was being rewarded. Her success was Astrid's success.

Only that had been enough to suffice her curiosity.

Malkia stared at the ceiling of the tent and watched as the light swept across the fabric. The suns were rising, and she suspected Damon would be in to see her soon. She reached toward Astrid and gently shook her.

Astrid eyelids fluttered, and she stretched, then smiled at Malkia. "I haven't slept that well in years," she whispered, her grin spreading across her face.

"It was a good night's sleep. I hope The Leader will continue to let us stay in here."

Astrid smirked and shook her head. "I doubt it. Unless you have more useful information for him, I guarantee this is a onetime opportunity. Of course, if you agree to marry him, you'll have your moments in his bed."

Malkia's jaw clenched. It terrified her to think this savage was edging his way into her heart.

She rose from the bed and dressed for the day, pulling on the clean shirt Damon had given her. Sweeping the brush through her long hair, she eased it into a bun at the back of her head. She did not know what she would do today, but if she was going to be working, she wanted her hair out of her face.

It wasn't long before she heard voices approaching her tent. Astrid brought her finger to her lips and Malkia nodded.

"I'm not making it easy for her. I want her to heal, so she will be useful to me. She is keeping secrets, and if I can get into her head, she will be easier to manipulate into divulging them." Damon's voice was nearly a whisper, but it carried easily into the tent.

Malkia shot Astrid a surprised glance, when a woman's voice responded. "You are a disgusting pig. Everyone knows you are just looking for someone else to marry. You don't deserve to be happy. And we both know she will not please you any more than the others."

The woman was the same one who had pulled Malkia's hair in Damon's tent. The contempt in her voice was clear. She really despised Damon, and from what Malkia had heard, it was for good reason. Why does he not let her go?

Damon chuckled. "Always the cynic, Genevieve. If Malkia will have me, I will allow you to leave, so consider that route before you discourage this union." He laughed louder. "Don't look so hopeful. Not yet. I don't have time for your nagging. Go attend to your duties and leave me alone."

Malkia's pulse quickened. She picked up the brush and ran it through Astrid's hair.

"Malkia, may I enter?" Damon asked, after several tense breaths.

"Yes, of course."

Damon stormed in, his jaw clenched, and brow furrowed, but as soon as he laid eyes on Malkia, his expression softened. A smile twitched on the edges of his lips. He glanced in Astrid's direction and motioned for her to leave.

As Astrid walked toward the door, Damon grabbed her forearm. "Please deliver breakfast for Malkia and me. We will work together today, and I don't want her distracted."

Astrid nodded at Damon and continued toward the door. Before she ducked through the doorway, she glanced back at Malkia with her lips pressed into a thin line. Malkia shrugged and turned her attention to Damon.

Damon ignored the strange exchange between the two women. He watched Malkia intently. His eyes danced with amusement as his gaze strayed down her body. She stepped backward and crossed her arms over her chest, uncomfortable from the way he examined her.

He blinked at her sudden movement, and his gaze snapped back to her face. Smiling at her again, he closed the gap between them and pulled her against his body. He pressed his soft lips against hers and parted her mouth with his tongue. Every muscle in her body tensed. This was not right. She pressed her hands against his body, but he held her tightly, never breaking the seal of their lips.

She sighed into his embrace. Why was she so weak? His affection exhilarated her and as much as she did not want to admit it out loud, her heart wanted him.

When he pulled away, Malkia's head swam with confusion. *What is it about him that makes me feel this way?*

Adoration pulsed in his eyes, and it was difficult to ignore the wanting look in them. She leaned into him and pressed her lips against his, refusing to think of anything but the heated energy mounting between them. He wrapped her in his arms and instinctively she wrapped her legs around his waist, kissing him with a fervent desire she had never known before now.

It was a few moments before her mind whirled back to reality. She unwrapped her legs and dropped to the ground, then turned away from him to hide the tears in her eyes.

"What's wrong?" Damon asked, snaking his arms around her from the back and squeezing her tightly.

She twisted around and pressed her face into his chest, gulping back a sob rising in her throat. She didn't know what she was doing. In one day, this man had shaken up her focus, while Dario was dead or looking for a way to save her. Why was she having these feelings for a man who was the reason for uprooting her life? He was a savage. A man hungry for power over her and her people.

A horrible ache throbbed in her heart, and she knew she had to escape as soon as possible. She pressed at her eyes, then slipped away from Damon, snatching a towel from the basin. She wiped her face and regained her composure.

"Damon, this cannot happen," she whispered, wringing the towel in her hands. "So much has happened in the last few days, and I do not trust my judgment right now. When you are near, my heart yearns for you and *that* is alarming. You are not a good person. You might have been at one time, but you're not anymore. I hate saying that out loud because I am afraid you will despise me, but the thought of you butchering others makes me sick to my stomach. I will never willingly be a part of that life."

Damon stared at her for a long time. He didn't appear angry, but his contentment had dissipated. Malkia was afraid he would take her away and lock her back in the cage, and she needed to be free and have his trust in order to escape. She should have played along, allowing him to have his way with her.

Astrid opened the tent door and entered with breakfast. Her eyes narrowed at their guarded stances, and Damon shook his head from the interruption but waited patiently as Astrid set their food and drinks down on the small table. She left without another glance their way.

Malkia sat on the little stool next to the table and ate, hoping Damon would either join and be happy again or leave.

He stood by the table for a few moments before sitting on the other stool. He watched her for several uncomfortable bites before finally eating his own food.

The food was delicious, and Malkia could not help but eat quickly. There were eggs, bread, and five strips of meat. She ate every single bite and gulped down the fresh pulpy juice. It tasted amazing, and she wanted to lick her fingers when she finished, but she refrained after realizing Damon was staring at her. She nibbled on her bottom lip and stood without a word.

He rose as well and grabbed her hand, tugging her toward the bed. At the bed's edge, he bent down and kissed her on the forehead, his lips lingering for a few breaths before he broke away. Malkia didn't know what that meant, but she feared it was her end. Instead, he picked her up and set her on the bed.

His fingers grazed across her face, running them over her cheeks and chin. "I want you to rest today. I will return throughout the day to check on you." He paused with a small grin, then kissed her hand. "Your hesitancy is noble, but unneeded. I know how I feel about you. You are in my every thought, and I cannot think of life without you. I'll prove it to you. When you fully recover, you will be free to leave, along with everyone else." His gaze dropped to the floor, and his brow furrowed. "There is blood on my hands, but none that was done by me, only those who follow me. Until I met you, my life seemed pointless, and I loathed every moment. If you will have me, I'll change."

Malkia eyed him, unsure how to respond. She needed his trust more than ever. "Can we please move slower?" she asked. "I need some time to wrap my mind around all of this. I have friends that might be waiting to rescue me, and I need to tell them to leave. Regardless, if you trust me or not, I won't be able to be by your side until I know they are safely away from this group."

A crimson flush rose in his cheeks, but when he spoke, his voice was calm. "Rest, Malkia. We can talk about all of this later when you have had time to heal." With that, he ducked through the tent opening and closed it afterward.

Fear bit at her heart. She had pressed it too far by talking about her friends. If Dario was alive, she had placed him in more danger. Cradling her head in her hands, her body shook as she wept. Now that Damon was gone, her heart ached for Dario, and she did not know how much longer she could play this charade. If Damon ever discovered she was in love with someone else, he might execute her or, even worse, track down Dario and end his life.

She fell back against the cushions, and she wrapped her arms around a feathered pillow.

Her worry turned to Mataya. How could Malkia protect the ones she loved the most, when Damon wanted her all to himself? The thought of him harming her sister or anyone else weighed heavily on her heart. Escaping was her only option.

She cried for a long time before her sore body settled down, and her mind drifted into slumber.

ELEVEN

War and Love

MALKIA DIDN'T HEAR Damon enter the tent, but when she woke, he was settled on the bed next to her. He stared unseeingly with a frown on his face, appearing lost and helpless. Malkia believed he really cared for her, and she wondered if he could ever change for the better or if his euphoric feeling would disappear after he had her around for a while. She feared his infatuation with her would be short-lived, and it made her desire to escape more intense.

Malkia sat up slowly, and Damon's focus turned to her. "How are you feeling? You nearly slept the day away."

"Really? It feels like I only slept a few minutes." She stretched and yawned. "But I feel a little better."

"You slept through lunch. I've been in and out a few times, and you didn't budge. It's nearing dinner. Will you accompany me on a walk? I have been doing a lot of thinking about what you said earlier, and I would like to talk with you further."

She nodded and slid out of the bed, and together they strolled outside.

Malkia tilted her face to the sky and closed her eyes. She loved to feel the suns' rays on her skin, and it reminded her of her final decision.

She grounded herself mentally for the upcoming discussion. His infatuation with her was disturbing and now that she had rested, her mind was clear. Dario was her choice.

After a few deep inhales, she opened her eyes and looked at Damon. "Now, I'm ready for that walk."

Damon gripped her hand and walked toward the east side of the campsite. They strode in silence, and Malkia kept her eyes out for Misty's cage. Not too long into the walk, she noticed a tree stump with a tent nearby. Although they were too far to see details, there appeared to be a metal cage peeking out from the bottom of the tent. That had to be Misty's prison.

She hoped Damon would head toward it, but he paused mid-step and turned north. Malkia sighed as they grew farther away. She snuck a glance back at the tent and made a mental note of its location.

As they strolled in silence, she noticed a group of men lounging around to the west of them. Their laughter and bantering permeated the air, catching Damon's attention as well. Without warning, one of them jumped up and punched the man directly across from him. The collision knocked him to the ground, and he roared with anger when he jumped to his feet and grabbed his sword.

"Really, Boomer? You want to brawl over—"

Boomer didn't let him finish. He swung his sword and nearly swiped the other man's face. Malkia glanced at Damon. His jaw clenched tightly, and an angry glare deepened the lines around his eyes, but he remained still. If someone did not intervene, one of those men would perish.

"Aren't you going to stop it?" Malkia asked, brushing her hand along his forearm.

His face muscles relaxed. "No," Damon replied with a deadpan expression.

It seemed like time stood still as the two men fought, but moments later, the man who had been hit swung his sword and struck Boomer in the head. He dropped to his knees while blood gushed from his wound. His eyes were gleaning with surprise and regret as the final blow came from behind and removed his head from the rest of his body.

Malkia gasped, hiding her face in her hands as Damon cheered with vigor. "Bravo, Turtle, your reflexes are improving more and more every day," he bellowed from the sidelines, loudly clapping his hands.

The group of men jumped to attention when they realized the leader had witnessed the fight. They rushed to clean up the blood and mess, apparently afraid of what his next reaction would be.

Damon sauntered toward the group with a grin on his face. "I admit, I would prefer you keep the massacres outside of this group, but he attacked you first, and it's magnificent to see you have improved tremendously on your sword fighting. Congratulations on the win, my friend."

When Damon reached Turtle, he slapped him on the back and curled his arm around his shoulder. He whispered something in his ear, and Turtle's concerned look turned into an ear-to-ear grin.

"Yes, sir," Turtle said, his eyes lighting up.

The men grabbed the body and the head and dragged them into the woods. Malkia lost sight of them when they entered the trees. She turned away and glanced back at the tent and the tree stub. She was going to escape this madness—and take Misty with her.

Damon returned to her side at that moment and clutched her hand. He walked north again, as if nothing had happened.

Malkia could not understand the change in his attitude. One minute he was loving her and saying he would change, and the next he was condoning the murder of one of his soldiers.

As they neared the forest, Damon halted and stared at Malkia. "I want you to marry me."

She attempted to keep a straight face, but she knew her expression gave away her surprise. She was astonished. He was moving too fast and hadn't even considered her request.

"I know you want to move slowly, but I've been thinking about this all day, and I know what I want. I have never felt so intrigued by a woman before, and I desire to be with you in every way possible. Marriage is unnecessary if you would just be with me." He paused, looking at her as if he expected her to answer his statement.

Malkia stared back at him with astonishment. "Wait. What? Did you hear anything I said earlier?"

"Don't answer just yet," he replied with a shrug of his shoulders. "Let me tell you my plans for our nuptials."

"No!" Malkia hollered. "Stop it, Damon. This is not fair. I cannot be with a man who allows that kind of brutality in his life." She waved her arm erratically toward Turtle and the decapitated Boomer.

Damon's eyes twinkled with delight. "I respect you and your need for marriage. We will seal the deal tomorrow." He nodded, as if she had already agreed. "There's no need to dally. I know what I desire, and *you* are it. My other wives are free to go once our union is complete. But I have changed my mind about leaving this group. These people are my family, and I won't throw away everything I have worked for. You can understand that."

Malkia was speechless. He had decided her life without even considering her feelings. "Do I have a say in this marriage?"

He continued as if she had said nothing. "Astrid will pamper you tonight. I have ordered some of the other women to stitch together a beautiful dress for you to wear, and they will bring it to you this evening. You and Astrid may stay in the tent again tonight and use it to prepare for the wedding. Then late morning we will wed."

He grabbed her hand again, his smile stretching across his face as he dragged her beside him. When they returned to her tent, Damon towed her inside. He stood still for a moment, then moved closer and kissed her hard on the lips.

Malkia grimaced. She stood as still as a statue while he kissed her. He leaned back and looked quizzically at her before gathering her into his arms and pressing his lips more forcefully against hers.

She shoved him away and backed toward the bed. "Why me?"

"You know why. I adore you. I have never met anyone as stunning and resilient as you." He paused for a moment, and when he spoke again, his voice darkened significantly. "I also know you are the leader of the group who escaped, and I am aware that the story you offered me when we first met, about the disappearing man, is false. You lied about the death of your family and friends, and I now know the larger part of your group is traveling east. The rest of your group has gone to meet with them, and your friends who remained have been circling this area since we captured you. You have a woman who can see through the sight of hawks, and you are conspiring with the pixies. Hm… Have

I left anything out?"

Malkia stared wide-eyed at him, trying to ignore the terror biting at her heart. "What are you talking about?"

He grabbed her around the waist and pressed her against the bed. "Don't lie to me again, Malkia. Was anything you told me the truth?"

"Yes-s-s-s," she stammered, her eyes wide and her breath coming in short. "Yes, there was a lot of truth. What do you want from me?"

"I want you. I want you tonight, but I respect you." He swept her hair out of her face and caressed her cheek with the palm of his hand. "I won't disrespect your choice to wait, but am claiming you, and if marrying you is how I will own you, then tomorrow we will become espoused. After we have consummated our marriage, we will gather our group and head east toward your people. Don't you want to tell your sweet sister the joyous news?"

Malkia squirmed against his hold, rage rising violently in her chest. "Who told you I have a sister?"

"It's amazing what a person can learn from someone who is deathly afraid of their life. Your friend eagerly divulged your secrets once we began cutting off parts of his body." Damon whistled, and a few moments later, Malkia heard rustling outside the tent.

They pushed the flap open, and one of the wolf-men barged in, dragging another man beside him. The wolf-man tossed the man to the floor, and he crumbled like a lame horse. Every muscle in Malkia's body tensed as a bloody Alex turned his face toward her.

TWELVE
Jailed Love

MALKIA RUSHED TO Alex and knelt on the floor in front of him. His face was swollen and bloody, with fresh bruises peppering his exposed flesh alongside several deep lacerations.

"What have they done to you?" Malkia cried.

"I'm so sorry, Malkia. They were going to take my entire hand and then they told me they would take one limb after another until I told them everything," Alex whimpered, tears brimming in his eyes.

He raised his hand, and Malkia saw he was missing three fingers. Only his thumb and pointer finger remained. Malkia glowered at Damon, with frigid hatred running through her veins. Damon's face showed no emotion, so she focused back on Alex and began wiping his face with the blanket that had fallen on the floor. Damon snatched the blanket, motioning for his wolf-man to take Alex away.

"No!" Malkia yelled. "Let him stay here with me. Please! He needs his wounds mended."

"One of the other women will tend to him. I don't want him with you. Who knows what other lies you two will devise? As well, I don't need you planning an escape plan. You are stuck with me, Malkia." He turned back toward the men. "Remove him, Barster."

Malkia eyed Alex. "Stay strong. I'll see you soon."

"Don't count on it," Damon muttered quietly.

After Barster took Alex away, Damon grabbed Malkia and sat her back on the bed. "I'm not going to even ask you why you lied to me. I know why. You think we would have slaughtered all your family and friends. And you know what, we probably would have executed some, but it would have been far less painful for everyone if you had just remained in your town. Now we have had to travel—quickly, might I add—to catch up. I discovered you covered your people's tracks, so now we must backtrack to find your group. It's a massive headache for me, but a necessary one. I would not be a gentleman if I did not include your family and friends in our big celebration."

"I don't want to marry you!" she screamed, her hands balling into fists and tears shining in her eyes.

He smiled. "You will change your mind. You know you have feelings for me. I saw it in your eyes, and I felt it in your kiss. You can't deny it."

"That's when I thought you had a chance to be a decent man!" She hollered at him as flames of anger shot through her. "Now I know you are just a barbaric savage who only cares about controlling others. You could not care less about me or my feelings. I'm just a possession to you, another shiny trophy for you to display. Are you going to shove me in a cage like you did to your other wives?"

Damon laughed. "You do not seem to understand, Malkia. I'm being generous by allowing you to live, let alone making you my wife. My people want to hunt your group down tonight and slaughter them all. I am the one restraining them. They understand, just by looking at you, why I want to marry you, but they are still hungry for blood, and after you deceived them, they would be delighted with yours."

Malkia's jaw clenched as she shoved Damon's hands away from her. "What? Was I supposed to come in here, after being torn away from my friends, and freely disclose the information you demanded?" Her pulse hammered in her neck as fury thundered within her. "Was I supposed to betray my family and friends so your tyrants would be pleased? You are right; I am their leader, and the last thing I would ever do is hand them over to you. As for my blood, they can have it. As long as they leave everyone else alone."

"They are not getting your blood," he said, a grin twitching on the edges of his lips. "You belong to me." He raised his hand in front of his face, his finger pointed to the ceiling." But I will give them the satisfaction of tracking down your group and taking the blood they want. I'm sure one of my men would love their hands all over your sister, especially if she is as delicious looking as yourself."

Malkia's entire body stiffened. "If anyone gets near my sister, I will rip their face off their body with my bare hands," she hissed, fear splintering her heart. "You will never hurt her or anyone else I love."

"We will see. As for the cages, I don't think there will be a need for you to stay in one unless you decide to cause problems. I still plan on setting my other wives free from our marriages. You are all I desire. They mean nothing to me. They never have—well, except for my first wife. Once upon a time, I believe we were—" He paused, staring off to the side, and shook his head. "It doesn't matter. The point is, you'll be my one and only wife, and you will house in my tent with me. Once we seize your group and I'm satisfied with our numbers, we will find a place to settle."

She glared at him with silent contempt.

He shrugged and leaned in closer. "You will learn to love me. It will take time, but I know it will happen. You are now a part of this family, and I want you to start acting like it."

"That will not happen," she muttered quietly.

Damon stepped toward the entryway. "I will pick up your dinner and send Astrid in to help you prepare for tomorrow. Make sure you receive plenty of sleep. There are guards posted at your tent to keep you safe, so don't even think about escaping. They are fast and mean. I wouldn't want to be caught in their teeth." He glanced at her one more time, and Malkia noticed a hint of sadness in his eyes.

She jumped off the bed, rushed toward him, and clutched his hands. "*Please,* Damon. I'll stay with you. I will love you forever if you just leave my friends and family alone. Please understand why I want to protect them. I would rather never see them again than have them hurt or killed. Please!"

Damon gazed down at her with the same tenderness from earlier. "It's too late, Malkia. If you had just been up front with me from the beginning, maybe I could save your friends, but now it's too late. I wish you would just be happy with me, no matter what. I know some day you will learn. You have to."

He frowned as he turned away from her and left without another word. Fear clawed through her gut as she stared desperately at the empty space in front of her. Sinking to her knees, she covered her face with her hands, her sobs shaking her entire body.

When her cries subsided, she climbed to her feet and walked the perimeter of the tent, searching for an escape route. With the flooring attached to the fabric walls, there was no way out other than the one entryway. She would have to cut a hole, but all she had was the bedding and furniture. Even if she broke a stool, she could not sharpen it enough to cut through the thick material.

She whirled around to rustling behind her.

Astrid stood by the table, staring at Malkia. "You should have just told him. He's going to destroy your family and friends."

Malkia shook her head. "I will stop him."

"No, you won't," Astrid said, stepping toward her. "He wants to tear you down, so you'll have no choice but to cling to him. He wants you. The buzz around the campsite is that once you have married, we will travel toward your group, and when we reach them, he ordered his warriors to terminate them all, women and children included. He wants to break you."

Malkia hung her head in defeat. "Astrid, what should I do?" A weight settled heavily on her heart. "I have to warn my group. I would die if anything happened to them."

Astrid glanced over her shoulder and motioned for Malkia to come closer. Then she whispered, "You have to escape tonight. You must do it as soon as the leader leaves. He won't return after that, and I can make it appear like you are in bed when his guard checks on you during the night."

"He will kill you." Malkia shivered at the thought of Damon's wrath.

"Not if you drug me. Once he leaves, I'll drink some water with some lakseed in it." She opened her jacket and pulled out a bag of herbs. "It won't take long for it to knock me out, so we will have to be quick. I'll show you how to escape the tent and find your friend they have captive. Luckily, he is in a tent instead of a cage, but he's tied up and guarded. Before you leave, we will create a body with pillows and then you will tuck me in and leave the cup on the table, with the residue of the lakseed." She grasped Malkia's wrist and pulled her even closer. Their foreheads nearly touched. "If I do this for you, promise me you will return for my mother. Promise you will save her from that disgusting pig who beats her every day."

Until this moment, Malkia had questioned Astrid's reasoning for helping her. Family was a convincing motivator.

"I promise. How will I know your mother?"

"She has a bright yellow scarf that her husband keeps tied around her neck. You can't miss her." Astrid's fingers tightened around Malkia's arm. "No matter what happens to me, promise you will save her and keep her safe."

"Yes, I promise. Absolutely. As soon as I can, she will be the first person we rescue."

With a curt nod, Astrid released Malkia's arm and stepped backward to give her space.

If they caught them, Damon would strangle them both. However, if she escaped, it was possible her people would have a fighting chance. With only three day's head start, it was imperative she reach them quickly to give them time to prepare.

"How do I slip away from the tent without the guards seeing me?" she asked, licking her chapped lips.

Astrid glanced at the entryway again, then slipped behind the bed, near the far wall. She pointed at the ground. "Here," she whispered. "I cut a hole in it while you were sleeping earlier. It's the only place in the tent where no one can see, and it's one of the few places blocked by a tree on the other side. You will have a tight fit squeezing by the tree, but you are thin enough, so if I can do it, you can. Once you leave, you will need to go north, past the leader's tent and five other smaller tents. Your friend's being held in a tent placed off in the distance from the last tent with a guard or two keeping watch in front."

"Two men are not a problem. Unless they are the wolf-men?" Malkia asked.

"No, he wouldn't put them there. They have been sniffing out your friends, and now a couple of them headed east, to see if they can catch up with your group. It's why you must leave tonight. Your group won't stand a chance." Astrid slinked back past the bed, then pointed at Malkia's dinner. "The leader is eating and will return soon. I'm going to go have my dinner and will come back to prepare you for the wedding tomorrow. Eat and follow my instructions exactly. I can only be your eyes and ears if I know you will listen to me."

"Astrid, thank you!" Malkia threw her arms around the woman's shoulders and squeezed her tightly.

Astrid stiffened from the embrace. "This wasn't out of the kindness of my heart. I need my mother to be safe."

Malkia stepped backward, patting herself on the chest. "I promise I will do whatever is needed to free her." It was now or never to find out more about Misty. "One question. Can you tell me if a girl named Misty is in this group?"

Astrid's eyes narrowed. "Where did you hear that name?"

"I heard some men talking about her the first day I was here. They said something about her being able to read minds or something like that. Is that really possible?"

Astrid chuckled, and her expression relaxed. "No, she can't read minds. I think there are a couple of people who believe that, but she can only read the minds of other people with telepathy. She told The Leader she heard someone a long time ago, but nothing since."

"Where is she?"

"To tell you the truth, I don't know. They move her around. The Leader doesn't want her found because he thinks when the time comes, she will be useful to him. For now, he drugs her, so she can't call for help, and locks her away with her mother." Astrid shook her head, moving toward the door. "Anyway, I have to leave. He will be here soon."

Astrid left, and as Malkia sat to eat, Damon sauntered back inside. He sank onto the stool across from her. "You haven't eaten."

"I haven't felt well." Malkia pushed her food around with her fingers, avoiding his stare.

"Do you want me to leave while you eat, or can I stay here and talk to you?"

"You can stay."

She nibbled on the cold ham and rice. It was hard to eat rice without a fork, but she was able to scoop it onto the ham and eat them together. As she ate, she felt Damon's eyes burning into her, but she refused to look at him. He had a hold on her that scared her and if she allowed him in again; she was afraid his spell on her heart would reactivate.

She continued to eat with her head bowed. When she was done, she rose and washed her hands in the cold water of the basin, keeping her back turned toward him. As she dried her hands, Damon reached around her waist and pulled her into him. He put his face down next to hers and kissed her neck.

"I can make you happy. Just give me a chance."

She choked back the harsh words she really wanted to say. When he talked to her like that, her heart melted. Why was she so weak? It made absolutely no sense, and she had to protect her people, even if it meant destroying this man's soul more than it already was.

"I don't have a choice. You are forcing me to give you a chance whether or not I want to."

Damon's breath quickened, and then he sighed in her ear. "Because I know you will be happy. I can protect you, and I can make your life easier." He stepped away from her. His fingers trailed over her upper back, tracing one of her scars from the day her family died. "What happened?"

Malkia pulled away, and she glanced his direction but did not look at his eyes. "Do you really care?"

He nodded, his brows furrowing into a scowl. "I do care. Please tell me."

Malkia's chin quivered. She turned away from him again to hide her emotions. "It was the worst day of my life, the nightmare of a day I can never forget." A tear slid down her cheek and she wiped at her eyes, then closed them. "It was the day my family was killed, and I survived against all odds." She white-knuckled the edge of the washbasin, and she opened her eyes to stare at the water. "An explosion demolished my house. My parents, husband, and baby girl died from the impact. I was thrown onto my sister and protected her from the blast, so you would have thought I would have died too, but I didn't. I woke up to this." She reached back and patted her scars. "It was the worst day of my life. Nothing you do can cause me more agony than that day."

She pushed past Damon and climbed onto the bed.

He stayed right behind her, and when she settled, he twisted her to face him. "Look at me."

She squirmed away from his grasp, but he was too quick. His grip tightened around her arms, and he pulled her close to him.

"I don't want to cause you pain. That's why I want you to be with me. Everything I do will be so you can remain with me forever and not have to worry about your family and friends. I have never felt this strongly about anyone in my life. Even when I should be furious with you, I can't. I want you to love me, just like I love you."

Malkia didn't respond.

"Please, Malkia. We will be good together." The desperation in his voice seemed genuine and a spark of hope lit up in Malkia's chest.

She leaned backward and took the risk of meeting his gaze. "Only if you protect my sister and people. Then I will be happy and promise to stay with you forever. Just leave my loved ones alone. That's all I ask."

His lips pursed in thought. "I'll do my best to keep them safe. No promises. If tomorrow goes well, I can then make a better decision." He turned toward the entryway, but then looked over his shoulder at her. "I will return before dusk to say goodnight."

Silence filled the tent after he left. Malkia fell backward against the cushions, eager for nightfall to arrive. She stared at the seam of the roof of her tent and tried to push away the trepidation churning in her gut. Her eyelids grew heavy as she imagined her escape going flawlessly. It had to work.

She closed her eyes and drifted into a fitful slumber.

THIRTEEN

Escape from the Savages

A RAINBOW OF colors swirled above Malkia as she strolled through a meadow of wildflowers. The anxiety she had been feeling for the past few days settled into a relaxing peace, and she marveled at the sudden change of scenery. Where were Damon and his followers?

Her fingers skimmed over the tops of the blossoms, and she spun around in a circle, laughing when a flock of birds rose in unison into the sky. If only Dario were here with her.

Out of nowhere, a torrent of black clouds swirled above her, and a flash of lightning struck a nearby brush. Drops of rain poured ferociously from the shadows above.

Using her jacket as cover, Malkia sprinted toward the tree line in search of shelter. It was useless. Her hair flattened against her face and it drenched her clothes within seconds. The water spilled endlessly down her cheeks and made it difficult to gain her bearings.

Frustration swirled at the edges of her mind as the safety of the trees grew farther away. She skidded to a halt, and the rain stopped. The umbrella of tree branches was as far away now as it had been when the rain had begun. She wiped her face and turned back to face the meadow.

She jumped in fright when the forest vegetation greeted her, instead of the floral shrubbery.

This isn't real. Am I dreaming?

Someone yelled, and she whirled in a circle, searching her surroundings. Through the brush, a figure sprinted toward her and when he grew closer, she realized it was Dario. He ran past her as if he could not see her, staring wide-eyed at something beyond her.

"Dario!" she yelled.

She turned to watch his receding back. That's when she noticed the two-headed dragon standing in his way. He gripped a large dagger in his right hand and he raised it between him and the beast. Malkia's breath stuttered in her throat, and she gulped to scream again at him, but a flood of feathers suddenly surrounded her, drifting like snow from the sky. Her gaze darted upward, and a familiar, bright light filled the space between the branches, illuminating the white feathers. She froze and could do nothing but watch the love of her life race toward danger.

He sped up and closed in on the dragon. It drew in a long breath and leaned forward, exhaling a funnel of fire toward Dario. The flames consumed everything in its path.

"No!" Malkia screamed, sitting up in bed.

It was darker outside, and she noticed candles had been lit in her tent.

Astrid hurried toward her from the basin, looking startled. "What's wrong?"

Malkia glanced at Astrid, with her pulse racing. She was still in the tent, and Dario wasn't being cooked by a dragon. Malkia let out a sigh of relief and fell back onto the cushions.

She pressed her palms into her chest to calm her heart. "I just had a bad dream. How late is it? Has he been back in to check on me?"

"No, not that late, but he will probably be in to check on you soon. You should wash and put on the nightgown he had cleaned for you. The dress you are to wear tomorrow is hanging there." Astrid pointed toward the table.

A long red dress hung from one of the tent's beams. Malkia stepped closer, grazing her fingers down the soft fabric. It was a strapless, snug-fitting corset up top and flowed like waves to the floor. The ties in the back ran from the backside all the way to the top. As beautiful as it was, it did not matter. She would not try it on since she wouldn't be there in the morning.

Malkia dropped the edges of the fabric and turned toward Astrid. "Did you bring everything needed for tonight?"

Astrid's gaze flashed toward the tent door and then back at Malkia. "Yes, everything is ready. Let's wash you and prepare for bed. The leader wants me to examine your bruises and make sure they are healing."

Malkia undressed and Astrid's fingers touched the bruise on her upper back. "The dress won't hide this."

"Good thing the dress won't be worn," Malkia replied with a sideways glance over her shoulder, then she climbed over the edge of the basin.

The steam from the water washed across Malkia's body as she eased herself down into the basin. She submerged her head and waited for her hair to follow. When she came up for air, Astrid handed her a piece of soap, then busied herself with tidying the nearly empty room.

Malkia still did not trust the woman, but her escape plan was all she had to hold on to hope.

The rest of her bath was uninterrupted and after she dressed in the silk nightgown Damon had picked for her, the two sat on the bed and combed one another's hair.

"Coming in," Damon said on the other side of the entryway.

Before Malkia or Astrid could respond, the flap was pushed to the side, and Damon entered. "Sleep well, Malkia. I will see you in the morning."

She glared at him. "Okay."

Damon stood quietly, as if he was waiting for something more. After several awkward moments, he shrugged and ducked out the way he had come.

Malkia and Astrid sprang into action. They blew out the candles, then packed the bed with Malkia's pillows, creating an illusion of a sleeping body. Wrapping up the towel, they put it down as Malkia's head and then used strips of rags to look like hair. In the dark, it appeared believable. Astrid lay in the bed, and Malkia fixed the blankets and cushions, so it appeared as if there were two bodies lying side by side.

Malkia gave Astrid the glass of water with the crushed lakseed in it, and after Astrid drank it, Malkia placed it back on the table where Damon would discover it later. She took what remained of the lakseed and put it on her side of the bed, hoping Damon would see them and realize it was all her doing.

They heard someone rustling outside. Malkia ducked behind the bed and waited until the guard checked in on them. She heard the fabric door slide open and then quickly slip back into place. Malkia peeked around the bed to make sure he had left before she rose.

After everything was in place, and she had dressed in her old clothes, she hugged Astrid. "Thank you again. I will return for you. Of course, you might head our way before I have the chance. Either way, I'll return to free you and your mother."

"My mother first," Astrid whispered. She smiled weakly, slowly falling into a deep sleep.

Malkia grabbed the knife Astrid had snuck in and then she ducked behind the bed again. She moved the cut tent fabric and peered at the tree bark on the other side. It was a tight squeeze. The tree was so close; she doubted there was enough space for her to fit. She glanced both ways and wiggled through, crouching halfway in and halfway out. The entire tent shuddered from the movement.

She exhaled slowly, waiting for the guards to capture her, but no one came. With shaky leg muscles, she pushed the rest of the way out and stood, pressing herself against the tree and sliding around it one tiny step after another.

The first thing she noticed was Damon's tent lit with candles. She crept forward. At the corner of her tent, she peeked around and breathed easier from the empty space.

Like a flash, she bounded to the trees near Damon's tent and hid behind the largest one. Damon's gruff voice greeted her, but she could not make out what he was saying.

It did not matter. She sprinted behind each tent until she could see the lone one off in the distance. Two guards stood unmoving in front, with a low fire illuminating their faces. It was enough light to reveal her if she was too close. It was best to stay inside the tree line and circle around to the back of Alex's prison.

The forest began about twenty yards from the tent. Malkia slipped underneath the dark umbrella of the trees and tiptoed across the dead leaves and twigs. She willed her body to be as light as a feather, and almost instantly, it felt like she was walking on air. Her footsteps were silent.

When she reached the spot behind Alex's tent, she pressed against a tree on the edge of the forest and watched with bated breath as someone jogged toward the guards. Damon's angry face appeared next to the fire.

Fear prickled down her spine. *Has he discovered my absence?*

Her gaze darted around, expecting to see the wolf-men sniffing her out, but the brush between her and the tent was empty. Damon yelled, and Malkia turned her attention back to him as he stepped closer to one guard. After he finished, he stomped away, heading toward his tent.

A sigh of relief escaped her lips, and she clapped her hand over her mouth. No one turned her way, so she stepped into the open space toward Alex.

A twig snapped behind her. She whipped around to put the knife between her and whomever was behind her, but they knocked out it from her grasp, and a shadowed hand pressed against her mouth, stifling her scream.

I was so close, she thought in defeat, struggling uselessly against the ironclad grip.

FOURTEEN
Freedom

MALKIA RECOGNIZED THE smell of the person holding her. Her stiff muscles relaxed and the hand on her mouth slowly loosened. She turned around and threw her arms around Dario's neck, then wept against his chest. With a quick squeeze from him, he leaned away and put his finger on her lips, turning to stare at Alex's tent.

Dario waved his hand to the side, shifted around her, and ran soundlessly toward the tent, with Levi next to him. They crouched as they grew closer, which slowed their pace but kept them out of the light. Malkia watched in amazement, overwhelmed with love for Dario and the rest of her group. They were her heroes.

A hand curled over her shoulder. She whipped around again and came face to face with Jayde. They threw their arms around each other without hesitation.

"You don't know how glad we are to see you," Jayde whispered in her ear.

Malkia wiped her face and sniffed. "I thought I would never see you all again. Did the rest of the group escape?"

Jayde nodded. "They stayed by the river until I finally woke that evening. I asked to come back. Kendrick forbade me at first." She smirked. "As if that would stop me. Jacob told Kendrick the pixies would stick close to you and give them updates so I could return and help. Of course, at that time, we didn't know you were taken. It was just before I headed back when the pixies told Jacob." She raked her hand through her hair, scanning the area. "I used my sight to find Dario, Levi, and Alex and headed back immediately. Once we found each other, we've been waiting for a chance to rescue you ever since."

Jayde stopped talking and focused on Dario and Levi. Malkia looked as well. They had made it to the tent and were finding a way to overtake the guards without being noticed by anyone else. Luckily, the embers from the fire were dwindling, but if anyone glanced that way, they would notice the struggle.

Malkia's nerves were overtaking her heart, and she really wanted to run out there and help them, but she knew she would make things worse. Jayde grabbed her arm and Malkia eased her friend to the ground as she fell into a trance. Before turning back to the men, Malkia wiped Jayde's hair from her face and planted a kiss on her forehead. She was lucky to know this woman.

Dario and Levi remained crouched behind the tent, and it appeared they were trying to cut into it. She looked back at Jayde and her pulse quickened as she waited for someone to do something. The silence was unnerving.

Many agonizing moments later, Jayde batted her eyes open. "The two wolf-men who stayed back from tracking our large group are in the leader's tent. They were on the other side of the campsite earlier, which is why we came over to Alex's tent. They have been tracking us for the past two days. When they captured Alex, it's because he saw them closing in on me, and he jumped out to distract them. He saved me." Jayde closed her eyes as she shook her head. "Do you know their leader's name?"

"Damon," Malkia replied, turning her attention to the men, not wanting to talk about Damon.

Jayde rested her head back against the tree behind her. "I saw you with him. I saw how he grabbed and kissed you. What was going on with that? Why did you allow him to kiss you?"

A weight settled on Malkia's heart. "Did you tell Dario?"

"Of course not. It would destroy him."

"Thank you." Malkia sighed, leaning against a nearby tree. "I didn't really have a choice. He's obsessed with me. I'm petrified for the moment he discovers my absence. He won't stop until he has me for himself."

Jayde rose from the ground. "And he knows where our group is?"

"Yes." Malkia ran her hands through her hair and drew in a long breath. "I tried reasoning with him. I tried convincing him to just have me and leave everyone else alone, but he is determined to be in control. He wants to take away my dignity and my strength while breaking my spirit, just like he breaks his horses." She shook her head, a frown forming on her face. "And you know what's funny? I feel a pull toward him. It makes little sense."

Malkia and Jayde both twisted toward the men at the sound of a quiet rustling. The men were returning, and Dario had Alex tossed over his shoulder. Levi was guarding Dario's back as they edged back to the women, and it appeared like the guards hadn't noticed their presence.

When they were within the safety of the trees, Malkia and Jayde helped Dario put Alex down on the ground. His hands were still tied, so she worked on loosening the knots.

Dario watched Malkia for a moment and then kneeled to help her. "We need to return to the pegasi and fly out of here." He covered her right hand with his.

"I can't leave yet," Malkia whispered in return, her heart thumping in her chest.

Everyone's shocked looks turned her way.

"Why not?" Levi asked, with a frown creasing the lines between his eyes.

Malkia's gaze flashed around, making sure they were not being followed. "There's a little girl over in that tent who is being tortured. I need to save her." She pointed north of Alex's tent at the tented cage she had seen earlier that day.

They each glanced in the direction she was pointing, and one by one, they shook their heads as they glared back at her. "Do you know what we have given up saving you?" Jayde asked, pressing her palms into her temples.

"You didn't save me," Malkia replied promptly, her annoyance flaring. "I freed myself. I am not leaving without her. Go to the pegasi, and I will meet you there as soon as I have her."

Dario blew out a frustrated breath. "You're as stubborn as an ox. I'll go with you. Can you two manage Alex?"

Levi and Jayde nodded. They propped Alex up, and each of them took a side. Malkia watched them as they headed away from her and Dario. She turned back toward Misty's cage and tiptoed her way through the brush and trees.

Malkia sensed Dario moving behind her. She didn't want to look at him until they had Misty and her mother. Too much judgment and she could not stomach the look of disappointment on his face.

They edged soundlessly through the vegetation for several minutes before she could see the cage clearer. There was a guard standing a few feet in front of it. Malkia pointed at it and nodded to tell Dario that was the one.

Dario shifted around Malkia and jogged to the other side of the cage. She tried to keep up, but realized Dario was purposely losing her.

She sprinted as fast as she could, slunk along the side of the cage, and glanced around the corner. Dario stood there with the guard lying at his feet. He was holding the keys to the cage and looking at her with frustration.

"Hurry, Malkia," Dario muttered. He unlocked the cage door and pulled it open.

Malkia realized at that moment it could be a trap, one she just made Dario walk right into. "Wait, Dario!" she quietly stammered as she raced toward him.

Just then, a frail woman poked her head out of the doorway. She saw Malkia and smiled weakly. "You must be Malkia. Misty said you were coming for her tonight. I didn't believe her, but here you are."

"How did she know I would come tonight?"

The woman wrapped a shawl around her thin shoulders. "My daughter connected with you."

Malkia did not understand. That was not how their ability worked, but she did not have time to talk about it. "Where is she?"

"She's inside. Please take her quickly." Misty's mother sunk to the ground and hung her head, no fight left in her. "Now. Before they send someone to check on us."

Dario didn't hesitate. He picked up the woman and moved her out of his way before ducking into the cage. His large stature made the tent look miniature. Malkia wrapped her arm around the girl's mother as she listened to the scuffling of feet inside the cage. A few seconds later, Dario emerged with a child in his arms.

"Let's go," he said, moving around the cage and back toward the trees.

Malkia curled her arm around the woman's waist and pulled her along beside her. They were rapidly falling behind Dario, but he did not notice. She whistled softly, and he glanced over his shoulder. He halted in his tracks and handed Misty to Malkia. He cradled the woman in his arms and sprinted toward the trees.

It took them a while to arrive at the other three. Malkia worried it had taken too long to rescue Alex, Misty, and her mother. Time was moving fast, and she was afraid they wouldn't be able to put enough distance between them and the savages before her absence was discovered.

When the pegasi were near, Malkia noticed Alex perched against a tree, his face white as a ghost. "Alex, can you ride on a pegasus?"

Alex's head wobbled as he stared at Malkia. "As long as… as long as someone holds onto me. I… feel… strange."

Malkia peered around at the others. "They have drugged him. Let's move out. I can't wait to put some distance between us and this place."

It was then Malkia saw her dear Parowan standing with the other pegasi. She sprinted to her beauty and examined her. She seemed fine and overjoyed to see Malkia as she nuzzled her neck.

"I missed you too, girl. Are you ready to leave this place?"

Parowan nodded as Malkia mounted her. She was happy to see her backpack hanging on the other side of Parowan's saddle. She grabbed it and threw it onto her back. Dario handed Misty to her, and he and Misty's mother mounted his pegasus. Alex pulled himself onto Levi's pegasus and leaned against him.

As they entered the skies, Malkia glanced back at the camp that had been her home for three days. A strange unease swirled in her stomach, and she hoped Astrid would not have to face Damon's wrath. The connection to that man still thundered in her mind, and Malkia turned to look at Dario to remember who she really loved. She had to tell him.

He threw her a tight smile. Misty's mother was leaning back against Dario's chest, and he was having difficulty keeping her propped up. He was angry with her for not leaving immediately, but they would work things out. They always did.

She smiled as the wind brushed by her face and reminded her she was free again.

FIFTEEN

Confessions

MALKIA AND HER friends reached the small group by morning. There were a lot of hugs, and joy blossomed within her. They were back together, and now they had to reach their large group in time to warn them.

The wolf-men had a significant head start, but her group had the skies on their side, so she wasn't too worried. After everyone had breakfast, Malkia asked Jayde to check on the savages' group to see what was happening.

"No need," Jacob announced, waving his hand in the air. "The pixies already told me what they saw when the savages' leader realized you were gone."

"Really? Why didn't you tell me?" Malkia asked, her brows furrowing.

Jacob brought his palms together and pressed his fingers against his chin. "I didn't think you would care so much. I figured I could tell you what their plans were after we had our morning meal."

"I'm sorry, Jacob. I do care." She leaned forward in her chair, rubbing her knees to warm them. "This man wants you all dead, and he wants to take me away. I'm his focus right now, and the thought of my life causing you all pain terrifies me. Please tell me what happened."

Jacob shifted in his seat and pulled his blanket around his shoulders. "When he discovered you your absence, he lost it. He nearly killed that woman who was with you, but for some odd reason, he held back. He walked away from her and summoned his two wolf-men and several of his soldiers into his tent. The pixies could hear them talking about leaving immediately and catching up to you, but then he said you would most likely be on a pegasus. He said he had an idea of where we were going and that the other two wolf-men would be making their way back to report to him their findings." Jacob stretched his legs in front of him as his gaze turned toward the sky. "He mentioned it was time to pack and move northeast, wanting to meet the wolf-men on their journey back. Then he composed himself in a rather odd and quiet way. His men even squirmed from his behavior. It was as if all his emotions disappeared, including his anger."

"Have they left?" Malkia asked.

Jacob shook his head. "An hour ago, they were still talking about their plans when they realized you probably took Alex with you. The wolf-men tore out of the tent and ran to his. They nearly ripped the tent apart when they found him gone, but their leader was not surprised. He knew you wouldn't leave without him."

"Does he know we have Misty and Cassida?" Malkia asked, referring to Misty's mother.

"I don't know. They didn't mention them. Did you leave the guard lying there, or did you hide him?" Jacob focused on Dario.

"We left him lying there," Dario replied, his eyes narrowing. "They have to know they are gone."

Cassida spoke up just then. "I'm sure they know we're gone. They probably discovered our disappearance first, which means he knows one of you has telepathy."

"She's right," Malkia muttered, wringing her hands together. "He's a clever man—too keen sometimes. I wish I could read his mind. I could always see his wheels turning, but I never knew what was going on in there. It's daunting to think what he's capable of doing."

"Well, then what is our plan?" Kelsey asked, her gaze flashing around the group. A slight look of irritation swept over her face, but she quickly masked it with concern.

Malkia seemed to be the only one who witnessed Kelsey's peculiar expression, but then she had always been a little different. "Our plan is to clean up this mess, cover our tracks, and depart. I want to reach our group as fast as possible. I can't wait to see Mataya and find Domesca. We have much to prepare, because Damon will chase after me and our group. Even if I left, he would still come after you. He knows it will make me cling to him because I believe I can stop him, but I know better. Nothing will stop him. Like I told Jayde, he wants to break me. He wants to destroy my spirit and then own what remains."

Malkia turned to Dario and walked over to him. He looked up at her and smiled sadly. "Can I speak with you alone?" she asked quietly.

He stood and wrapped his fingers around her hand, and she led him away from the rest of the group. When they were out of ear's reach, she stopped and gazed up at the man who was not only her hero, but held her heart in his hands. How had she let it wait this long before she told him how she felt?

"Dario, I have been wrestling with my feelings for a long time. I realized when I was captured and being manipulated into caring for Damon that there was only one man I loved." She paused and checked to make sure the rest of the group was not eavesdropping.

A frown slid across Dario's face.

"Dario," Malkia whispered as she inhaled a deep breath. "I love you. I love you more than words can say. I didn't realize I could love someone this much again, but I do. Your face gave me the strength to hold on and find—"

Dario gathered her in his arms and pressed his lips to hers, shutting her up. Goosebumps traveled down her spine, and a yearning grew in her chest. Their embrace lasted only a few moments, but when they pulled apart, it felt like an eternity had passed by. A smile twitched on her lips, and Dario grinned back at her.

"Yay!" Jayde yelled, clapping her hands.

Malkia and Dario burst into laughter, and both turned to look at their friends who had stopped packing and were watching them. Then they looked back at each other, and Dario winked.

"I love you, Malkia, more than my own life and would do anything for you. I hope you know that." He ran his thumb tenderly down her cheek.

"I do." She grinned, closing her eyes. "I wish I had allowed myself to feel this way before now. I guess there's one good thing that has transpired out of my imprisonment."

Dario planted a kiss on Malkia's forehead and pulled her against his body. She laid her head against his chest and let him hold her. She needed this, and she deserved to be loved again.

Malkia tilted her head back to look at him. "Damon will be furious if he found out about you. It scares me to think what he would do."

"I'm not afraid of that man. My strength and speed outmatch his abilities. He needs thoughtless dogs to do his bidding in order to accomplish anything. When he comes for you, I will let him know who I am and that he does not have a chance of taking you again." His eyes glazed over in thought before refocusing on her. "And we will devise a plan to imprison his dogs, so we won't have to worry about them. They could be of some use in the future."

Malkia inhaled sharply. "They're so fast though, faster than you."

"But they're not smart." Dario shook his head, giving her a squeeze. "They were easy to fool out in the forest once we established their whereabouts. Although they might be fast and strong, they don't think things through very well. That's why they grovel on their leader's floor. They know they would never survive without his instructions. He's the intelligent one, but like I said, he doesn't possess the total package. He requires those dogs' strength and speed."

"Are you positive? There were a few times he seemed to imply that he had a significant ability that could extinguish our group." Malkia chewed on her bottom lip. "I never figured it out, but from the speed he gained on our people, I think he might at least have some kind of power on his side."

"He might, but it still isn't as illustrious as my abilities, or what our group possesses." Dario playfully rubbed his nose across hers. "I'm not worried. Let's pack and go meet up with our group. I'm looking forward to Domesca and having a safe roof over your head."

Malkia grinned, stepping away from him. "Me too. Let's leave."

They joined the rest of the group to clean up and pack their belongings. Weariness from traveling all night wreaked Malkia's clarity, but her exhaustion did not come close to everyone else's. Alex was healing, thanks to Damion, and Porter had completely healed. The drugs had made its way out of Misty, and she was feeling like herself again.

When they arrived to Parowan, Dario leaned down and sealed his lips over Malkia's. Another smile lifted his cheeks. "I love you so much, Malkia. You've made me the happiest man alive." He nuzzled her neck before picking her up and setting her on Parowan's back. He mounted his pegasus, Brit, and they all flew out of their small camp area and into the sky, heading toward the rest of their group.

As they flew, Malkia moved Parowan next to Jayde's pegasus. "Did you see anything at the savage's camp before we left?"

Jayde shook her head. "I caught a glimpse of them packing up, but nothing of importance. I didn't see Damon or your friend. When we stop to let the pegasi rest, I'll check again."

"Okay, I just wanted to make sure."

The group of them flew in silence until lunchtime, gaining significant ground. They reached a mountain range and found a small waterfall where they agreed to rest and eat.

Malkia and Dario found a quiet spot near the waterfall and settled next to one another on the ground.

"Dario, I have to tell you something," she said, brushing her arm against his.

He put his hands around her waist and lifted her to him. She rested her cheek against his chest.

"What's up?" he asked.

Malkia gulped, her throat suddenly constricting. "I kissed Damon. Actually, I kissed him several times. Well, I probably only kissed him twice, but *he* kissed me several times. I had some moments of weakness, and I saw the good in him. It was difficult to not allow him close to me." She paused, closing her eyes, and snuggling in closer, sadness tearing at her chest. "However, I knew from the beginning you were the one. I knew before his advances that I was returning to be with you. I allowed him to kiss me because I wanted to have him trust me. It was a means to an end, and that is all I ever allowed him to do. He was going to make me marry him. Did you know that?"

"No, I didn't," Dario muttered, his voice barely a whisper.

She didn't dare look up as she continued to explain her circumstances while imprisoned. "He had a dress stitched for me, and this morning, he was going to force me to marry him. He said if that was the only way I would allow him to be with me, then so be it. I escaped not only to warn you guys but to escape a union I didn't want. I could only think of you."

Dario was quiet for a minute before he hugged Malkia tightly. "If you think it would upset me, because you did what was necessary to stay on his good side, then you are wrong. I don't blame you. Even if you had feelings for him for a minute, I don't care. To know I was in your thoughts, and I had your heart, is proof enough of your devotion for me. I don't care what happened with you and that barbarian, as long as he didn't hurt you."

Malkia exhaled slowly, squeezing him back. "Thank you, Dario. I wanted to be honest with you."

"Well, I'm thrilled you didn't marry him." He chuckled, nibbling on the top of her shoulder.

Malkia ran the tips of her fingers over the stubble on Dario's chin. "Me too."

They nestled in with one another, and slowly, Malkia drifted off as she listened to the bubbling waterfall. She was content, lying on his chest. Dario closed his eyes, so she snuggled in, allowing sleep to take over her body.

"Malkia, wake up. It's time to go." Dario was kneeling next to her when she opened her eyes. "Did you have a good nap?"

She nodded as she yawned and stretched. "The best I've had in a while. How did you move?"

Dario laughed. "You're light as a feather, and you sleep like a rock. I picked you up, moved, and laid you back down."

She grinned, propping herself on her elbows. "Is everyone else ready to depart?"

"Most everyone," Dario replied, nodding. "A few of them are still waking."

He rose from the ground, holding out his hand. He helped her up, and she fixed her clothes and ran her fingers through her hair so she wouldn't look like a complete disaster.

"You look beautiful," Dario said, watching her prep herself.

"Maybe to you, but I can guarantee I'm a mess."

"Nope, not in the slightest." He frowned, pointing at her back. "But I saw your bruise on your back. I hope you don't mind; I took a little peek after your shirt slid up a bit. That bruise is horrendous. Is that what those dogs gave you, after knocking you off Parowan?"

"Oh, yes," Malkia said, touching her lower back. "It's not that bad anymore. I have them on my legs, arms, and stomach as well. The first couple of days were painful, but today, I finally feel better."

Dario cracked his knuckles, then rubbed his palms together. "I can't wait to get a hold of those dogs, especially the one who wounded you. I about died when I saw him smash you off Parowan. And he was fast. Then I saw the other one hit you before you recovered from the first blow. I have played that moment repeatedly in my head."

"You nearly died trying to save me after I told you not to do it," Malkia snapped. Her brows pulled together in a scowl.

Dario laughed again, arching a sly brow. "Not a chance! My healing abilities had me up and running before they were out of sight. I saw them with you, and I knew they had captured you. I also heard you scream. Never do that again. If you see me shot by an arrow, you run the other way."

She rolled her eyes. "You know I won't do that, but if it ever happens again, I will do my best not to get caught, as long as I become your hero."

They had been strolling toward the rest of the group, and Dario halted. He picked Malkia up in an embrace and nuzzled her neck. "You are already my hero."

Malkia giggled and hugged him back. She wished she had opened up to him years ago, when she first realized his attraction to her. She would have been less lonely and far more satisfied with life.

Dario set her down, giving her another kiss on the forehead, and they continued their walk to the rest of the group and the pegasi.

"Are you two going to need a room?" Damion asked, a grin twitching on the edges of his lips.

Dario laughed. "Absolutely."

Malkia's smile widened, and her gaze swept over the group. "Ha, he wishes!"

"You two are adorable." Jayde's hands settled on her hips.

"Oh, boy," Dario grumbled, walking toward Brit. "I think we are too old for that."

"Speak for yourself!" Malkia shot back at him, her spirits soaring. She turned and focused on Jayde. "Did you see what was going on with Damon's group?"

Jayde nodded, pulling her hair back into a ponytail. "Yes, I did. I saw Damon. He still had a stone-faced expression, but he's making everyone hurry. I noticed when they had everything packed, their trailers no longer touched the ground. One hawk had to dive to the ground and double-check, but sure enough, the trailers were floating. An older woman stood behind each one for a moment before they lifted. I really think this is how they have gained on us." She coughed and cleared her throat. "They have a witch accompanying them."

Fear twisted in Malkia's gut as her eyes widened. "Are you serious? I haven't heard of a witch sighting since I was a kid," she said, chewing on her thumbnail. "I never saw a witch while I was there. What did she look like?"

"She had gray, short hair. Her body, frail and shriveled. That's the best description I can provide for you. The hawks are having a difficult time flying too close after one of their own was slain, especially now that they know you have someone with my ability." Jayde shuddered. Her fingers hovered over the opening of her saddlebags as if she were deep in thought. Then she shot Malkia a quick glance. "I'm sure it will delight your boyfriend to capture me."

Malkia gripped Jayde's arm. "Too bad he won't have a chance." She shook her head. "I don't remember this woman at all. Of course, they held me in a cage and then a tent for most of the time I was there, so I don't remember seeing many women. If she is a witch, that could explain a great deal. The trailers floating would help them travel faster. I wonder what other spells this woman knows." She strolled over to Parowan. "Did you see anything else?"

Malkia mounted her pegasus and helped Misty up in front of her. Jayde and Cassida both mounted Jayde's pegasus, and the beasts took off into the sky.

Jayde pulled up next to Malkia and continued their conversation. "After they packed and they put the women and children in their cages, they began heading our way. At first, they were slow, but they didn't take long to speed up. Damon was on a horse, along with the other men and a few women. The witch climbed into a trailer and closed the curtain. I'm sure traveling is far less bumpy with the trailers floating off the ground. That's all I could see. They haven't been traveling long. We have time on our side. They have to pass over the mountains and remain with the trails, unless they have some other superpower we haven't seen."

"I wouldn't be surprised. Damon seems to be full of secrets. And he was mad at me because of mine." Her tone was laced with a hint of sarcasm. "Thanks, Jayde, I'm grateful for you." She patted Misty's hand, which was wrapped around her waist. "I think we all are."

Jayde winked at Misty and fell back to talk to Kelsey.

SIXTEEN
Pixie Delight

RAIN CAME UNEXPECTEDLY. The small group huddled in the thick of the trees, with their pegasi standing beside them. The clouds had rolled in without warning and caught them off guard. They had cleared the mountain and were gaining on their group, but the storm was slowing them down.

Jayde had fallen into a trance again. It only made Jacob anxious, because he hadn't heard from the pixies since the morning.

Malkia leaned forward and squeezed Jacob's arm. "Relax. It will be fine."

"That's easy for you to say," Jacob snapped, his head held between his hands. "You're on cloud nine right now. The rest of us have been in a horrible state since you were taken."

"Jacob, that isn't fair," Kelsey said, leaning over Dario to punch Jacob's leg. "She has been through enough. She had to play charades with the man who wants us all dead. If she hadn't kept her cool, she might be dead right now."

Dario and Kelsey had been whispering their conversation since the rains began, but it wouldn't be the first time those two had been cozy. Malkia trusted both, but for the first time, she felt a pang of jealousy from their tight friendship.

She stole a glance at Dario, but his eyes were closed. "Thanks, Kelsey, but he's somewhat right. It was much easier for me. I could sleep in a bed. It sucked playing Damon's games, but I wasn't being tortured. However, we still have to keep our heads on straight." She turned back toward Jacob, rubbing the side of her arm that was still tender with a bruise. "Jacob, the pixies will appear as soon as they are able. Remember, they were caught in this rain as well. They know where to find you."

Jayde's trance dissipated, and her eyes snapped open. "They're coming fast, again, but we still have a good head start. This rain has just reached them, and they've stopped and are held up in their trailers. Damon was furious at the delay, but he calmed when the witch came out of her trailer and whispered something to him. He actually smiled. I do not know what she said, but his smile scared me. She must know something."

"I wonder if she can see things like you can," Porter whispered.

Malkia groaned, her chest tightening with fear. "I hope not. Jayde and Jacob are our best weapons right now. If they have something similar, we could be in big trouble."

Jayde shook her head. "I don't know what she knows, but it pleased him. He hid in his trailer for a few minutes, but then he came out and sat on his horse in the rain. He also sent out his other two wolf-men. I watched where they were going, and it seems they were moving toward their two friends, who were on their way back. I'm not sure what they have discovered, but they must have news, or they wouldn't be returning, right?"

"Who knows?" Dario interrupted, and finally opening his eyes. He rubbed his temples as a look of annoyance flitted across his face. "Good news. The rain is letting up. We could at least walk with the pegasi." He rose and pulled Kelsey to her feet, never looking Malkia's way.

Had she angered him?

"Sounds great," Kendrick said, steering his pegasus away from the group.

Dario walked away with Kelsey beside him, whispering once again. Swallowing her jealousy, Malkia joined the others, petting Parowan before throwing her leg over the beast's back. They trudged through the sludge, searching for a less muddy trail that would allow the pegasi a chance to dry off.

Dario was finally alone, and Misty had asked to ride with Kelsey. Malkia trotted Parowan next to Brit.

"Do you have a headache?" Malkia asked.

Dario turned to look at her. His expression hardened. "Something like that. The storm has not been good for me."

"Can Damion help you?"

"No," Dario snapped.

Malkia was taken aback. "No need to be rude. Why are you acting like this?"

Dario drew in a long breath, before looking her way again. His expression had softened, and a tight smile surfaced on his lips. "I am not feeling well. Give me some time to heal myself and then we can talk."

"You know I'm here for you," Malkia replied, pulling back on the reins and putting space between them again.

As she grew farther away, Kelsey moved in next to Dario, throwing a glance at Malkia over her shoulder. Misty looked as well and Malkia sensed the barrier go up between their minds. For the first time, confusion swirled through Malkia's thoughts, second guessing her decision to open up to Dario. She had given her heart to him, just to have Kelsey move in like the jealous ex-lover. Did they have a history before they came to live in her town?

Malkia looked away from the trio and focused on the search for drier land.

They walked for some time before the rain stopped. The suns peeked out from the clouds, and the smaller one was setting. They stopped for a break and let the pegasi shake off and clean themselves. Malkia removed her horse brush from her pack, and after the beast finished shaking off, she ran it down Parowan's coat. Parowan enjoyed the attention, and it gave Malkia some time to think about their next move.

Jacob spoke up behind her. "The pixies are here. I'm going to speak with them. I'll let you know what they say."

Malkia was thankful they finally came. She glanced behind her. "Hopefully, they have more information. Thanks, Jacob."

He sprinted away just as Dario approached Malkia. He wrapped his arms around her waist and kissed her neck. "I feel better now."

His mood swings were giving her whiplash, but she stopped brushing Parowan and curled her arms around Dario's neck, pushing away the weird vibes between him and Kelsey. Standing on her toes, she reached up and planted a kiss on his lips. Dario's face lit up, just like Parowan's had. Malkia couldn't help but laugh.

"What's so funny?" he asked, leaning back to see her better.

A gleam of deviltry swept over her face. "Nothing, I'm glad you feel better. If I knew you would make me this happy during the run for our lives, I would have done this ages ago."

"I'm not one to say, 'I told you so,' but—I told you so!" He winked at her, a sly smile curving his lips.

"You were so right. I can't wait to end this foolishness and be able to spend time with you alone, without someone bugging us every two minutes."

Dario wrapped his arms around her waist and picked her up. She wrapped her legs around him, puckering up for another kiss. Instead, she screamed with delight when he nuzzled her neck with his whiskers, and they both glanced at the others and found them staring in their direction. Dario set her down, and Malkia blushed.

"They're going to grow weary of our mushiness," Malkia whispered, feeling drunk with happiness.

"I'm sure they are already sick of it, but who cares? This is our moment. Who cares what they all think?"

"You care what Kelsey thinks," The words came out before Malkia could stop them.

Dario stiffened before stepping away from her and folding his arms over his chest. "She's just a friend. Are you jealous?"

"Maybe, a little." She was internally hitting herself.

"And this is coming from the woman who was kissing another man recently," he replied with venom laced in his tone.

A prick of annoyance surfaced in her chest. "Is that how"

Jacob ran up to them, interrupting the tense conversation. "The pixies have information, but they would like you to hear it from them. They are under those trees." He pointed to the thick brush off in the distance.

Malkia shot Dario a guarded look. He had turned away and Kelsey was staring at him. What was up with those two?

Jacob grabbed her arm, and she reluctantly followed him. As she entered the thickest part, the illumination of the pixies filled her with warmth and, after being drenched by the rain, she welcomed it. Jacob stood beside her and put his hand on her arm to help keep her grounded.

The same pixie who had touched her face a few days before spoke. "Hello, Malkia. Zana is my name."

"It is a pleasure, Zana." Malkia bowed her head slightly.

The edges of Zana's lips quirked upward. "We were just informing Jacob everything we have learned. I had sent some of my own to check on your group, while I summoned others to monitor those who follow you. Your sister is well."

Malkia breathed a sigh of relief.

"They are only a few days away from the castle. Your friend, Tatum, has led them safely and seems to be keeping his word. They are anxious and frightened, but the strong ones, including your sister, are keeping everyone calm." Zana moved forward, stopping a few feet away. "The savages have a witch, as you already know. She has hexed Alex."

At this point, Malkia was not surprised. "Is he leading them to us?"

Zana gave a curt nod. "Yes. The witch is experienced and not of this moon. She can track you with this powerful curse she placed on Alex, but the spell was not functioning until the rain began." Her wings fluttered for a moment as her words melted into Malkia's panicked heart. "Once the wolf-men return to their camp, he will send them after you. He is aware you ride on pegasi, and can out-fly his wolf-men, but he's hoping to outsmart you. He is also aware of our help, along with the hawks', but he believes his witch is far more powerful." The pixie backed up a couple of feet and continued. "Despite his potent feelings for you, they are not honorable—at least not at this time."

The other pixies all buzzed with excitement, but Zana flicked her wing to silence them. Malkia looked around in confusion.

Another pixie rushed forward and whispered in Zana's ear. She shook her head fervently and shooed the pixie away. "Damon is obsessed with you, and he will stop at nothing until he has you again. His people acknowledge it, and being loyal to him, they believe they must find you. It means as much to them as it does to him, so beware of the wolf-men. They will not hesitate to execute anyone standing in their way. You have time on your side, but without knowing their next move, even that can be taken. The first order of business would be to take care of Alex."

Malkia's eyes widened, and she took a few slow steps backward. "What do you mean, take care of Alex?"

Zana smiled, clearly understanding her mistake. "I don't mean any harm to Alex. You will require your own witch, one who can block the spell. You must be quick so it will throw them off your trail."

Malkia shook her head, a chill running down her spine. "Where will we find a witch?"

The pixie held out a necklace with a large, clear pendant. "Take this necklace and wear it around your neck against your heart. When a trustworthy witch is near, it will glow blue, but if there is one near who only means harm to others, it will turn black. Wear the necklace, and it will guide you to one who will assist you."

Malkia's fingers wrapped around the necklace and jumped when it gave her a slight shock. Her startled gaze traveled from the pendant back to Zana, who motioned for her to put it on. Malkia eased the chain around her neck.

Zana nodded her approval. "We will continue to keep an eye on the savages for you. I will always be near, unless the rains begin again." She turned her attention to Jacob, her eyes softening, and a smile twitched the edges of her lips. "Jacob, there's no need to worry. I will appear as soon as I am able." With that, she turned and disappeared into the forest.

Malkia looked at Jacob, who was still holding her arm. "We will need to address this problem."

"Alex could be the reason they catch us. We have to leave him here," Jacob replied with furrowed brows. He crossed his arms over his chest.

"Are you insane?" Malkia's breath caught in her throat as she choked on her disgust. "We can't just abandon him."

"That's what those savages are counting on. They know you will never leave him, even if you knew he was going to be the death of all of us." Jacob gritted his teeth.

A twig snapped under Malkia's foot, and she jumped from the noise. "That's not the point." Her heart bumped against her chest, and she forced down a rising sick feeling. "Did you not hear what she said? We need to find a witch who will block this spell. We have to do what she says."

"I think we should vote on it." Jacob jutted his chin out, looking away from her. "I'm tired of running. I want to return to my family and end this insanity."

"Do you really think their chase will end once we reach our group?" Malkia placed her hand on Jacob's shoulder, urging him to look at her. "Damon is bound and determined to destroy us, and from the way you are talking, I believe he is already succeeding."

Jacob stood quietly for a moment and then nodded. "You're right. I'm struggling to handle this in a dignified manner. I miss my family, and the thought of those wolf-men even coming close to them is making me crazy."

"I know, Jacob. I feel the same way, but we must handle this properly. Let's go tell everyone else what we have learned and then we will plan our next move. If finding a witch is too hard, then we will forget about it and return to the group, anyway. Damon already has a good idea of where we are going. By the time we find a witch, we might have wasted more time than we have, and this whole thing will be for nothing."

They left the shelter of the trees, jogging to meet their group. As they approached everyone, Dario and Kendrick stood. They looked worried, and after seeing Jacob's and Malkia's faces, both their foreheads furrowed with concern.

"What happened?" Kendrick asked, looking from Malkia, then back to Jacob.

"Good news and bad news," Malkia said. "Which would you all like first?"

"Bad news," Porter replied, raising his hand.

Kelsey glared at Porter. "I think I would rather have the good news, but whatever."

Malkia didn't want them arguing over what came first. "The bad news is we are being tracked. Alex has had a spell put on him by the witch in Damon's group."

Silence filled the space around them as each of them turned to stare at Alex.

"Now what?" Jayde asked first, tears welling in her eyes.

"The pixies gave me this pendant." Malkia lifted the necklace and showed everyone. "It will guide me to find a witch who will help us. If we can find one, they can put a block on the evil witch's spell and then there won't be a problem. However, after discussing it with Jacob, we don't think we should seek one out. For the time being, we continue on our way back to our group, and if we find one on the way, we can intervene with the spell. Damon already knows our group is heading northeast, and his wolf-men might have tracked them down, so trying to find a witch will be a waste of time. I really think putting a spell on Alex was a backup plan." She glanced around at the group. "What do you all want to do?"

Alex spoke before anyone else could respond. "I remember something eerie happening. A feeble old lady stood over me, muttering bizarre words, but I thought it was a dream." He shook his head, his gaze focusing on Malkia. "I hate that I have put you all in danger. I would stay back if it came down to it."

"Don't get all heroic," Kendrick blurted, softly punching Alex in the arm. "None of us want to desert you. We'll do whatever it takes to block the spell. For now, I agree with Malkia. We need to continue toward our group and make it to Domesca. Let's not give those savages any more power against us."

"How does everyone else feel about moving on, with all of us, and rushing to catch our group?" Malkia asked, clasping her hands together in front of her chest.

Everyone raised their hands. Alex appeared a little perplexed, but Kelsey nudged him, and he smiled warily. Maybe Malkia's apprehension toward Kelsey was only because it involved Dario. Kelsey had a soft heart for everyone.

Malkia rose, beckoning for them to follow. "Let's hurry. I'm eager to see my sister and the rest of our people."

"Wait," Kelsey said. "What's the good news?"

Malkia stopped in her tracks. "Oh, yes. The pixies said our people are doing well. They are about three days away from Domesca, and they are progressing quickly."

The tension in the group melted from the news.

"That's a relief," Porter said, bouncing up from his seat. "I was wondering if we were going to be checking on them soon."

Jayde rose quietly and slipped away from the group. Malkia watched as she found a rock to sit against and closed her eyes. A few moments later, she slipped into a trance. Malkia walked toward her, hoping to receive good news from her as well.

When Jayde finally came out of her trance, she looked at Malkia and smiled. "Everyone *is* doing well. It looks like they are preparing to stop for the night. I also took a quick glance at Damon's group. They're trudging slowly through the mud but are gaining ground. The wolf-men are still running toward one another. I couldn't find the two heading back to the savages, but I found the two racing toward our group." She paused, wringing her hands together. "Can we please go?"

"Absolutely. We only have a few more hours before it will be too dark to fly, so let's leave now."

Malkia helped Jayde up from the ground, and they returned to the rest of the group. They mounted their pegasi, and they flew off into the quickly darkening sky.

SEVENTEEN
Beast Showdown

MALKIA BOLTED INTO a seated position and glanced around at the others sleeping by the fire. Her heart was beating out of her chest, and she remembered why she had awakened.

The two wolf-men Jayde could not find weren't heading toward the other two mutts. They were tracking her down.

Her gaze flashed to Damion who was nodding off, even though he was on watch. She jumped to her feet, and he jerked awake, leaping to his feet in a dazed confusion.

"What's wrong?" Damion demanded, his gaze darting around the campsite.

She searched for Jayde as she stepped around Dario. "I just realized something," she whispered. "I need to wake Jayde." She rushed to her friend and gently shook her. It took a few moments, but Jayde's eyes finally fluttered open.

She gazed up at Malkia and Damion with half-opened eyes and then realized it was still nighttime. Shifting to her knees, she glanced beyond the two hovering over her, then focused on Malkia. "What's wrong?" she asked.

"I need you to find all four wolf-men." Malkia inhaled sharply and raked her hands through her hair. "I need you to find them right now."

"Why?" Jayde asked, then her eyes widened. Fear spread across her face as it dawned on her why she had not seen the other two wolf-men. "They are coming here, aren't they?" she whispered, her question hanging in the tense air around them.

Malkia nodded. "I think so. They must have met already and sent the two heading back to Damon in our direction. We have to know for sure, right now."

Jayde rose, her brows furrowing with frustration. "It's so difficult to find them if I do not know where to start."

"Start at the place we stopped before now and then go backward toward their group," Malkia suggested, pushing against her chest as it tightened with worry.

Jayde fervently nodded. "Give me a moment. I need to calm down first." She bounced spryly to a large rock and sagged against it as she eased to the ground. She took three deep breaths and put her head in between her legs. After a few moments, she peered up at Malkia and Damion before focusing on the fire and falling into a trance.

Damion's eyes widened as if he realized what the commotion was all about. "Do you mean those dogs are on their way to us right now?"

Malkia stepped toward Jayde. "I don't know for sure, but I think so," she muttered. She rolled her neck from side to side, stretching away the tension. "Call it a gut feeling, but I don't want to dismiss it. They cannot find us when we are in the air, so the best they can assume is where the witch told Damon we were when we met with the pixies. If they find our last stop, they could easily run toward the direction of our large group and catch up with us that way."

"What about throwing them off by walking in a different direction for a few hours and then flying away?" he asked, stepping over to the edge of the sleeping group and peering into the darkness.

Malkia shook her head vigorously, her gaze flashing around at the dancing shadows. "That will only throw them off momentarily, and we'll have wasted precious time returning to the group. We have to know where they are, so we can make the best move."

She knelt in front of Jayde, watching her friend's eyes twitch back and forth. It was eerie to see her ability in motion, but extremely mesmerizing as well. Malkia could only guess how wonderful and at the same time burdensome her ability was.

A few minutes later, Jayde withdrew from the trance, and dread rushed across her expression. "I can't find them, Malkia." Her voice quivered. "They're resting or they know I am searching for them. I can't find the other two either. They haven't reached our group, nor have they returned to Damon's. He's still moving, even though it is the middle of the night, and he's gaining significant ground. He is a little more than a half day behind us, even with us using pegasi."

Malkia looked back at the sleeping group. "We have to leave now. They might already have our scent and direction. For all we know, the other two wolf-men are circling around to grab us. Let's wake the others and leave."

Damion did not hesitate, poking at each one and telling them to wake. Malkia hurried to Dario's side as he stood. He appeared confused as he searched the darkness.

"What did I miss?" he grumbled, rubbing his eyes.

"Jayde can't find the wolf-men." Malkia straightened her stance and rubbed her palms down her hips, wiping away her panicked sweat. "I can guarantee the reason she couldn't see the other two yesterday is because they are heading our way. Now that they are unseen, I know it. And the other two could very well be circling around to corner us. It's not about catching our large group. They will chase them after they take me back and eradicate all of you. We have to leave now."

Dario scanned over the dark area around them, and he focused on the pegasi. If the wolf-men slaughtered the pegasi, they would all be doomed. Malkia knew he was thinking the same thing. They had to fly into the air and stay there until they knew where those dogs were.

"Let's go!" Dario barked at the others.

They extinguished the fire, gathered their belongings as quickly as they could, and packed everything on their pegasi. Malkia grew more anxious as time passed. She kept looking over her shoulder, her ears catching every rustle. They were all tense and quiet, but they worked quickly. Finally, they were able to rush into the air, flying away from the area below.

Dario pulled up next to Malkia. "We should head in a different direction for a little while. Maybe go east for an hour and then look for them again. They won't be searching for us in that direction. They'll think we went north to catch up with our group."

"I'm good with that," Malkia said, nodding. "I feel like Damon pulled a fast one on us, and it makes me angry, at him and myself. I don't know if I can make the right decisions for this group right now, so I'm happy to let you decide."

"Don't beat yourself up over this. He outwitted us for a moment, but he underestimated your sixth sense. Your intuition is amplified more than others, and he doesn't know or understand that. I'm glad to suggest different moves, but the leadership is yours, and it will remain yours."

Malkia sighed. "Well, then please give me all the suggestions you can think of. I'm fresh out of them myself." She was tired and felt foolish. They had been close to being overtaken. If they had stayed there until morning, she knew they would have had a quick and unpleasant surprise waiting for them. The thought of it made her stomach churn.

Misty peered back at Malkia, sending her thoughts to her. *I despise The Leader. I hate him, so bad.*

I do too. He is a horrible person. But she really did not hate him, and it ate at her when she realized this truth.

Misty leaned back on Malkia and closed her eyes. Malkia's heart hurt for the girl. She had seen too much violence and pain in her brief life.

Malkia followed Dario as he led the group east, away from the wolf-men and Damon. Hopefully, by the time the first sun rose, they could find the dogs and have a better idea on what steps to take next.

They flew along quietly for almost an hour before they found an open area to land the pegasi. They didn't want to be in an area with hiding spots where the wolf-men could sneak up on them. The first sun was peeking above the horizon just after they landed, giving them the confidence to be out in the open.

Jayde leaped off her pegasus and sat in the middle of the field. She immediately fell into her trance as the rest of the group dismounted and sat near her.

Jayde was in her trance for over five minutes before she came out of it. "I found them." She exhaled slowly. "Two of them are closing in on our last campsite right now. They were hiding in the trees as much as possible, and they didn't emerge into the open until it was absolutely necessary. As for the other two, they are still on their way to our group and are closing in on them fast." She rose from the ground, signaling for the group to follow suit. "We have to stop them."

Malkia looked at Dario, who was already standing. "Move out, folks," he instructed, helping Malkia off the ground.

"Wait." Kendrick waved his hand around. "What's our plan? We can't just ride into these wolf-men and expect to end them. Does anyone know how to catch them off guard? Malkia, did you see anything while you were captive that would help capture these dogs?"

Malkia shook her head, and her lips set in a grim line. "No, I didn't notice anything. As Dario has told me, they are senseless, but ruthless. They have no remorse, and they won't hesitate to kill any of us. The only piece of advice I can give any of you is don't hesitate. We will have to advance on them quickly and quietly. Injuring them in the beginning is futile because once they know we are onto them, their speed will outmatch all of ours. Any ideas on how to mask our scent?"

"We need to kill a ritter," Porter said. He scratched his chin before leaning back and looking up at the group.

Everyone stopped and stared at him.

"Why?" Malkia asked.

"When I was young, and my dad and I ran into that dead ritter, it had the most rancid stench." He scrunched his nose from the memory, creasing the fine lines between his eyes. "My dad told me, if I was ever in trouble with an animal, other than a ritter, and I ran into a dead one like we had, then I could mask my scent with their blood. The animal will withdraw, not only because they fear them, but because their odor is nearly unbearable. If we have a ritter's blood to disguise our smell, they won't think anything of it, and we will be able to sneak up on them."

"Where do we find a ritter?" Alex asked with a smirk.

"They are everywhere," Dario replied, jabbing his thumb toward the forest. "They only surface from their holes when they hunt. It could be complicated tracking one down, but if we catch one, I think Porter could have saved the day."

"We don't have time, do we?" Kelsey asked. "I thought we had to hurry."

Dario and she exchanged uneasy glances, and Malkia could not decipher the meaning. There was no time to worry about their secret messages, but when they reached Domesca, Dario would need to explain himself. His strange behavior, combined with Kelsey suddenly clinging to him, was not what she had signed up for.

"We do," Malkia replied, bouncing on her toes. "But if we can catch one quickly, it will be worth it. Dario, do you have any ideas?"

"Actually, I do. Let's fly the pegasi to the forest north of us." Dario glanced at Alex, pursing his lips to the side in thought. "Alex, you still have blood on your clothes, and your wounds are healing. The ritters will smell the blood and withdraw from their holes. Once we catch one of them, we must move straightaway because it's possible others will come. Alex, are you willing to do this?"

"Absolutely, let's just hurry." Alex nodded his head enthusiastically. "I'm sick of waiting to return to everybody."

This time when they mounted their pegasi, they did it in silence. The lives of their families depended on them not making a mistake. Malkia felt the tension thicken in the air between her and the others. If they failed, all bets were off, and she feared life would never return to the peace she had known for the past nine years.

Dario had been right. The ritter caught Alex's scent almost immediately. He wiped his blood on leaves and walked through the trees, silently signaling to the team whenever he heard movement.Everyone else strategically placed themselves in different trees around the area, ready with their bows and arrows.

The rustling branches caught Malkia's ears and moments later, a beast came into view, ambling toward Alex. She whistled and pointed, signaling the others. Alex stopped in his tracks and waited. The ritter barreled toward him, but he did not budge, having full trust in his friends.

Dario shot first and struck the ritter in the side. The blow did not phase the beast, but Porter's arrow was right behind Dario's and penetrated the beast's flesh near its neck. The ritter slowed but almost immediately picked up speed again. Malkia drew her arrow back, and she and Kelsey shot at the same time. Their arrows thrashed into its hind leg and back.

The ritter's leg caved under its weight, and it tumbled to the ground just before he reached Alex. Shock and fear took over his face as the ritter skidded to a halt directly in front of him. That had been close. He drew out his knife and sunk it into the eye of the beast. The ritter snapped at Alex but missed, so Alex gripped his other knife and stabbed the beast's neck. The ritter jerked back suddenly, striking violently against the ground.

Everyone else climbed out of their trees and ran to the ritter. It smelled awful. Malkia held her nose and breathed through her mouth. It was a bulky beast, but not too large for Dario and Kendrick to carry. They threw the shoulders and hind legs over their shoulders and hurried toward their pegasi and Jayde.

After the men put the ritter on the ground, Porter and Alex used their knives to dig into its stomach, and they each pulled out a different organ. Porter handed Malkia something that appeared like a liver. She wiped the smell all over her body, dry heaving several times before her stomach finally calmed.

Then they spread it all over their pegasi's bodies. Parowan flicked her tail at Malkia and shot her several dirty looks. Malkia finally smacked her on the backside and told her to knock it off. Reluctantly, she mellowed out, but the pegasi made it clear the stench displeased them.

It took them over an hour to kill the ritter and smear its guts and blood over them, and they were back in the air. Jayde had taken a moment to find the whereabouts of the two wolf-men heading toward their group. They were only a couple hours' ride from them, even with the dogs running.

Dario seemed distracted, and Malkia wondered if he was mad at her. She continued to stay next to him during the flight, but he refused to look her way. She did not like his silence because it made her second-guess everything she thought was right.

After they had flown for some time, Jayde's pegasus flew up next to Malkia's. "We should gain on them soon. Is there a way someone could hold on to me while I check their whereabouts?"

"No, we're going to have to land." Malkia pointed down at the terrain. "Let's put them down right near that stream coming up. Just make sure the pegasi don't wash off."

Malkia led the way, and one by one, the pegasi landed. Jayde slid off Izzy and leaned against a tree. A few moments later, she was in her trance and Malkia sat next to her, waiting.

The rest of the group dismounted and whispered to each other. Jacob walked off into the trees, looking for the pixies, and Dario stood over Malkia and Jayde. After a minute, he knelt and curled his arm around Malkia. He didn't say anything, but he was clearly upset about something. She was about to ask when Jayde's eyes opened.

"They are closer than I thought," Jayde said, nibbling on her bottom lip. "They are less than an hour ahead of us. I'm not sure if they stopped to rest, but they are running right now. I checked on our group as well. They're still a day ahead of us, which is good. The farther away from them, the better for now."

Just as she finished, Jacob sprinted toward them. "The pixies were here. They told me Damon is moving fast. The witch must have placed a spell on their horses and livestock. They move quicker than normal animals, not as fast as the dogs but fast enough to only be behind us by half a day. The other wolf-men are with them. Once they found our camp deserted, they raced back toward their camp and gave Damon the news." He turned to face Malkia as he folded his arms over his chest.

"Apparently, he planned on having you back with him by now, but he has decided to move forward and catch up with our people. They're still tracking Alex, but Damon has realized this doesn't give him much of a lead because he can't see what we're doing, and he knows he won't be able to catch up with you before we reach our people. The one thing he emphasized was that those other dogs better reach them before we do so he can take your sister hostage."

Malkia jumped to her feet. "Let's go then. We are less than an hour behind the dogs. Let's close in, kill them, find our group, and move onto Domesca. We'll be safe there."

Malkia was on the warpath. She would not allow those filthy dogs to lay a hand on her sister. She would execute them with her own hands before she allowed that to happen. Her mind focused, and she quieted, like Dario, as they flew toward the wolf-men.

EIGHTEEN
Wolf-man Blaze

"THEY'RE COMING," JAYDE whispered to Malkia and Porter. Her foot dangled from the branch she perched against.

Malkia waved at Dario, who was in a tree across the path the dogs were on. Dario waved at the others, who could see him. With her bow in one hand and an arrow in the other, Malkia positioned herself with a perfect view of the area below.

The scuffle of the running wolf-men was quiet but noticeable. Their agile speed was not decreasing, and they obviously were not worried about any creatures they might run into.

Jayde drew her bow, followed by Porter and Malkia, waiting for the sighting of the dogs. They spotted the mutts at the same time. Jayde's arrow released first, with Porter's and Malkia's following close behind. They quickly reloaded.

One struck the nearest wolf-man several times, and he tumbled like a boulder across the dirt, while the other dodged each arrow and kept going, then jumped at the tree with Kendrick in it. Dario shot off another arrow, followed by Porter. The overly large, hairy man dodged the first one, but the next arrow pulled him down when it slashed into his upper thigh. He howled and whimpered as he hobbled back to his companion.

Dario, Kendrick, and Alex jumped from their trees, and each shot another arrow. One hit the dog who had fallen. Shock spread across his features, and he face-planted into the ground. His fight was over.

The wolf-man, who was hobbling, dodged two other arrows while limping toward his companion.

His abilities must be more advanced than the other. Malkia climbed from the tree she was in and watched with amazement.

The wolf-man yanked the arrow out of his leg, howling at the sky as he dropped the bloody object to the ground. As he passed by his friend, he grabbed his arm and hauled him alongside him. Dario reloaded his bow with a stony expression and gritted his teeth when the arrow released. It struck the wolf-man in the shoulder.

The wolf-man howled again, then whipped around and glared at Malkia before turning his furious expression toward Dario. Hatred spewed like flames from his eyes. Dropping his friend, he turned and galloped away in the direction of Damon's group. Alex and Kendrick raced after him, preparing to shoot again, but the dog disappeared into the brush before they had a chance.

The group circled the dying wolf-man. He was still breathing. Alex and Kendrick shoved him to his back, and he stared at them with watery eyes. Malkia gulped. Even a man determined to kill the ones she loved could pull at her heartstrings.She was weak.The wolf-man blinked several times, turning to Dario, as he grimaced in pain. "You promised," he muttered, his gaze never leaving Dario.

Dario released another arrow, slicing through the wolf-man's chest. His last breath whistled from his lungs.

Jayde turned away and covered her face with her hands. A somber expression slid over Kendrick's face, and Alex shot Dario a disgusted look.

"It had to be done," Malkia whispered, touching Dario's arm.

He glanced her way. Everyone else did as well, waiting for her to tell them what to do next. She stared at the dead wolf-man. They had to discard his body.

"Let's burn it," she said, staring at the corpse. "Start a fire and throw him in it. He might have been horrid, but he deserves to plead his case to the Alethieans. The other will either perish on his way back or get there and tell Damon we killed one of his dogs. Safety is more imperative for our group than ever before."

She didn't have to say it twice. They built the fire in haste and tossed the wolf-man in as soon as the flames were large enough. They watched in silence as the fire enveloped his body. It felt surreal. Malkia couldn't believe they had slain the wolf-man. He was a living person, human or not, despite his peculiar and advanced abilities. It made it difficult to wrap her mind around their actions. She had to keep reminding herself they were protecting their group.

Several calm moments passed before anyone moved. Jayde edged away from the group and sat against a tree. Malkia watched as she closed her eyes, falling into one of her trances.

Her gaze swept to Dario, who was staring back at her. He smiled briefly and looked away. It was time to hash out what was bothering him. Malkia walked behind the others and grabbed Dario's hand. "We need to talk."

Dario nodded his head and did not argue. She drew him away from the group but in eyeshot of Jayde.

"What's wrong?" she asked. "You have been acting strange off and on for days now."

His eyes watered, and he glanced away from her, wiping at his face. When he looked back at her, she knew why he was upset. "You think Damon is going to take me away, don't you?"

Dario stared at his feet, nodding. "He's determined, isn't he? I'm afraid they're going to come for you, and I won't be able to stop him." He stuffed his hands into his pants pockets and kicked at a pebble near his feet. "The thought of his dirty hands on you again makes me ill. I can't think of anything else but getting you away from him. If I didn't care about the rest of our group, I would take you away from this place. I am torn and struggling to decide."

Malkia grabbed Dario's chin and forced him to look at her. "I love you. We are going to win this war. We are going to fight side by side and end this madman's journey. Damon will die before I allow him to have me. I will execute him with my own hands if it comes down to it. I'm with you, and there's nothing Damon can do to convince me otherwise. If he wants a war, he will receive one."

She rose on her toes and pressed her lips against his. He pulled her against his body and returned the kiss. They were hungry for each other, and the emotions of their circumstances made their desire more intense. It wasn't until Malkia heard Jayde's voice that she pulled away from Dario.

"Malkia?" Jayde mumbled again.

Malkia and Dario turned to find Jayde standing a few feet away.

She was staring at the others and diverting her eyes. "I wanted to tell you what I saw."

"Yes, yes. Sorry," Malkia stammered, smoothing her clothes, and pushing back a flush creeping up her face.

As they walked together, Malkia noticed Jayde's worn expression. The trances were taking a toll again.

"I checked on our group," Jayde said when they reached the others. She wrung her hands together and avoided everyone's eyes. "We are so close. About a half-day flight for us. We could be with them by early morning. I also checked on the wounded dog. He's running slowly, and it looks like he is losing blood, but he's headed back to his group. Damon is not far behind us, less than half a day." She turned and looked at Malkia with desperation in her eyes. "Can we leave now? I would rather fly all night long so we can be with our loved ones tomorrow."

"Yes, of course. Let's go," Malkia said softly, curling her hand over her friend's shoulder. "Does anyone else need anything before we leave?"

Each shook their heads and headed back toward their pegasi and the ones who had stayed behind. Malkia stood by herself, watching the flames eat away at the flesh of the wolf-man. She knew this was it. Once Damon received word of his dead dog, the war would officially start. They could not run anymore. They would have to hurry to Domesca and convince Jasper to put the lives of his people on the line to protect hers.

Dario clutched Malkia's hand. She smiled at him, and they followed the rest of the group to the pegasi. They were all tired, and a melancholy mood settled over them. It was hard to not feel sad when they knew this was the beginning.

Malkia thought of her family and friends waiting for them a few hours away. They were in the dark about how awful their circumstances had become, and she wasn't looking forward to the moment when she had to make their lives worse. Dread snaked up from her stomach and encased her heart as she thought of their future and the disaster they had created.

NINETEEN
Dysfunction Among Friends

THE FIRST SUN rose in the east as they flew toward their group. It had taken them all night to put distance between them and the dead wolf-man, and Malkia was hoping to see her people soon. Jayde had seen where they were and the path they were on, but there were still no signs of them.

Malkia gave Dario a questioning look. Worry was consuming her every thought. She thought they would have run into someone by now. *Where were the lookouts? They had to have someone watching for intruders or savages.*

Then she saw it, smoke rising toward the sky.

"There they are!" Malkia exclaimed, pointing at the smoke.

The others cheered. Relief spread through her mind. They would finally be together again.

Not long after, they landed in the clearing next to everyone and the crowd swarmed them, with cheers rumbling through the masses. Malkia bounded off Parowan, searching for Mataya. They overwhelmed her with hugs and pats on her back, but her sister did not come. Panic beat against her chest and she pushed through the group until she broke through. Mataya stood on the outskirts with Justin, shielding the sun with her hand and searching the crowd.

"Mataya!" Malkia yelled.

Mataya's gaze darted Malkia's direction. When their eyes locked, Mataya screamed and raced toward her sister. They met half-way and threw their arms around one another, squishing themselves into the embrace. Sobs rose from both of their throats, and as Malkia tried to pull away from Mataya to get a good look at her, her sister clung onto her harder. Malkia laughed with delight, cradling Mataya. It did her heart good to hold her little sister again, and she knew she would never want to leave her again.

After several minutes of crying and hugging, Mataya slowly unraveled her arms from Malkia. It was time to address the masses. She gripped Mataya's hand, and they walked toward the campsite where most of the others were gathering.

As they reached the camp, Malkia noticed the crowd was looking around for someone. It only took a few seconds to realize that someone was her. She grinned and pulled Mataya toward the group, laughing as they all applauded.

Dario waved, standing with Jayde and Porter. She walked toward them and motioned for them to follow. As she reached the center of the group, she searched for something that would put her above everyone so they could see her. There was nothing around, but then Dario tossed her on his shoulders. She squealed with delight, knowing how ridiculous she looked.

Once she steadied, her smile turned to the crowd. "It's so good to see all of you again!"

The group cheered, and she raised her hand to settle them down.

"We have flown all night just so we could reunite sooner. The thought of you all being so close was all we needed to push ourselves toward you." She swallowed hard and closed her eyes for a moment, trying to steady her shaky breath. When she opened her eyes again, the joy she had been feeling disappeared. She hated she had to do this. "However, we have not returned with good news. I'm regretful to say, but our plan didn't work out the way we had hoped. The savages are moving our way, and they have magic on their side, which is increasing their speed. We will need to pack up this camp and depart as quickly as possible."

The happiness on their faces melted into wide-eyed, sheer panic. People spoke to one another in hushed tones, and others yelled questions at Malkia and the others who had been with her. Several more ran toward their tents and were already pulling them down.

Malkia held up her hand again. "Please, no questions right now. I will answer as many questions as I can as soon as we depart. It is more important we leave."

Dario helped her slide off his shoulders as the rest of the group rushed toward their tents to clean up.

"That did not go well." Malkia rubbed her temples, then pressed her palms into her eyes. After several breaths, she glanced at Mataya. "Where's your tent?"

"Right there," Mataya said, pointing at a tent at the edge of the campsite.

"Let's pull it down and start helping others. The faster we are out of here, the sooner I can give you answers."

Mataya nodded as Justin began cleaning out her tent. Malkia looked at Dario and Jayde, who were still standing next to her. "Dario, help your group. If you see Skye and Curtis, please send them my way so I can fill them in. Same with Tatum. I would like to speak with him." She was surprised Skye had not been there to greet her.

Dario nodded and walked away without another word. It did not surprise Malkia when Kelsey stepped out of the shadows and joined Dario. Now that she thought about it, this was how they had always been, but only now was it bothering her. Their constant whispering grated on her nerves.

From the opposite direction, Skye appeared and raced toward Malkia. They embraced, and Malkia wanted nothing more than to find a quiet spot and tell her best friend everything she had been through.

Skye ran her hands over Malkia's hair. "I missed you, girl. I was so worried. Why did it take so long to catch up to us?"

"It's a long story, but… I can give you the short version."

Malkia motioned for all of them to come closer. "The savages took me."

Mataya drew in a sharp breath and Skye slowly shook her head, but neither said a word.

"I realize you probably haven't seen Alex, or you would have asked me what happened to him. They captured him about a day after me. It was a dreadful situation, as I seemed to have caught the eye of the leader. Obsessed is a better word. My capture has made the situation worse. He's determined to apprehend me again and extinguish all of you in the process."

Skye's eyes widened, and an unexpected look of icy disdain spread across her expression.

Malkia squirmed under Skye's judgmental gaze, so she focused on Mataya. "I'm not telling you this to scare you. I am telling you to make you understand how important it is we continue… quickly. Domesca will be the safest place and probably our only chance to survive. We could split up our group and everyone head in different directions, but he will capture someone and do whatever he wants to them in order to find me. He's a disturbed man, with only power and control on his mind." She closed her eyes and pinched the top of her nose to ward off an incoming headache. Someone touched her arm, and her eyelids fluttered several times before she could focus on her sister.

"How long do we have?" Mataya asked.

"Several hours, maybe half a day. They have trackers they call wolf-men. They're atrocious and wild. Two of them were on their way here when we stopped them. We slaughtered one of them and seriously injured the other. I'm hoping he'll die before he reaches Damon, their leader. But I will have Jayde check to see where he is at as soon as we are close to leaving." Malkia shuffled her feet awkwardly and picked at a loose piece of thread from Mataya's tent. "That's the short version, but there is a lot more to it."

Skye shook her head and doubled over, laughing. "You mean this leader of theirs is pursuing you? Why would he want you? What did you say or do that made him want to come after you?" Her laughter stopped abruptly, and she stared intently at Malkia as her lips set in a grim line.

"What do you mean, what did I do?" Malkia asked, placing her hands on her hips. "One of his wolf-men launched themselves at me, and after nearly killing Dario, they took me to their camp. He questioned me and I *lied* through my teeth to keep him off your trail. His obsession began immediately, and I did nothing to cause it." She paused, her eyes narrowing to slits. "What is going on here? Why am I being attacked for doing everything I could to protect my people?"

Skye growled softly. "You should have stayed with him. Then he wouldn't be chasing us."

Malkia's and Mataya's jaws dropped at Skye's words. Malkia couldn't believe her best friend would suggest such a thing.

"But I would never leave *you*," Malkia whispered, swallowing the hurt that threatened to turn into tears.

Skye's expression hardened.

"Skye, what's your problem?" Mataya spat at her. "Why would you even think of Malkia not returning?"

"Mataya, don't be naïve." Skye pointed at herself, frustration crinkling her eyes. "*I'm* thinking of the rest of our people. I love Malkia, but I also love everyone else, and now she has put us all in danger. If she had remained, they wouldn't be pursuing us right now. They would never have found out where we were. She is a traitor… and a liar."

"Stop it!" Alex yelled from behind Malkia.

Malkia whipped around and shook her head. Alex ignored her.

"Malkia didn't tell them where we were." His voice trembled, and he pushed his way past Justin to get closer to Skye. "I did. She saved me from them. Do you see my hand, Skye?" He lifted his hand in front of his face. "They cut off three of my fingers. So yes, I caved. I was the weak one. Malkia escaped and helped everyone free me. She would not leave me. *She* does not abandon anyone. They were coming for you, even if Malkia stayed. Damon was going to force her to marry him and then they were going to come exterminate all of you and make her watch as the wolf-men murdered Mataya. He wants to break and destroy Malkia's spirit so she will never have the guts to leave him. So, Skye, maybe you should wait for the entire story before you throw stones. Malkia is the victor in this story, and don't you forget it."

Skye stood silent, shifting on her feet, and looking at the ground. When she glanced up, she had tears running down her face. "But did he ever threaten to cut off her fingers? She had the chance to draw him away, and she failed."

"Why does it matter if he threatened her with the same torture as me?" A crimson flush rose in Alex's cheeks. "He used the love of her sister and people to torture her in other ways. She still escaped and make it back to you. Your anger is misdirected, and I don't understand why."

Skye hiccupped and threw a desperate look in Malkia's direction before pivoting on her heel and sprinting away. Malkia watched her go, not sure if she should follow or let her be alone.

Alex grabbed her shoulder. "She has her reasons to be angry, but we really need to focus on leaving."

"You're right," Malkia said, turning her attention back to the tent. "Thank you for saying that, Alex. It was unnecessary, but I appreciate it."

"You are too modest," Alex replied, patting her on the back as he walked away. "You really were the hero this time. Don't let anyone take that away from you."

Malkia shot him a tight smile, but he was already gone. "I should go talk to Skye."

Mataya grabbed her arm, holding her back. "Malkia, she doesn't deserve your sympathy. She should have waited to hear what happened," she hissed.

"She's afraid, Mataya. It doesn't mean she doesn't care or love me. I need to talk to her and give her the entire story... but it will have to wait." Glancing around the campsite, she noticed their belongings were far from being packed. "We need to finish taking down your tent, pack everything, and go help others. I'm going to make my rounds and then I will return."

Malkia began walking away, but turned back and hugged Mataya again. "I love you, sis. Thank you for believing in me, no matter what. I will come find you as soon as I know our timetable."

She backed away, staring at Mataya one last time, before turning toward the rest of the group. The exhaustion of her emotions was consuming her, and she knew it was time to ground her soul and find some peace. She searched the surrounding area, looking for tree coverage that would conceal her.

From the corner of her eye, she noticed movement just inside the tree line of the forest. She squinted at the brush, but nothing moved. Dread washed over her. Could Damon already be here?

Dashing toward the forest, she was intent on reaching the trees and stopping whoever was in there before they alarmed or harmed her people. As she entered the forest, silence surrounded her and even the tree branches had stilled. She quickly glanced back at her group, anxiety filling every cell in her body.

A rustle from the vegetation startled her, and as she turned toward it, a dark silhouette shifted behind the curtain of leaves. In her gut, she knew it was one of the wolf-men. She drew out her daggers from their sheaths and sprinted toward the savage, determined to wound it before he had the chance to come after her people. When she burst through the brush, she skidded to a halt. She was too late.

"Come with me, Malkia, or he has ordered me to slit as many throats as I can before your group slays me," Barster growled, holding his sharp claws next to Jayde's throat.

Malkia stared hard at Jayde, Skye's hurtful words playing through her mind like a broken record. She had no choice but to follow Damon's orders. Tears welled in her eyes as she thought of Mataya and Dario. This was the only way.

She held up her hands to surrender. "Okay, I'll go with you. Just free my friend without hurting her, and I'll come with you willingly."

Barster growled, tightening his grip on Jayde. "Don't give me any conditions. Slowly move toward us before I rip her head off. After the stunt you pulled yesterday, I would gladly kill everyone in your group. You murdered my brother, and for that, *you* will pay."

Malkia gingerly stepped toward Barster, suspecting he would not harm her until they arrived to Damon. Jayde mouthed the word "no" as Malkia grew closer, but she ignored her friend and asked the Light Beings for a smooth exchange.

As soon as Malkia was within arm's length, Barster struck Jayde on the back of the head with his fist. She tumbled headfirst into the dirt, unmoving. Malkia wrenched forward to check on her friend, but the mutt yanked her backward, clutching Malkia firmly around the waist. He tore through the brush and sprinted in the opposite direction from her group. A sob escaped her lips when she realized it was probably the last time she would see her family and friends.

Barster reached around her and shoved what smelled like lakseed into her mouth. After several uncomfortable minutes, the drugged blackness edged across her eyes and her muscles unwillingly relaxed.

TWENTY

A Light at the End of the Tunnel

IT WAS DARK when Malkia woke. Her eyes fluttered open to the stars twinkling above her. Trees swayed in the soft wind, and she heard the rustling of brush nearby. She pushed against the ground to sit up, but her head pulsed to the rhythm of her heart, and white specks floated across her eyesight. Easing back down, she tried to remember if Barster had hit her in the head too. She reached up with her hand to check the top of her head.

"Careful, you're going to mess up my lovely bandaging job," a strange, gruff voice said. He gripped her hand before she touched her wound.

Malkia sat up in haste and scooted backward. A rush of blood shot to her head, and a dizzy spell flooded her eyes. She cradled her head in between her bent legs and inhaled several times before the sensation passed.

The warmth from a fire pressed against her skin and she tilted her head slightly to find several sleeping people on the other side of the flames. She turned slowly to face a large man with a dark, full beard sitting a few feet away from her.

"Who are you?" she whispered, her question quivering across her lips. Trepidation washed down her spine. "And where am I? What happened to the dog who had me?"

A weary smile formed on the man's lips. "He's dead, Malkia. We killed him." He pointed at her head. "And I apologize for the damage to your head. When he dropped you, your head struck a rock. I tried to bandage it up as best I could, but I'm no doctor. As for who I am, my name is Cormac. We're all from Domesca." He jabbed his thumb at those sleeping around the fire. "Jasper sent us to find you and lead you to our city once your messengers arrived. We saw your dog friend drinking from the stream and stopped when we noticed he had you bound. When he spotted us, he attacked my friend before we had a chance to ask what was going on. So—" He shrugged and grinned. "We took him out."

Malkia's eyes narrowed. "Just like that, you killed him? And how did you know my name?"

Cormac's smile spread across his face again. "You don't remember me, do you?"

Malkia examined his face again, trying to remember who he was. "I'm sorry, I don't."

"That's okay." He leaned back on his hands, staring intently at Malkia. "I wasn't visible to you as much as you were to me, but I am one of Jasper's guards. I was there every time you had dinner or drinks with him." He chuckled, a sparkle gleaming in his dark eyes. "You had quite the many admirers in our city, including Jasper, and you're difficult to forget. As for killing the dog, it wasn't easy. The sucker was fast, but unfortunately for him, so is my buddy over there. He didn't go down immediately, but we were able to finish the job. I'm assuming he's one of the savages Dominique and Nedra told us about?"

"Yes, he was. I owe you my life." Malkia wrung her hands together, cringing when she thought back to the mutt's hands gripping her body. "He was taking me to their leader, who struggles with boundaries. I'm not sure what he has planned for me, but I'm positive it wouldn't be roses and candlelight dinners." She shuddered, kneading her thumbs against her temples. "I'm sorry I can't remember you. Domesca was one of many places I visited last year, and it's difficult to keep all the faces straight. I won't make that mistake again."

Cormac ran his fingers down his beard. "There is nothing better than being remembered by a stunning lady like yourself."

Malkia relaxed her shoulders and took in her surroundings. They were deep in the thick of the forest, snuggled into a mini clearing. It was perfect for a small camp and seemed to keep them concealed. Malkia was grateful for these men who had saved her. It was confirmation the Light Beings were really watching over her.

She turned back toward Cormac. "How close are we to sunrise?"

"The second sun set not too long ago. Do you have any idea where your people are?"

Malkia nodded. "We were heading north once they packed. That was late this morning. When Barster caught me, he had to head southwest to return to his group, so I'm presuming my group is northeast. But I don't know what they decided once my absence was discovered. I would have to know how far the mutt ran before you met up with him."

"It was late afternoon when we spotted him. We have seen no one else since then, but I noticed hawks circling above us just after sunset."

Cormac tilted his head back, searching the sky. "Maybe that was your friends. They could be on their way to retrieve you right now. I hope they realize we are the good guys."

"If the hawks were circling us, that was Jayde, which means she's safe. Thank Theia. She is the one who knew the identity of my captor, so you might have a chance." Malkia winked, her lips forming a sly grin.

Cormac burst into laughter, then ducked his head and quieted when the others stirred. "I like you, Malkia," he said, his tone hushed to nearly a whisper.

Malkia pulled her knees up to her chest and wrapped her arms around them. "It's nice to have a friendly face around. I'm tired of these dogs taking me away from my friends. Trust me, I think you are wonderful yourself. Thanks again for being in the right place at the right time."

"You're welcome. Now maybe we should try to lie down for a bit. I need to wake my friend so he can take watch duty."

"I can't sleep," Malkia replied quickly. "I would be happy to keep your friend company. Plus, who's going to stop my friends from destroying you while you sleep?"

"Good point," Cormac said jokingly, laughing again. "I guess it's your turn to protect us."

Malkia grinned to herself as she watched Cormac shake one man awake. The man perched himself on his elbows and looked at Cormac. Malkia couldn't hear what was being said, but the man glanced at her and waved. He nodded at Cormac as he stood and strolled toward her. He was large like his friend, but was beardless. His auburn hair hung slightly in his face, and Malkia guessed from his smoother complexion he was younger than Cormac.

"Hi, Malkia. Name is Kolten." He reached down to grasp Malkia's wrist. "It's good to see you're awake. We were worried about you."

She held onto his wrist to greet him. "It's good to meet you, Kolten. I feel fine. My head hurts, but I guarantee you it's far better than the alternative. I was just telling Cormac how grateful I am to your team. I would be in the grips of a monster right now if it weren't for you."

"No problem. We were happy to take care of that mutt for you."

Cormac walked up next to Kolten and leaned down toward Malkia. "I'm going to go sleep for a while. Make sure you keep this boy in line for me. He might not listen to me very well, but you might have the magic he needs to stay alert."

Kolten laughed, and Malkia smiled. "Good night, Cormac. I will keep an eye on him for you."

Kolten sunk cross-legged next to Malkia and waited until Cormac snuggled into his bedding before turning her way. "How surprised were you to see us rather than that beast of a dog?"

"Surprised, for sure. Delighted, as well." She stretched her legs in front of her and shook out the numbness prickling through them. "Two down, two to go."

Kolten's jaw dropped. "There are two more?"

Malkia nodded and straightened her posture. "As far as I know, there were four total. My team eliminated one of them yesterday. Now that you slayed Barster, there are two remaining. They're horrible savages. I'm not one to kill, but for my family and friends, I will do what it takes to keep them safe."

"Absolutely. A woman after my heart." He grinned, twirling the edge of his large knife on the ground in front of him.

Malkia changed the subject. "What do you do in Domesca?"

"I'm one of Jasper's guards, like Cormac."

"If Jasper is sending out his guards, who is going to guard him?"

Kolten laughed loudly and then realized how loud he had been and slapped his hand over his mouth. They both looked around at his friends, but they didn't seem to be bothered by the outburst.

"I guess being a guard for Jasper isn't really being a guard," Kolten whispered. "We're more like the head of his army, and we get the pleasure of hanging out with Jasper during the day. He doesn't really need guarding, but we are usually talking politics and strategies during the day."

"Why did Jasper think it was important to send his guards to help us to Domesca?"

"He never said why." Kolten shook his head, leaning forward. "After speaking with your friends, he organized our small team to find all of you. He said he felt it was important you had help. Jasper is our leader for a reason. He sees things no one else does. We trust him to make accurate decisions for our city, and so far, he hasn't failed us. I trust him with my life, and if he said we needed to help you, then it was the right move." He paused and stared into the fire. "And as usual, he was right."

Her stomach knotted with worry for her people as her gaze flitted across the darkened forest. "Did you know we already have someone from your city who is helping us find our way to Domesca?"

"Really?" He focused back on her, shaking his head again. "No, we weren't aware. Who is it?"

"His name is Tatum. He's a dragon slayer from Domesca."

Kolten looked like he was deep in thought for a few moments. Then his face softened, and he chuckled.

Malkia's brows knitted together. "What's so funny?"

"If it's the Tatum I think you are talking about, he's been missing for months now. His family didn't even know where he went. He used to be a dragon slayer a long time ago, but there haven't been sightings for ages now. What has that old gizzard been up to?"

"Slaying dragons," a voice in the trees grumbled loudly.

Kolten and Malkia jumped to their feet and faced the voice in the trees. Two figures stepped out of the protection of the shadows, walking toward them. Malkia recognized one figure immediately. She jogged toward Dario, threw herself into his arms, and held onto him with everything she had. She was laughing and crying and when Dario peeled her away from him; she reached up and kissed his mouth hard.

"After that greeting, I guess I can forgive you for getting captured again," Dario teased, tickling her sides with his fingertips.

Malkia punched him on the shoulder and then kissed him again. It thrilled her to see the man she adored. Malkia glanced over at the other man and noticed it was Tatum. "Tatum, if you're here, who's leading everyone?"

"They stopped for the night. After we found Jayde, we moved immediately. Once Jayde was feeling up to finding you, we made camp. We really made little progress, which is reckless."

"I agree," Malkia said. She chewed on her fingernail, an alarm ringing in her mind. "We should leave. Damon's group can't be too far behind us. Good news though, these men saved me from one of Damon's dogs, and they killed him. Only two more to go."

Dario's facial expression froze, his eyes glazing over for a moment when she finished speaking, but he relaxed and gave her a curt nod before she could comment.

Malkia looked back at Kolten, who was quietly watching the joyous reunion. Tatum was suspiciously eyeing him.

"Do I know you?" Tatum asked.

"Yes, old man." Kolten stepped forward and grasped Tatum's wrist. "I'm one of Jasper's guards. Jasper sent us here to help bring Malkia's group to Domesca. She was just telling me you were with them."

Tatum nodded, his eyes softening. "I recognize you now." He turned toward Malkia. "Well, if we are going to depart, we better do it soon."

Dario's jaw clenched, clearly agitated again. His gaze flashed around, as if he was searching for something or someone. "Jayde viewed Damon's group before we left to find you. They're only a half day behind our people and closing in on this campsite. It will take us some time by pegasus to catch up with everyone, and we aren't sure if Damon has stopped for the night." His gaze finally rested on Malkia, frustration creasing the corners of his eyes.

Malkia stared back for a moment, unsure of what disturbed him, aside from the obvious. There was something more going on, but now was not the time to address it. She turned to face the guards. "Kolten, do you think your men would mind if we woke them?"

"Not if the savages are on our heels. I'll wake them right now."

Malkia led Dario away from the others. "You're my hero again. I knew you would come for me. What did Skye say about all of this?"

Dario shook his head, his stance becoming rigid as he pulled away from her and crossed his arms over his chest. "When she found out you had been taken again, all she did was cry, along with Mataya. She never said why, but since you are asking, it has sparked my curiosity. What is going on with you two?"

"It's a silly story and kind of girl drama. I wouldn't bore you with it. I'm sure she will be okay." She winked at him, hoping to spark his smile again.

He relaxed slightly but remained stone-faced. "Hmm… Yeah, I think I would rather not know. I'm fine without the girl drama."

Malkia was uneasy about his sudden change in demeanor, but she pushed away her nagging thoughts. The other three men were waking, and Kolten was filling them in with the details. It only took them a few minutes to gather their items and join them.

Cormac introduced the three other men as Damari, Knox, and Lucan. After a quick hello and thank-you, they all mounted their pegasi and headed toward Malkia's group.

"Jayde, will you glance at Damon's group before we leave?" Malkia asked quietly, not wanting anyone else to interrupt them.

"Absolutely, I was planning on it." She stepped toward Malkia, a frown covering her face. "I'm so glad you aren't hurt. When I came to and realized you were gone, my heart fell to my feet. But when I saw these men with you instead of the dog, I was praying they would be friends instead of Damon's group. I cannot tell you how overjoyed I was to see you safe."

A lackluster smile played on Malkia's lips. "Thanks, Jayde. I'm just happy he didn't hurt you worse than he did."

Jayde hugged Malkia for the third time since she returned, then Jayde sat next to the tree they were standing under and fell into a trance. Malkia watched Dario as he spoke to Curtis and Skye. He seemed tired. He rubbed the thick stubble under his chin, and his jaw clenched from frustration or fear. Malkia couldn't tell which one it was, or if it was both. Scanning over the rest of her people, she saw Tatum and the other men from Domesca speaking with a small group near Dario, while the rest were finishing packing their horses and pegasi.

Malkia and her rescuers had returned to her group a little less than an hour before and had been greeted warmly. The group had pulled together and was nearly ready before Malkia ground herself. Jacob hadn't heard from the pixies for nearly a day, and their absence was worrisome. She needed to know Damon's whereabouts and if he had sent the other two wolf-men after them as well.

Jayde stirred, drawing Malkia's attention back to her. "They've stopped." She exhaled with relief. "My view was skewed, but I could see their group. The horses are sleeping, with only a few people guarding. I couldn't find Damon, or the witch, or even the dogs. They could hide in the trees though, and who knows where Damon and the witch are, but I would guess they are several hours behind us."

Malkia wrinkled her nose at the mention of the dogs and their tendency to disappear. "Cormac says the Domesca people are more than willing to protect and defend our group. I will feel a hundred times better once we reach the safety of their walls." She reached down and helped Jayde to her feet.

Turning toward the rest of the group, Malkia noticed more of her people were gathering, murmuring to one another. She jogged toward them and was happy to see smiles when she got close.

She raised her hand in the air. "I'm not sure if everyone can hear me, but I wanted to say a few things before we depart," Malkia announced loudly.

The large group quieted and focused on her. "I'm not sure who has spoken to the men who rescued me, but I wanted to provide the details they have given to me. Jasper has graciously offered us his protection and home, as well as sent these men to assist us safely to the city. We have almost a two-day ride to reach our new home, but that's if we stop for the night. I'm asking that we leave now, in the middle of the night, because my capture caused us to fall behind on our schedule. I apologize for the lack of sleep. However, we will be able to stop tonight if we all agree to wake early and push through the next night, so we can reach Domesca sooner. If we can, we could be there by this time that night. What does everyone think?"

Most nodded their heads, with a few voicing their yeses. They were exhausted, but eager to be safe again. Malkia smiled in reply. They had hope, and at that moment, hope was all they needed.

It didn't take long for the group to be on their way. Malkia was at the front with the Domesca men, Mataya and Dario. She grinned at Dario when he reached over and grabbed her hand. He was his old self again.

Mataya chuckled. "You finally did it?" she asked with a sly grin.

Malkia glanced at her. "Did what?"

Mataya nodded toward Malkia's and Dario's hands. "Gave into the madness."

Dario winked at Malkia when she turned his way. "Absolutely," the two said in unison.

TWENTY-ONE

Strategic Planning

THE GROUP TRAVELED through the night and into the next day without incident, and Malkia relaxed enough to enjoy the journey again. Although they hadn't heard from the pixies, so Jacob's nerves created some stress. Malkia and Jayde had both done what they could to keep him calm, but he had stormed off in a rage, and they hadn't heard from him for a better part of the day.

The group rode through several decrepit and abandoned towns and cities. Many watched with wide eyes as they witnessed nature's aggressive vengeance: the vegetation overtaking the buildings, giving them a haunted and mysterious appearance. Malkia yearned to explore the shattered settlements and discover what part of their old life remained, but they had to keep trekking and ignore the surrounding history.

It was nearing dinnertime when Jacob finally raced up behind Malkia. "The pixies are here. I can sense their presence." He panted, continuing without catching his breath. "Can we stop for a moment?"

Malkia waved at the Domesca men. "Will you continue to lead my people? We're going to stop for a moment and speak with the pixies."

"No problem, but don't be too long. Catch up as soon as you can,"

Cormac replied, pulling his pegasi ahead of the group.

Malkia nodded and slowed Parowan. Jacob, Mataya, and Dario followed her off the path and into the trees. Jacob dismounted and jogged toward a thick part of the forest, where he could have some privacy.

Malkia turned toward Dario and Mataya. "I hope they bring good news," she said and sighed heavily with the anxiety swirling inside her mind.

"Me too," Dario whispered, his forehead creased with worry.

The silence consumed all three of them as they watched the still vegetation Jacob had disappeared into. Malkia studied their surroundings, her eyes occasionally falling on Dario. He had closed his eyes, and his expression had relaxed, but there was an odd change to his appearance. His eyes fluttered open and without looking her way, he slid off Brit and turned his back toward Malkia. She continued to stare at him, trying to pinpoint what had shifted.

Jacob emerged from his concealment a few minutes later, appearing relieved, although his frown remained. Malkia's heart skipped a beat, petrified by what the pixies had divulged.

"They had a spell placed on them," Jacob muttered. He wiped his hands down the sides of his pants. "There has never existed a witch powerful enough to hex the pixies, so they are perplexed by how it happened. However, their concern for our people has amplified, as well as for their own assemblage."

"How did they stop the spell?" Mataya asked.

"They didn't," Jacob replied, looking over his shoulder. "Another witch sensed the evil of the spell and blocked it. They aren't sure how long it will hold, but they had to warn us before her barricade disintegrates. The spell returns them to their dwellings, and they're unable to leave. The pixies are distraught over this predicament, and they've said the only way to break the hex is to stop Damon's witch."

"Where's the witch who blocked the spell?" Malkia asked, remembering Alex and the curse on him. She curled her fingers around the pendant hanging from her neck.

"She's in the forest, close to here. The pixies asked if she could block the spell on Alex, but she said she is not powerful enough. She is struggling to block the spell on the pixies, and an additional barricade would make them both impossible."

Malkia raked her hands through her hair and looked back at the road they had journeyed on. "Were the pixies able to see anything before they came here?"

Jacob nodded. "Yes, they did. Damon's group is gaining on us. They have this witch nearly flying. They aren't as fast as us when we are up in the air, but they are quicker than us when we are traveling on the ground." He leaned back on his heels, frustration crinkling his brow. "As of now, it doesn't look like they will catch up to us, but they won't be far behind us when we do reach Domesca."

Malkia and Dario glanced at each other and then back at Jacob.

"What are the pixies' plans?" Dario asked.

Jacob's gaze flashed around at the forest surrounding them. "They're going to send some of their group to take one more look at Damon's." His gaze rested on Dario, who nervously tapped his foot repeatedly against the dirt. "After they report back to me, they're going to continue to do what they've been doing until the block can no longer hold. After that, it will be up to us to stop this witch. We will need to find more witches. If we have enough of them, their powers could stop this powerful one and, if possible, remove her powers. It's complicated, they say, but doable."

Malkia grimaced, holding up the pendant that was glowing blue. "I don't know how we will have time to find several witches. This necklace they gave me has done nothing until now, which is probably from the witch who is hiding in the forest. I just don't know how we will make this work."

"We'll figure out something," Dario said, mounting Brit again. "Jacob, tell the pixies thank you. We better catch up with the rest of our group."

Jacob vanished in the thick of the vegetation for a moment. When he returned, he mounted his pegasus, and the four of them caught the tail end of their group after a few clicks down the road. Malkia raced Parowan toward the front, where the Domesca men led.

"We have a problem," Malkia said, riding next to Cormac.

The muscles in his face stiffened. "What kind of problem?"

"Damon's witch is increasing their speed. They are catching up, and if we continue at this pace, we will have them nipping at our feet when we reach Domesca." Malkia breathed in deeply, her heart threatening to jump from her chest.

"Well, then we need to speed up our pace." Cormac raised a sly brow. "Do you have any ideas? Because I might have a few."

Malkia nodded. "I was thinking we should immediately send some people by pegasus, to prepare Jasper and your people. Then we should put as many children as we can on pegasi and fly them to Domesca first. The rest of us can take the horses. We can load up on everything we can carry, leaving the rest behind."

"Do we have enough pegasi for all these children?" Cormac asked. "Safely, we could only place one child with one adult."

Shaking her head, she leaned forward, keeping her voice down. "We could have an older child and a younger child and only send a few parents with them. I know it will be hard for them to separate from their kids, but this is our best chance."

"That might work." Cormac's eyes narrowed with thought, his lips setting into a thin line. "When we stop for dinner, we could organize it. We will send the few adults, along with a child each, to warn Jasper. Then we can organize the children and pegasi."

"But we can't send the children off into the night," Dario said, coming from behind Malkia and placing himself between her and Cormac. "It would be too risky for one of those older children to fall behind or lose sight of the others."

"He's right," Cormac replied, eyeing Malkia. "We wouldn't be able to send the children until morning. My suggestion is to stop briefly for dinner. Ride on until late into the evening and then rest for the greatest part of the night. Let everyone sleep, but before light, we should be up and on our way. As soon as the first sun rises, we could send the children off with a few adults."

"That's sounds like the best plan," Malkia said in agreement, looking back at the tired group. "We should break for dinner soon. I would like to have the small group gone as soon as we finish eating."

Cormac nodded, pointing forward. "There's a small, abandoned town coming up. It isn't much and has housed no residents since the wars, but there's a small building we could eat in. I've stopped there a few times on my travels. It will work perfectly to shelter everyone from the heat and provide you a platform to speak to everyone."

"Fantastic," Malkia replied, shoving her hair out of her face and giving him a wry smile. "How long until we reach it?"

"I would say it is only a mile or so away." Cormac raised himself off the back of his pegasus, squinting his eyes at the road ahead. "We should be there shortly."

Malkia nodded, and they continued in silence. She was deep in her thoughts, looking for ways to break up her group without having parents angry and hurt.

Kolten pulled his pegasus up next to hers. "Malkia, can I speak to you?" His voice was barely a whisper.

She pivoted to face him. "Absolutely, what's on your mind?"

"It needs to be private." Koleton's gaze flashed around at the others. "Can I have some time when we stop for dinner?"

Malkia nodded, smiling. "Sure. As soon as we stop, we can take a few minutes."

"Thank you."

Cormac was correct. The town had been deserted for a long time. The houses and buildings were crumbling, and the grass was towering with weeds and vines snaking throughout the dwellings. Very few windows were intact, and Malkia had a feeling it wouldn't take much to shatter them.

The building Cormac had spoken of was probably the most stable of all the structures. It seemed to have been constructed later than the others, and it possessed the latest advances to keep it from collapsing.

Most of the windows were blown out, but the building itself was completely intact.

When Malkia dismounted Parowan, Kolten was standing a few feet away, waiting to speak with her. Everyone else was busy helping others, so she beckoned him to come closer and they strolled toward the building together.

Kolten looked over his shoulder, making sure they were alone before he spoke. "My sister is a witch."

Malkia glanced at him with a surprised look on her face.

He raised his finger to his lips. "I didn't want to tell you in front of anyone because it is a secret." His eyes narrowed. "There are five witches in my community, and one of them is my sister. She is afraid if Jasper discovers them, he will either banish them or use them for things they aren't willing to do. I've tried reasoning with her, but she's petrified. Jasper is a decent man. I know he would not exile her." He paused, stealing a look behind them. "I heard Jacob saying Damon's witch is potent and is keeping the pixies prisoners, along with helping Damon speed up his group. He also mentioned something about her hexing Alex. I don't know how powerful these five witches are, but I know they are respectable. They could help."

Malkia forced a smile at Kolten and curled her arm around his back. "I'm sorry you feel like this needs to be a secret, but I can understand your desire to protect your sister. I won't divulge this information to anyone. Will you go with the first group of people back to Domesca and speak with your sister about the incoming problem?

"Yes, of course."

"Good. Between the five of them, they might stop her. Beg them to help, and if they agree, prepare them for the fight of their lives."

Koleton patted Malkia on the shoulder. "I will do whatever I can to convince them."

"Let's get this show on the road," Dario said as he strolled up to them. His gaze flashed toward Koleton with a gleam of contempt surfacing, but it quickly dissipated.

She pursed her lips and waited for him to look her way, but he never did. Did he not like Koleton?

Her questions for Dario would have to wait. She focused on the building and noticed most of her group was already inside, preparing to eat. She smiled at Kolten, then followed Dario into the building with everyone else. Cormac had already pulled a makeshift stage together and motioned for Malkia.

When she climbed on top of the platform, she was happy to see the gathering below her. She clapped her hands several times. "We did excellent! We are nearly to Domesca, and Damon's group remains behind us. I'm so grateful to all of you, for sticking by me and the rest of our people. I know I'm not perfect, but I hope you all know I am always thinking of what is best for us as a group."

"You did great!" someone yelled from the group.

Malkia's smiled widened as she scanned over the crowd. "Thanks. I hope you all feel that way. And I hope you still feel that way once I tell you what has occurred."

The room grew quiet, and all eyes were on her.

"We have found out Damon's group is speeding up, and there's a chance they will catch up to us if we continue on the route we are on."

The silence grew, and everyone's eyes widened.

She continued, wringing her hands together. "But we have a plan, and with everyone's cooperation, I know we can make it work. After dinner, I'll be sending a small group of people on pegasi to warn Jasper and his people of Damon's whereabouts. I have asked Kolten to lead that group. This cluster will comprise three other adults carrying three children with them as well. And if Kolten doesn't mind, I would like to send a child with him."

She glanced at Kolten, and he nodded his approval. Looking back at her people, she breathed in deeply before proceeding. "We will continue on, after this group has departed, and we will ride until late into the night. I know we have been moving for nearly two days straight, but I'm asking that we only stop for a few hours before we continue. That will give us some rest and maybe a few hours of sleep. I know it is painful to think about, but once we reach Domesca, we will all be able to rest until Damon reaches the castle."

The chatter from the crowd grew quickly, and Malkia couldn't speak over the shouting. She looked at Dario for help and he whistled loudly, securing the group's attention.

Malkia straightened her posture, standing tall over the multitude. "What I'm about to ask will be difficult, but I think it is the best plan we can plan. I want to remove the children, sending them to Domesca as quickly as possible. I'm asking for all pegasi. When the first sun rises in the morning, I want two children, one older and one younger, to take a pegasus and fly to Domesca."

People shouted at her while others sobbed in reply, clasping their children to them. Dario whistled again, but the noise didn't stop.

"Stop talking!" Cormac bellowed at the crowd.

The horde immediately quieted, focusing on Cormac.

"What's wrong with all of you? Malkia has done nothing but risk her neck for every one of you. Show her some respect by shutting up and allowing her to finish. Her plan is the best we could think up, so unless any of you have a better idea, keep your pie holes shut!"

"Thank you, Cormac," Malkia replied gratefully. As she turned back to face her group, her eyebrows furrowed with sadness. "I want at least three or four adults to travel with the children. Maybe even eight would be better. We have a lot of kids, and I want to ensure their safety. One of the Domesca men will accompany the children, along with two or three of our own men. The rest of the adults should be women, especially if you are pregnant. We can also send pregnant women tonight. By show of hands, how many women are with child?"

Five hands shot up, and two more came up slowly. Both women looked around at the group and then at their husbands.

Malkia nodded. "We have seven pregnant women. Let's send two of them tonight and five of them in the morning. Does that sound fair to everyone else?"

More heads nodded, and this time, the crowd remained quiet. Malkia relaxed. Finally, they were getting somewhere.

"Here's the plan. We will finish dinner. Afterward, we will send three adults, two of them being out of the pregnant women, and four children. They will take as many supplies as their pegasi can handle and follow Kolten to Domesca. When they arrive, they will inform Jasper of Damon's witch and his two wolf-men and that his group is closing in on us. The rest of us will continue until late into the night. We will only stop for a few hours to rest. At first light, we will send the second group. This group will consist of the rest of the pegasi, all the children, and as many adults as we can send. They'll follow Knox to Domesca and take shelter until the rest of us arrive. Once the second group has departed, we will race to Domesca on the horses that remain. Luckily, if I did the math right, we should have enough horses for everyone. Does anyone have questions, concerns, or ideas?"

It was silent for a few moments until one of the older children slowly raised their hand.

"Yes, Penny?"

"Can I choose to stay here with my parents? I don't want to leave them," the child asked.

"Penny, I would prefer you went onto Domesca with the rest of the children. You're one of the older children, and you would be a great help to the younger ones. It would be nice to know we had someone like you to assist with the kids once you arrived in Domesca."

Another woman in the back raised her hand.

"What's your question, Ashlyn?"

"What about mothers who are nursing or have small children and babies?"

"They'll go with their children. If you have a baby, carry them in their pouch and hold a smaller child on a pegasus. Make sure the baby is secure so you will be able to hold on to the other child if needed."

Another woman raised her hand. "What if our children are older but we don't want to be separated?"

"It depends on the number of seats left. Our goal is to deliver the children to a safe place and make it easier for us on the ground to ride hard so we can put some distance between our people and Damon's group." Malkia inhaled deeply a few times, her eyes closing for her to compose herself as she straightened her stature. "Do you understand where I'm coming from? This is a group effort, and we all have to be unified to make it work."

The woman nodded and stared at her hands. The group was quiet for a moment, and one by one, people whispered to one another.

Malkia cleared her throat. "I'm going to assume the whispering means there are no more questions. Please come to me if any of you think of better ideas. We will depart in the next twenty minutes. Eat quickly. We already know Kolten is leaving with two of the pregnant women. I will need one more man to volunteer to go, along with four children." Her gaze swept over the crowd. "First come first serve."

Dario helped Malkia from the platform, and she hurried to one exit, needing some air. Dario, Cormac, and Mataya followed. When she neared the exit, one of the pregnant women approached her.

"Malkia?" She held out her hand. "I would like to go with this first group. I also have two other children. Can they be two of the kids to go first?"

"Absolutely, Trina." Malkia's lips set into thin lines, and she stared intently at the woman. "What about your husband? Would he like to go with this group?"

"He said he would, but he thinks someone else should receive the spot if his whole family may be in the first group. We don't want to be too selfish," Trina explained with a weary smile.

"You're not being selfish, just proactive. Do you see anyone else over here asking to go?"

Trina looked around and noticed everyone was eating and talking among themselves. No one else was taking this moment to be a part of the first group. "If no one else volunteers, my husband would gladly be in this group. But let someone else take it if they ask."

"Okay, Trina. Be prepared to leave in the next twenty minutes."

"We will be." Trina walked away.

It disappointed Malkia that they could not grasp the seriousness of this situation. Dario put his arm around her and gave her a side hug. "They'll come around. It's a lot to take in. Separating from a child is painful."

"I know it is, Dario," Malkia whispered sadly. "I understand their pain all too well. It would just be nice if they understood mine as well. I'm only doing this to protect them, not hurt them."

"We know you are, and they'll understand soon enough. They haven't seen Damon and his group like we have. I'm sure they almost feel like they are running from our illusion. They are doing everything by faith, and sometimes that is difficult. Be patient. They will come around."

"Thanks, Dario." Malkia looked back at her group and smiled when she noticed another pregnant woman strolling toward her with two children. It appeared as if her first group would be complete and on their way.

TWENTY-TWO

Domesca

WHAT REMAINED OF Malkia's group raced through the forest, following Cormac, Damari, and Lucan toward Domesca. The second group had taken off hours ago, and they had left their trailers back in the town they had the meeting. Both suns had risen, and Malkia was feeling free as a bird as their horses whipped across broken roads toward safety.

Malkia asked Jayde to look at Damon's group before they separated, and she'd said he was still gaining on them. He was mere hours behind them and hurtling through the deserted towns and forests. Malkia was content with the plan they had decided on, especially after Jayde told her how close Damon was. The wolf-men stayed close to Damon but were nipping on her team's heels at the same time. It was unnerving.

"It's just over these hills," Cormac affirmed, pulling up next to Malkia and Dario as they slowed to a walk.

"So close," Malkia quietly whispered. She peered behind her at the exhausted and restless group. Worry knotted in her gut, but hope was too close to stop now. The group continued to climb up the hill they were on.

"We will make it," Dario assured Malkia. "He's not behind us yet, and we only have another hour of travel."

"I know," Malkia replied, forcing a smile. "I'm just worried we will be at war before we prepare Jasper."

"The others will have arrived by now, and Jasper will prepare our people," Cormac stated. "I told Kolten to move everyone into the safety of the castle walls before we arrive and to organize our military and weapons. We will be ready as soon as we arrive."

"I apologize for bringing this upon your people, Cormac," Malkia said with an apologetic tone. She steered her horse around a fallen tree. "They don't deserve this war."

"Don't be sorry, Malkia. They would have eventually found us, and who knows how much more resilient they would've been by then. This is for the best. We will fight side by side and end this situation before it becomes out of hand. If I know Jasper, he has already alerted the towns nearest to us, which means we will have more than enough people to fight this war."

"I still feel awful, but thank you for trying to make me feel better." Malkia patted the side of her chestnut horse. "We had better keep moving."

They eased their horses back into a run, and Dario whistled to alert the rest of the group to do the same. It would not be long before they reached Domesca, and Malkia was overly excited to stop running.

A yawn overtook her face as Malkia watched her friends reunite with their families. They had just reached Domesca, and her energy was drained and she felt emotionally fragile. The long journey was over, but she knew the hard road was now beginning.

She grabbed Dario's hand. There were tears threatening to overtake her, and she knew she would need his strength to pull herself together and be strong for their people. She didn't think she would have the energy to face Damon and his savages. All she wanted to do was find a dark corner, curl into a ball, and sleep away the war coming their way.

Dario pulled her close and squeezed her. It was easy to let him protect her, but she feared by letting him protect her, Damon would not stop until Dario was dead.

She wrapped her arms around him, and he swung her up off the ground and carried her away from the chaos. He walked up the stairs to the room Cormac had told her was hers when they had first arrived at the castle. Someone warmly decorated it with colorful paintings and murals, and the bed was plush and warm. Malkia already felt at home.

Dario laid her on the bed and kissed her forehead. "Get some rest. I'll wake you when we hear anything about Damon and his group."

She didn't resist. Her eyes were already closing before he walked away.

Malkia woke in a panic. She sprung into a sitting position and glanced around the room. One candle had been lit on the nightstand, but besides that, it enveloped her in darkness. It had to be late in the night, considering nightfall was later during the warm season.

She jumped out of bed and nearly tripped over her own feet as she hurried toward the door. When she pulled it open, she faced more darkness.

The silence was eerie, and Malkia's stomach flip-flopped as she thought of the possibilities. Had Damon already invaded? Her heart jumped into her throat when quiet footsteps reached her ears. They were coming her way. She ducked back into her room and softly shut the door.

She looked for a place to hide and decided behind the door was her best option. In haste, she slid into her position, but not before she grabbed another candlestick sitting on the wardrobe nearby. She waited for the footsteps to fade away. Unfortunately, they stopped outside her door. She watched the doorknob turn, and the door creak open. When she was ready to hit the intruder on the head, she noticed his silhouette.

It was Dario. "You—you scared me to death!" she exclaimed, placing her free hand over her heart.

Dario jumped, looking over his shoulder at Malkia. He noticed the candlestick in her hand and burst into laughter.

"This isn't funny," Malkia grumbled. Her chest tightened with frustration. "Why is it so late, and why have I not been awakened before now?"

Dario grabbed Malkia around the waist and pulled her against him. He gave her a quick kiss on the mouth and smiled wickedly. "Did you really think you were going to take me down with a candlestick?"

Malkia pouted. "I had to use something. It was dead quiet in this place, and I did not know what time it was or where everybody had gone. For all I knew, Damon had already taken the place over, and he was coming for me."

"What did I tell you?" he asked, nuzzling her neck with his whiskers. "I will never let that slimeball put one of his greasy fingers on you again. I will protect you, no matter what."

Malkia smiled halfheartedly. Dario didn't understand how much his protection terrified her. Damon was vicious, and the thought of the two of them fighting because of her made her sick to her stomach. She set the candlestick back on the wardrobe and wiped her tears before she turned back toward Dario.

"What is happening with Damon?"

"We asked Jayde to take a quick look before she took a nap. She was exhausted, just like you, if not worse. She found Damon's group and said they'd stopped. They had set up camp a few clicks away, and the dogs had returned to Damon. We're not positive what their plan is, but we heard from the pixies, and Jasper wants you to hear what they had to say. Are you ready to come join the group?"

"Dario, why didn't you wake me up earlier?" She gritted her teeth, her annoyance flaring. "I should have been a part of this planning group from the beginning."

"Because you and I are a team now, and you needed your sleep. I promise you won't be left out of anything. Whatever I hear, you will hear, and I hope vice versa from you."

Malkia bit her lip, her irritation melting away. It was hard to stay mad at him. "Yes, of course."

Dario pulled her back in his arms. "I love you, sweet Malkia."

Malkia melted in his embrace for a moment, then pulled away.

"Will you take me to Jasper, please?"

"Follow me." He took her hand and led her out of the room.

When they reached the rest of the group, Malkia was happy to see so many people gathered. Mataya settled next to Justin, and Skye was sitting with Curtis. They waved her over.

"Malkia, it's so good to see you!" Jasper exclaimed, bounding up from his seat. "I was sorry I didn't greet you when you first arrived, but they told me you found a warm bed to sleep in."

She hugged Jasper when he reached her side. "It overjoyed me to have a safe and warm place to sleep. Thank you, Jasper, for taking care of my people."

Jasper released Malkia and looked her in the eyes. "No, thank you for thinking of us. I heard of this group about a month ago, but didn't realize how vengeful they had become. I'm glad we have the resources to keep you safe—and fight them as well. Our neighboring friends arrived yesterday, and we've been watching and planning ever since."

Malkia smiled and nodded. Jasper returned to his seat, and Dario led her to Mataya. Malkia sat next to her sister and leaned into her embrace.

"Did you sleep well?" Mataya asked.

"Yes." Malkia nodded. "I don't think I have slept that well since before we found out about Damon's group. How about you?"

Mataya smiled widely, her eyes twinkling for the first time in weeks. "It was lovely to arrive early today and spend some time walking around and familiarizing myself with the area. I also got a fabulous nap in a warm and soft bed. The best sleep I've had since we left."

"Malkia?" Jasper asked, interrupting.

Malkia turned toward Jasper and the others.

"I thought you would like to know what we have done to prepare and maybe hear about our special secrets that will give us an advantage over these savages," Jasper said, once he had Malkia's attention.

"Oh, yes! Absolutely!" She scooted to the edge of her seat.

"First, Jacob heard from the pixies. The witch who is protecting them is growing weak and will need help soon. They've informed Jacob that Damon and his group are planning for battle. They stopped about an hour from the castle, and he has sent out trackers, along with his dogs, to find other people willing to join the fight. His dogs have been close to the castle, and they've returned to give Damon the details. They overheard him demanding to overtake our castle and capture the people, along with finding you. He has ordered them not to hurt you, but they can exterminate anyone who stands in their path."

Malkia sat in silence. Feeling like a burden, she simply stared back, unable to form the right words.

Jasper leaned forward, tapping his fingers on the arm of his chair. "I know that look. Don't get any ideas about leaving, thinking you will protect us."

Mataya squeezed Malkia's arm.

"He will invade, no matter what." Jasper pointed around the room. "You're a part of this group and we will protect you, along with everyone else here. We are bigger than Damon's group, and we have the protection of the castle."

"I know, Jasper, but the man scares me." Malkia shuddered, recalling his outlandish behavior. "I think he has lost his mind. The thought of him hurting or slaughtering anyone because of me is terrifying."

"I don't want to sound rude, but this was going to happen whether or not you were his obsession." Jasper cleared his throat. "He would have eventually come our way. It is better we end this now than endure it later, when he's far more powerful. Don't beat yourself up over this. I guarantee you did us a favor by bringing him to us now."

Malkia saw a glimmer of something in Jasper's eyes when he spoke, and it made her uneasy. He winked at her, giving her a smile of reassurance. Instinct told her he knew more about Damon, her, and this situation that no one else knew.

"To continue…" Jasper settled back into his chair. "The pixies have given us a lot of information about the whereabouts of Damon's trackers and dogs. They've been eavesdropping on Damon's conversation. He's threatening to execute your friend, Astrid, and her mother as well."

Malkia winced when he mentioned Astrid. "I should've saved them. I should have never left them there with him."

"Don't be so hard on yourself," Jasper replied. "You cannot save the whole moon. We'll do what we can to rescue them and everyone else but you cannot put any deaths on yourself unless you are the one committing the murder."

Malkia closed her eyes, exhaling slowly. "What else did the pixies say?"

Jasper smiled when she opened her eyes again. "They said you have a great destiny and that we have to keep you safe. I already knew those things, but the pixie's confirmation is reassuring. They are cognizant of you and your future. Their wise words have made this battle even more important than it was before."

Everyone's attention turned toward Malkia. It was as if she had grown a third eye. The surprised look on her face was hard to hide, and she suddenly felt very overwhelmed. "What do you mean? And how would you know?" she questioned, shaking her head. "I'm just a normal person wanting a normal life. I didn't ask for anything great, and I don't understand how you or the pixies have come to that conclusion."

Jasper smiled again. He stood and motioned for her to follow him. She rose to her feet, but then stopped and glanced at Dario and Mataya.

"Jasper, where are we going?" Malkia asked, not wanting to go without those two.

"I have something to show you. The pixies want you to know where you really came from."

The whispers in the group grew loud as she walked toward Jasper. "Jasper, this is insane. Tell me what you—"

"Malkia, don't be afraid. Take this leap of faith with me," Jasper said as he grabbed her hand. He peered over her shoulder at Mataya and Dario. "You two are more than welcome to come, but let's keep the circle small. This is going to be very emotional for Malkia, and for you too, Mataya."

Jasper didn't act concerned by the whispers or the curiosity of the others. He waited patiently as Mataya and Dario joined them, and then he led them out of the room and down the hallway. On his way down the hall, he grabbed a lantern and continued down several corridors until they reached a large door. He motioned for a guard to open it.

Malkia clutched Dario's hand as they waited, and her anxiety grew, especially when the door opened all the way.

A large stone staircase opened, leading down into the lower levels of his castle. It was dark, but the guard used a torch to light what appeared as a small shelf on the wall. When it lit, the fire raced down the whole staircase along the shelf, illuminating the way down.

The place petrified Malkia. It went down to a place she could not see, but as Jasper gripped her hand again, she noticed compassion in his eyes. Although he made her feel uneasy, she had a feeling it was only because he was nudging her into the unknown and out of her comfort zone.

There was a voice within encouraging her to trust him. It was imperative she followed him. Whatever was down in the abyss of his vault held the answers to her unspoken questions. The ones that kept her awake at night and those that haunted her dreams when she slept.

Finally. The answers to her forgotten past.

TWENTY-THREE

A Past Revealed

AS THEY DESCENDED the enormous staircase, Malkia thought of her childhood friend, Palma. She was the only one in their town who had telepathy and they had been the best of friends. It had all come to a screeching halt after the wars. Palma had disappeared. Malkia had searched her friend's home and the town for her, but she was never found, and their connection had been severed.

Palma's dad had died several years before, and her mom had perished the same way Malkia's parents had died. Her brother had moved away a few years before, and Malkia did not know where he had gone. With no significant other and only her mother's destroyed house as her known safe haven, Malkia believed her best friend had faced the same fate as all the others. They never found her body, and if she had survived and left before the bombs hit their town, she had obviously decided not to return.

Malkia had mourned Palma right along with her family. Over the years, before the wars started, she had met others with telepathy, but they had all disappeared as well. Malkia felt alone after the chaos ended, and even more so when people began rebuilding their lives. When they had asked her to lead them, she had only accepted to keep her mind from wandering into despair and loneliness.

After all this time, why was Palma at the forefront of her thoughts?

The staircase kept winding, and it seemed like it would never end. Malkia was growing anxious to find out what was at the bottom. Dario squeezed her hand and smiled at her. Malkia tried to catch Jasper's expression, but he was a couple of steps ahead of them.

Mataya clutched Malkia's other hand and was shaking, so Malkia cradled her close. "Everything is going to be fine, dear sister."

"I have an awful feeling in the pit of my stomach. I feel like I'm about to lose you."

"Don't be silly, Mataya. You will never lose me."

Jasper shot Malkia a sideways glance. She sighed, not understanding why he was being so mysterious. *Was Mataya going to lose her? Were they all stepping into a trap?*

"Jasper, how much farther?" Dario asked.

"Just another bend, and we should be there," Jasper replied, glancing over his shoulder. "There's no need to be afraid, Mataya. Your sister is right; everything will be fine. You're all in safe hands. I apologize for the vague answers to what is down here, but I know you wouldn't understand if I told you. This is something you have to see, to understand and believe."

They rounded the next bend and came to a large corridor. They strolled down the hallway toward another large door. The guard who had accompanied them opened it. Malkia's pulse quickened as the door moved slowly.

Jasper walked ahead of everyone, over the threshold and into the darkness. Malkia shot Dario an apprehensive glance, then jogged after

Jasper. She had to know what was in there. She had to know why he believed she was greater than she really was.

She eased up close to Jasper and heard Dario and Mataya walking behind her. After a moment, Jasper stopped and nodded at his guard. The guard walked around the four of them and pulled down on a lever. Instantly, the room filled with light and a quiet buzzing noise.

The three guests each stepped back, taken aback by the bright lights.

The room was large. It was wired with electricity, and right in the middle was a small ship. However, this was not a ship that floated in the water. It appeared identical to the spaceships the sky people flew.

Malkia's mind raced along with her heart. She glanced at Dario and Mataya, whose eyes were both wide with shock and confusion.

"Jasper?" Malkia quizzically whispered.

He was smiling as he peered at Malkia. "When you first came here last year, I knew who you were. You're different. Did you know that?"

Malkia shook her head, but then stopped and slowly nodded.

"Have you always felt you belonged somewhere else?"

Malkia stared at him, wondering how he knew. "I never told a soul how I felt. How did you know?"

"I come from the same place as you do. I've been able to stop the incantation that was placed on my memory, but I'm still not as powerful as you are. You're meant to do great things, considering you have the coveted gift of telepathy. It is why they hid you all here, and it's why most of you disappeared during the wars."

Malkia's eyes brimmed with tears, her face scrunching with frustration. "What are you talking about? This is my home!"

Jasper shook his head. "You were born on a different moon. Before the sky people made their presence known to Esaki, they placed a few dozen of their children here to protect them. You and I were a part of them. They put a spell on us to forget. It also blocked our powers. The only one they couldn't halt was telepathy. Misty is a daughter of one boy they placed here, and she inherited her ability from him. They took him away after the wars, but they could not lock onto Misty, along with three others. When they locked on you, Esta's essence interrupted the signal, and they took her without you. Something similar happened to Misty. She should have gone with her father, but it only took him."

"Wait. What? Esta's alive?" Malkia looked at Mataya, then feeling weak, she collapsed to the ground, her body shaking uncontrollably. Her sobs grew loud as she thought of her life and her baby. How was this possible?

Dario curled his arms around her, pulling her into an embrace.

"Jasper, that's enough. This is way too much for anyone to handle," Dario bellowed, throwing him a disgusted glare.

Malkia shook her head and spoke even louder. "No! I want to hear it all. I want to know where my baby is. I want to know why you didn't tell me all of this last year and why my parents didn't return for me." Her face heated with fury, as she realized her whole life had been a lie. Her parents had deceived her, and her birth parents had abandoned her. Jasper had lied to her.

Everything was a lie.

Jasper didn't appear upset, nor did he seem to worry about her anger. He inspected the spaceship and motioned for Malkia to go aboard. "Malkia, I didn't have the right to tell you. I'm only divulging this to you now because they asked it of me. I wanted to tell you, but they said you were meant to remain on Esaki."

"Who's 'they'?" Malkia asked, growing angrier.

"Your parents. They have Esta, along with Palma. Did you know you two are sisters?"

Malkia climbed to her feet, clenching her hands into fists to push away the fury rising in her chest. "Jasper, for the sake of my sanity and your life, stop telling me bits and pieces and spit out everything."

Jasper smiled, although his tired eyes told a grimmer story. "To tell you the truth, I don't know that much. The entire group of them are mysterious. My parents abandoned me as well. I don't mean to be offensive, but this is not all about you. I found out in a far more disturbing way than you, so please take a step back and allow me to explain as much as I can. It won't be long until you speak to them and then you can yell at them yourself."

Malkia realized she was nose-to-nose with Jasper. Taking the few steps back, she reclined back to the ground and cradled her head between her legs. Dario was by her side, along with Mataya.

Her sister cried as she put her arms around her. "Don't let them take you away from me," Mataya pleaded in between sobs.

"Never. Never," Malkia replied, grabbing her sister's chin and forcing Mataya to look into her eyes.

Her attention returned to Jasper. "Tell me everything you know. I'm ready."

Jasper nodded, sagging against the wall for support. "Here is all I know. Our moon was attacked when we were children. They wanted the telepathic children, not only because they thought these children could read everyone's minds, but also because of their various other powers. I don't know what other powers you possess, and we won't know until your parents remove the spell on you. In my experience, you won't only remember all your powers, but you will remember your life on our home moon, Eris. We lived in the most amazing place, far more stunning than Esaki. When the creatures from a nearby moon began kidnapping the gifted children, our parents brought us here. It was a secret mission, and only the parents they found for us knew of our existence and reasons for placing us here."

Jasper quieted, and Malkia cradled her head back between her legs. Confusion flooded her mind as anger and hurt waded through her stomach, oozing toward her heart. She peeked at Mataya and realized that no matter the depth of her anger, she was grateful to have her as her sister. She couldn't be mad without wishing away her family and friends. Malkia wiped her tears away and rose with the help of Dario.

She helped her sister off the ground and gave her an enormous hug. "I'm the luckiest person in the universe. You're my sister, even when it wasn't supposed to happen. I'm so blessed."

Mataya sobbed again, clinging to Malkia. "I love you, Malkia. You're all I have."

"And I'm never leaving you," Malkia said, stroking her sister's hair.

Jasper cleared his throat. "After they realized they had left you here, they believed there had to be a reason. They watched you to see how you would respond to your grief, and it amazed them how the townspeople flocked to you. They knew you were meant to lead and lead you did. You had your settlement back to working order in only a few short months. And by the year anniversary of your parents' death, your town was fully functional and content. Your parents believed, for the time being, this had to remain your home."

Malkia growled again before she spoke. "Then why did they not return my baby?"

Jasper wrung his hands together, shaking his head. "To tell you the truth, I don't know. That will be something to ask them."

"When will that be?"

"I don't know that either. They said to bring you down here and when they could safely transmit to the spaceship, you would already be here. But to tell you the truth, it could be days before we hear from them."

Malkia swallowed back the knot of dread in her throat. "So we just wait? I have to stay down in this dungeon and wait until someone can tell me who I really am?"

"I don't think so." Jasper straightened his stature as he stepped toward her. "Let's return upstairs, finish planning our attack on Damon, and maybe find a way to block the spell put on you."

"How did you break the spell on you?" Dario asked, his eyes narrowing as he folded his arms over his chest.

"My parents broke it. The only ones who can break it are your birth parents, but you can block it if you find a powerful witch."

"If we found a witch that strong, it wouldn't be me they would help," Malkia said. "They would need to help the pixies by stopping Damon's witch."

Jasper shook his head. "Malkia, you don't understand. If we blocked the spell on you and you remembered all your powers, I am confident you could stop Damon on your own."

Malkia's mind raced as she thought of the possibility, but then returned to reality as she glared at Jasper. "I don't know who told you this, but I'm tired of hearing it. Keeping my people safe has been my only focus. I don't know the people who stole my daughter, but all this nonsense is insane. I'll find a witch to stop the spell on me and then you will see I am not extraordinary. Afterward, I will have that witch help the pixies and end this fiasco with Damon."

Jasper remained poised and unmoved by her speech, but he did nod his head and move toward the corridor that led them back to the windy staircase. Malkia grabbed Dario's and Mataya's hands, and they followed Jasper together.

They hadn't quite reached the door when the ground and walls around them quivered and then convulsed. The three of them halted in their tracks and glanced at one another with panic in each of their expressions.

Damon had made his first move.

TWENTY-FOUR

Magical Saviors

MALKIA LEAPED FORWARD and sprinted across the hard floor. She passed Jasper and the guard as she pushed her long legs to move faster up the staircase and bolted over the threshold leading to the main corridor. Everyone else had fallen behind and the staircase was dark behind her.

As she raced down the hallway, a raised piece of marble stabbed the edge of her toe and she stumbled forward, nearly toppling face first into the incoming wall. She braced herself against the stone structure and caught her breath. As she did, there was another blow, and the walls and floor shook around her, crumbling in several areas.

Malkia was desperate to reach her people. She had to find Kolten. He was the one who knew those witches and would be the one to help her.

"Malkia, wait! I have something else I must tell you!" Jasper yelled.

Malkia glanced over her shoulder, barely seeing Jasper and Mataya, who were running as fast as they could toward her. Dario was only a few yards away, but considering his ability of speed, it surprised her he hadn't torn past her.

She shook her head in reply.

"Damon is one of us!" Jasper yelled again, his breath coming in short.

Malkia skidded to a halt and whirled around to face the small group behind her. Her mind was once again going a million miles an hour, and she wasn't sure she heard him right. *What did he say? Damon is one of us?*

"Jasper, are you serious?" Malkia yelled, even though they had nearly reached her.

"Yes, I found out after Dominique and Nedra arrived." Jasper panted, trying to catch his breath. "It's like our people knew what was transpiring. They contacted me the next day and explained who he was."

"And who is he?" Malkia whispered, not wanting to face the truth.

"He's the other man who they hid here, as a child, just like you and me. His children inherited his powers as well, but they were maliciously murdered. He believes the sky people are to blame, even though he knows he's one of them."

Malkia's eyes widened. "Who told him?"

"His parents," Jasper replied, wiping the sweat from his forehead, his chest rising and falling with rapid breaths. "Not his birth parents, but his Esaki parents. They told him when he was a teenager that he could be powerful if he found a witch to block the curse. He didn't believe them. In fact, he thought they had lost their minds. When he was old enough, he left them and never returned. Then he met this witch, the one who is helping him." Jasper leaned backward against the wall. "His kids had just been slain, and he felt like he was going insane. He remembered what his parents had told him, so he asked the witch to block the spell. From what our people claim, it's a hard spell to stop. Most witches take a long time to even sense its presence, but she figured it out and has blocked the spell for years."

"What are his powers?" Dario asked.

"He can manipulate a person's mind without them suspecting a thing. He has a way of diving into your head, without reading it, of course, and making people do what he wants." Jasper turned toward Malkia. "I'm sure you witnessed that firsthand. Those people are senseless for following him. He's vicious, unmerciful, and full of hate, but he has them all wrapped around his finger—even his first wife. She despises him but does exactly what he says with little argument. Even you were pulled in for a moment, but somehow you escaped his leash. That's not only what intrigues him about you, but he desperately wants to control you."

Nausea swirled like a tornado in Malkia's gut. Now she knew why he'd had such a powerful grip on her. Why had she been able to break away? She wondered if it was when she saw what had happened to Alex... or was it before that? She'd wanted to escape from the beginning, but for a few moments, she had considered staying with him—willingly. Why was she able to resist when others could not?

Malkia stepped away, unable to tear her thoughts away from her former captivity.

The strikes to the castle had ceased, but she had a dreadful feeling it was taking a significant effort on everyone's part to stop him. She sighed and looked at the other three, who were following silently beside her. "We must develop a strategy to stop him. I must find a witch right now. The rest of you need to create a block to protect this fortress. I still possess the pendant the pixies gave me, and now I understand its importance more than ever. I also need to find Kolten. Do any of you know where he is?"

Jasper appeared surprised at the mention of Kolten's name. "I'm sure he's somewhere in the castle because everyone is here. He has a mother and sister he's protecting. His quarters are on the third floor. I can take you there if you would like."

Malkia nodded. "Yes, that would be great. But once I find him, I really have to speak to him privately."

Jasper flinched, but then nodded in reply.

When the four of them reached the large room where they had departed not so long ago, it was nearly empty. Malkia wasn't surprised but was more eager to find Kolten and convince his sister to help her. Maybe she didn't possess these magical powers Jasper mentioned, but to dismiss the idea entirely would be a disservice to both her people and those trying to help them. It wasn't a risk she was willing to take after all that had transpired. If there were powers lying dormant within her, she owed it to everyone to rise to her greatness.

"Let's go, Jasper," Malkia urged, gripping his forearm. "Dario and Mataya, I think I know how to block my spell. I will catch up with you soon."

Jasper touched Malkia's hand. "I really should find out what is going on with my people. They have obviously hit the castle with something, and I would like to know the damage before I go hunting for Kolten," he said, showing irritation for the first time.

"Why would you need to hunt for me?" a low voice spoke behind them.

They all whirled around to where Kolten and three women stood behind them.

Malkia smiled, stepping toward the four of them. "Kolten, there you are. Can we talk in private for a moment?"

Jasper left halfway through her last sentence, followed by Dario. Mataya kissed Malkia on the cheek and ran toward Justin, who was waving at her from the other side of the room.

The women stayed behind Koleton as he approached. "I need to speak with you as well. I wanted to introduce these ladies to you."

Malkia smiled and reached out to grasp their wrists. "Hi, I'm Malkia."

"Name is Kacey," the first woman said with a curtsy after exchanging the formal greeting. Her black hair hung past her waist, straight and shiny as spun silk.

"Bella," the second woman said. Her sky-blue eyes were so bright, they sparkled in contrast with her olive skin.

"Nice to meet you," Malkia replied.

"This is my sister, Tandi," Koleton said, tugging the last woman forward.

She reached out her hand, and Malkia grasped her wrist. "You look like twins."

Tandi smirked, running her fingers through the edges of her auburn hair. "I hear that a lot. Koleton was blessed with feminine features and the beauty that turns heads."

Malkia pressed her lips together to suppress her laughter when Koleton's face turned beet red.

"Don't be jealous, sister," he replied with a glare. "It's not my fault men and women alike follow me like puppy dogs. My charm is irresistible."

Kacey pushed Koleton and Tandi flicked him on the cheek.

"Don't mind them, Malkia. They have manners, I promise." Koleton wrapped his arm around Tandi's shoulders and rubbed his knuckles on top of her head.

Tandi scrunched her nose and shoved him away.

"Stop messing around. We have work to do. Did you forget?" Tandi asked, giving her brother a sharp look. She fixed her hair and smiled at Malkia. "Koleton claims you need a spell blocked."

"That would be helpful," Malkia replied, a weary smile rising on her lips. She pulled her hair back from her face and twisted it into a knot on top of her head. "I've had a spell on me since I was five years old. I can't remember my life before then, nor what other powers I supposedly possess. Jasper believes once I remember my abilities, I will be able to stop Damon on my own." *If I know how to use them.* Doubt lingered like a dark cloud.

The three witches looked at each other, their lips setting in thin lines as they focused on Malkia again. Bella spoke up, sweeping her golden blonde locks behind her shoulders.

"We don't think it is wise, making people more powerful than they already are. Maybe there is a reason they took those powers from your mind."

"I agree, except the reason they hid my powers from me was to protect me from creatures who were trying to abduct me. If I am able, I will stop Damon. If you don't want me to tap into my powers afterward, then stop blocking it. The only people who can completely take away the enchantment on me are my birth parents, and since I do not know how to contact them, you're my only hope at this moment." Malkia remembered the pendant the pixies had given her. It was still around her neck, but had fallen beneath her shirt and jacket. She lifted it out and stared at it. The stone was a bright blue color, and she could not help but grin.

"Where did you find that?" Bella demanded, recognition dawning on her face.

Malkia held it out for the others to see better. "The pixies gave it to me. They said it would help me find a witch who would help me."

Bella glanced at Tandi and Kacey again. They nodded in unison. "The pixies would only give you that pendant if you weren't from this moon. That pendant is from the sky people, and it only works if you have their blood running through your body. It senses evil and good in witches and has long been missing from the eyes of civilization. Being the pixies had possession of it explains a lot."

Malkia's eyes had widened in surprise. "You mean the pixies already knew I didn't belong here?"

"Looks that way," Tandi replied, looking at Kolten. "Kolten, would you go speak with Ashya and Pastua? They did not want to help, but maybe they will change their minds if they know the pendant and pixies are a part of this."

"Yes, your majesty." Kolten winked, his confident smile spreading across his face. "Where should I meet you ladies?"

"My room," Tandi replied, turning back toward Malkia.

"Let's go see what we can do for you, Malkia." Bella grabbed her hand and pulled her toward the door.

They wound up several flights of stairs before trekking down a cold and dark corridor. Tapestries with dragons and Light Beings, along with several creatures Malkia had never seen before, hung on the walls. One creature had talons that could wrap around her head, while another's razor-sharp teeth reminded her of the wolf-men. Were these creatures real, like the dragons?

"Here we are." Tandi stopped in front of a wooden door etched with flowers. She pushed it open.

Tandi led the way in and motioned for the other three to take a seat around a small table. "Malkia, we're going to try to sense the spell placed on you. It might take us a while to find it, but since there are three of us, I'm hoping it will be quick. The best thing you can do is lie on the bed, close your eyes, and let us do our work. We'll do whatever it takes to block the spell if we can find it."

Malkia did as she was told. She reclined on the bed and looked up at the three women she was trusting with her life. Under normal circumstances, she would be terrified, but she was more determined than ever to find out if there was a spell to block. If, by chance, she possessed what Jasper claimed, then possibly she could save her people. And if he was right about that, then maybe... just maybe, her baby Esta could still be alive.

She closed her eyes as the witches circled her. She felt the cushions shift when they climbed on the bed. They didn't touch her, but she sensed their hands hovering above her body.

No one spoke for several moments. The air was calm and relaxing, and Malkia felt light, as if she were floating. She didn't dare open her eyes, but wanted to see what was transpiring. Resisting the temptation, she focused on seeing Esta again. The possibility flooded her chest with warmth.

After a few minutes, their quiet whispering penetrated the air, but she couldn't make out what they were saying. Only words of another language, and as they spoke, she drifted off to sleep.

Moments later, Malkia's eyes sprung open. The three women were standing around the bed, looking at her.

"What happened?" she whispered.

"We found the spell. They hid it well. We've been at it for nearly an hour," Bella grumbled. She stifled a yawn with her hand.

"An hour? It felt like minutes to me."

"We put you in a trance. It's the only way to calm your mind and body enough to find the spell," Tandi replied, wringing her hands together. "The enchantment is going to be challenging. I'm not sure how Damon's witch has the strength to block his spell while still performing other incantations. One of us can barricade your spell, but we will have to take turns as it tires us quickly."

"I'll hurry," Malkia answered, perching herself up on her elbows. "At least I hope I can make this quick. Have there been any more attacks on the castle?"

"No," Kacey answered as she rubbed her forearms. "Ashya and Pastua have been holding them back, but it won't be long before they will require assistance."

Malkia bit her lip. "Does Jasper know they're doing this?"

"No, he doesn't," Tandi replied, shaking her head. "And unless they say they want him to know, it has to stay between us. They're terrified of persecution, as we all are. Witches have a poor reputation for being evil and vindictive, but most of us aren't." Her gaze swept to the other two witches, and they nodded at one another. "Malkia, we have agreed to block this spell so we can identify your abilities, and then we will decide whether we'll continue to block it. Are you ready?"

"Absolutely." She nodded her head, reclining back onto the bed. "And I'm fine with whatever you decide. Just let me stop Damon, and you can do whatever you want after that."

The three women walked back to the table with the chairs. Tandi pulled several jars filled with herbs from the shelves next to it and placed them on the table. They whispered among themselves as they mixed the items together on a plate. After they finished, they returned to their places around Malkia, with Tandi holding the plate.

"Just close your eyes," Bella instructed. "When you come to, hopefully the spell has been blocked."

"Am I going to be placed in a trance again?"

"Actually, we'll be putting you to sleep," Bella replied, setting her hand on Malkia's forehead. "It makes it easier for us to do our work if you are in your most relaxed state. Don't worry, we will take good care of you."

Malkia nodded and closed her eyes. After a few breaths the whispering begun, followed by silence.

TWENTY-FIVE
A Life Remembered

MALKIA'S EYES FLUTTERED open. Feeling relaxed and content, it was hard to come back to reality. The three witches were gathered around the table with Kolten. She lay there for a few minutes, attaining her bearings and allowing her body to awaken slowly.

She had believed nothing would change, but without even moving, she knew there was a difference. An intense awareness ebbed and flowed around her, and she reached out to see if the air would move from her touch. Her fingers glided through the candlelight and a rainbow of colors swirled against the darkness. Her pulse quickened with delight.

The conversation at the table hit her ears, and it seemed as if it were taking place next to her. They were whispering, unaware she had awakened. The aroma in the air smelled ambrosial and bright, as if the light itself was tangible. Magic coursed through her veins, and she held her hands in front of her, half-expecting them to glow. They looked normal, but she felt the power pumping like fire in her veins.

Her mind was open. Most of all, her worries about Damon had dissolved, and her ill feelings toward her birth parents seemed non-existent.

A quiet giggle escaped her lips, and as the sensation of it tickled her chest, she burst with laughter. Joy and peace danced through her mind, and an awareness surrounded her unlike anything she had experienced before. She sat up and beamed at the four at the table.

"Did you drug me?" Malkia asked and chuckled again at the shrill sound of her voice.

Kolten eyed her like she had lost her mind, and the three women shook their heads, too shocked to reply.

"What's going on with me? I feel like I'm high." She giggled, looking over her body as if it were the most magnificent object she had ever laid eyes on. "But definitely in a good way. My mind is free of clutter and chaos. Wow!"

She cradled her head in her hands as memories of her early childhood raced back to her. She remembered her birth moon, along with her parents and sister. Recollection swept through her mind, including their journey to Esaki and her distraught young mind as her parents abandoned her with strangers. A sob escaped Malkia's lips.

"What's wrong, Malkia?" Bella exclaimed.

Malkia glanced at the three women, tears running down her cheeks. "You did it. You blocked the spell. I remember everything. My moon, my parents, my sister... and even my voyage to this moon. I feel incredible, like I'm floating in the clouds. And I no longer feel angry at anyone."

Relief spread along Bella's features as she stepped toward Malkia. "Kacey is the one blocking it right now. We are hoping to pass it to one another so we can take shifts, but it is exhausting and difficult to hold on to. Maybe you should begin as soon as possible, and finish this," she advised, wringing her hands together.

"Give me a minute." Malkia's gaze shifted around the room. "I need a few moments by myself to gather my memories. Would you mind if I had some privacy?"

"No problem," Kolten replied, rising from his chair. "We will be right outside if you need us."

Once she was alone, Malkia sat on the bed in amazement. Her body seemed foreign but at the same time so familiar. She felt as light as a feather. Her abilities remained a mystery, but an inner knowing tugged at her thoughts, and she suspected it would not take much to remember.

Closing her eyes, she fantasized herself flying away from this place. She imagined herself so light, not even gravity could keep her on the ground. As she opened her eyes, she already knew she was no longer sitting on the bed. She was hovering about ten feet above it. Her head lightly bumped the ceiling, and she laughed. She could defy gravity, and the thought of it made her giddy inside.

She focused on the four standing in the hallway, and as soon as she did, she heard them speaking. Their thoughts remained private, but she easily could hear their conversation. They were discussing her, and the witches were still apprehensive about her power.

Intruding on their privacy was not the direction she wanted to take, but at least it gave her an idea of her capabilities. She abandoned their exchange and focused on Mataya. Immediately, she could hear her speaking, followed by Justin responding. She didn't know where they were, but she knew they weren't close. A cloudy vision of Mataya came into view and then it vanished. Malkia's thoughts raced with all the possibilities, and it was difficult to focus.

Her mind turned to Damon.

She dropped back to the bed as Damon's image appeared before her, as clear as the room she was in. She gasped with surprise. The vision disappeared as soon as she hit the bed. Why was she able to see Damon? Her focus turned to Jasper, and she saw him speaking with some of his men, down in the large room the meeting had been in.

"There must be a deeper connection to us three," she told herself, sorting through the reasons she could see some and not others. "But why was Mataya obscured?"

She scooted off the bed and nearly leaped to the door. The four others were still waiting on the other side when she opened it.

"I figured out a few of my powers." Malkia slipped into the corridor. "I know you ladies are worried about me being too powerful, and to tell you the truth, I probably am, but with my advanced abilities I believe it is possible I can stop Damon on my own."

"Don't leave us in suspense. What can you do?" Tandi's gaze washed over Malkia's body, like she was searching for a change.

Malkia's smile spread across her face. Thinking of her body being light as a feather, she floated above the ground. She burst into laughter, watching the shock in everyone's expressions.

"Amazing, right?" Malkia exclaimed, spreading her arms wide. "Also, if I focus on Damon, I can see and hear him. I know exactly what's going on. He don't believe he can hide from me. I can hear and see Jasper and my sister, and I am able to hear all of you from afar, but I cannot see you. I am wondering if it has something to do with my connection to these people."

"Are those the only powers you possess?" Kolten asked, his brows bumping together in a scowl.

"Isn't that enough?" Malkia asked, laughing at his serious expression. "I still have my telepathy, but it only works with others with telepathy. Oh my! I must be able to see Misty."

Malkia settled back to the ground and focused on Misty. Immediately, an image of the little girl was in front of her. She was with her mom at the far end of the castle. She smiled at Malkia, like she knew she was there, and then waved happily. Malkia waved back before returning to Kolten and the witches.

"I wonder if I can hear Astrid," Malkia said and closed her eyes in concentration. She heard weeping and what sounded like one of the mutt's yelling, in his scratchy, deep voice. Malkia focused on Damon and Astrid, and instantly she could see them both. They were in a tent, with Astrid tied to a post, lying on the ground and sobbing. Blood dripped from her mouth onto her torn and dirty clothing. Damon was looking at Astrid with no emotion, and the dog was yelling and jumping around her as he barked in her face.

Malkia cried out. "No! I'm coming for you, Astrid. If you can hear me, I'm coming for you."

As she spoke, Damon's gaze snapped to her, and his eyes widened just as the vision disappeared.

She focused back on Kolten and the women. "I have to rescue her. They are hurting her." She balled her hands into fists. "How could Damon be so evil?"

"Wait, Malkia." Kolten grabbed her arm before she could leave. "We have to come up with a plan. Don't go do anything imprudent."

Tears threatened to spill, but she quickly wiped them from her eyes. "I can see where Damon is and hear anyone I want to hear. I can swoop in there, grab Astrid, and flee."

"How do you know it's not a trap?" Koleton took hold of her other arm and gripped them tightly, forcing her to look him in the eyes. "How do you know Damon doesn't already know what your abilities are? What if he has been told, and this is a snare? Don't be a fool. I know you are smarter than this."

Malkia listened, nodding her head slightly when he finished. "You're right, Kolten. I must keep a level head. Maybe Jasper will have a plan ready for us." She shook herself free from his grip and turned to the three women. "Are you willing to disclose your magic to Jasper and the others? It is more important now than ever before."

Tandi gulped and stepped backward with a slight shake of her head.

Bella nodded and grabbed Tandi's hand. "We can do this." She turned and took Kacey's hand as well. "Jasper has always been good to us and Malkia is right. We are powerful, magical beings. Why would we continue dimming our light?"

"I'm in," Kacey whispered, linking arms with Bella. "We can do this, Tandi."

Tandi looked at Koleton, who nodded encouragingly.

She blew out a long breath, then gripped Bella's forearm with her free hand. "Let's do this."

The five of them sprinted all the way to the large conference room. Jasper was there, speaking with Dario and a few other men and women. They glanced up when Malkia entered the room.

"Was everything figured out?" Jasper asked, even though Malkia could tell he already knew.

"Yes," Malkia said, hurrying toward the group. "I have ideas to stop Damon, but before we begin, these women have some things to disclose."

Malkia turned toward the witches and nodded. Jasper excused the others. Dario and he followed the group to a secluded table in the corner. Jasper sat quietly and rested his arms on the table while everyone else gathered around.

"We are witches," Tandi said in haste, her eyes darting around at each person.

Jasper's expression remained steady, not appearing surprised or displeased. A smile surfaced on his lips, and after a few seconds, he chuckled, shaking his head as he eyed each woman. He already knew. Kolten was clearly shocked, as his jaw dropped, while the women's faces scrunched into scowls.

"I'm sorry, ladies." Jasper licked his lips. "Not trying to be rude, but your serious faces were priceless. I already knew you were witches, and I've known for some time now. I also know your two friends who are holding off Damon are witches as well. Speaking to me about your private matters had to be done on your terms, and it would not be fair for me to demand your help."

Malkia's eyes widened, and she breathed in sharply. "Of course, it would've been fair! These women have been petrified that you would run them out of town because people are afraid of witches, and this whole time you have known. Geez, Jasper, you're driving me insane. I've met no one, aside from Damon, who has infuriated me as you do. You have changed since I met you last year."

"Much has occurred since you last graced us with your presence. Discovering my true identity has given me the power and freedom to shift into a higher state of being. I am not required to push another into their full potential, but you are right, it would have served us all better if I had done so." Jasper leaned forward and looked at Tandi, Bella, and Kacey. "I apologize, ladies. My waiting was only to respect your privacy."

Bella sunk into a chair next to Jasper. "It wasn't your responsibility, but if we had known we would have been safe, coming forward would have been easier. Our city should be a sanctuary for all witches."

"Agreed." Jasper patted Bella's hand, then turned to Malkia. "Are you really angry?"

Malkia had watched the exchange with quiet admiration for the women. Anger was far from her mind, even when she had spoken harshly to Jasper. What she was feeling was different from anything she had felt before. Fury, maybe. Joy, possibly. Passion was too weak of a description, but it was the closest emotion she could attach to what she was feeling.

"It doesn't really matter what I feel." Malkia shook her head and glared at Jasper. "What matters is these women could have been helping from the beginning, but you chose to keep quiet and wait for them to approach. Your style of leadership differs from mine. I'm not passive, and maybe that's a reckless attribute, but I feel people respond better if you're more open with them instead of using mind games."

Jasper shrugged his shoulders and rose to his feet. "It is done. Let's move on. Have you discovered your powers?"

"Yes," she said with a wide smile. She couldn't help herself.

Dario spoke for the first time, his expression strangely aloof. He folded his arms across his chest. "What can you do?"

Malkia rose on her toes and planted a kiss on his cheek, ignoring his guarded pose. "I'll show you. It's more fun that way."

She imagined herself flying and giggled when her toes dangled above the table. Dario's eyes widened and his arms fell to his sides, and Jasper's smile widened. Glancing around the room, she rose even higher, but only made it a few feet when the castle juddered and the surrounding walls cracked from the pressure.

Everyone braced themselves as pieces of stone fell around them.

Malkia lowered back down and whirled toward the front of the castle. "It's time."

TWENTY-SIX
Miracle Child

INJURED PEOPLE STUMBLED into their path as they tore down the corridors toward the front of the castle. Several were covered in blood and lacerations. Their screams echoed against the stone walls, cutting through Malkia's heart.

A boulder had toppled onto a woman, crushing her leg, sending Malkia back to the last moment she saw her Esaki mom alive. She swooped toward the woman and flung the stone away from her leg as if it were a pebble. The woman grabbed Malkia's hand.

"Thank you."

"Can you walk?"

"I think so," she said, climbing to her feet and hobbling forward.

"Then help the others," Jasper said from behind Malkia.

The woman nodded and limped away.

"Kacey, are you still the one blocking the spell?" Malkia asked, as they began their run again.

"Yes, but I need to hand it over soon. I'm exhausted."

"Would it be better if the one who is blocking it stayed away from the main scene, somewhere quiet?" Jasper asked, slowing to a jog.

"Probably," Tandi replied.

"Kacey, pass it to Tandi," Jasper stated, halting in his tracks. "Tandi, make your way to the back of the castle, to my quarters. I'll send two guards with you. Stay there and keep all your focus on Malkia. How many hours before you will need to be relieved?"

Tandi's brows scrunched with thought, and she wiped the back of her hand across her forehead. "Two at the most, just to be on the safe side."

Jasper nodded. "Good, we hopefully won't need more than that, but if we do, Bella will relieve you. Kacey, exchange it in the privacy of my quarters, then get the rest you need. Return when you are ready. These guards will accompany you, and one of them will be with you at all times."

Jasper summoned the nearest guards and disclosed his orders. The four of them rushed to the back of the castle while Malkia, Bella, Dario, and Jasper continued toward the front entrance.

Malkia needed to see Damon before she could devise a plan. As soon as she saw a private room, she motioned for the others to follow her. "Give me a moment to find Damon. I can stop him easier if I know where he is and who he has with him."

"Is that another one of your abilities?" Dario asked.

"Yes, but I can only see certain people. I can hear others, but I'm not sure why or if it is everyone." Malkia sagged against the wall for balance, thinking of Damon. The vision of him appeared instantly. He stood near her, his back turned to her as he surveyed the castle.

He was yelling at a woman who was standing a few feet in front of him. "Destroy those witches now. I want them dead."

The old woman didn't flinch at his icy words but continued to stare at the castle in deep concentration. Malkia heard her muttering but could not make out the words she spoke.

Malkia pinpointed Damon's position and how far he was from the castle. He was away from his camp, and he had both dogs with him and several other men and women. It would not be easy to sneak up on him. She could fly in, but she didn't know if she had the strength to hold him. If only she could cause a diversion or, better yet, freeze the people around him. Malkia smirked. Now *that* power would be useful.

She turned in a circle, searching for an area she could use for cover, when her gaze rested on the witch. She was staring at Malkia. The witch mumbled an incantation and pointed her fingers at Malkia. Ducking behind Damon just in time, she watched as the spell rushed by her, a current of dark green. This witch was far more powerful than she expected. Malkia dropped the vision.

"His witch saw me," Malkia sputtered, shaking her head. "How did she know I was there?"

"She must be a warlock," Bella whispered, fear spreading across her face. "I've never met one before, but I've heard about them. They originated on your home moon. Their powers are endless and if that is who is trying to break into the castle, she will succeed. I must warn the others."

"Wait," Jasper said, throwing up his hands before Bella could run off. "Let's not be hasty. I think Malkia can rectify this. Perhaps she doesn't know it yet."

Malkia's eyes narrowed, her nose crinkling with frustration. "What are you talking about? I can fly... and see and hear people without them being near. I have telepathy, but only with others who share my ability.

What else am I capable of doing?"

"Think about it for a moment. Remember being a child on our moon. You had to have known then. According to your parents, you are one of the few—" He paused, searching her eyes. "One of the few who could destroy all humankind if you desired. You must have more abilities, and you need to focus on them right now. You are stronger than this warlock."

Malkia inhaled sharply, her eyes narrowing as bitterness filled her mouth. "The way you said that... I'm not comfortable having these abilities," she hissed, a flush creeping up her face.

"Malkia." Jasper's voice rose an octave as he straightened his posture. "Quit having these weak thoughts. We don't have time for your feebleness. Figure out what you can do and perform it now, before that witch dismantles this entire fortress and executes everyone inside."

His gaze never left hers. It was finally making sense. Their people were superior to the Esaki inhabitants, and it was their job to protect them from the tyranny of those who came from Eris. Jasper acted as if he was better than those around him, but he only wanted to keep his people safe. He needed her because he was not as powerful.

Dario glared at Jasper, balling his hands into fists at his side. Malkia reached over and clutched his hand. "It's okay, Dario. He's right. I need two minutes to myself." She turned to Bella. "Can you push back on Damon's witch and buy me time?"

"I will try." Bella patted Malkia's shoulder and left the room with Jasper behind her.

Dario wrapped his arms around Malkia and kissed her hard on the lips. "You're my universe. Please don't do anything senseless, and for the love of Theia, please keep yourself safe."

Malkia kissed Dario on the tip of his nose. "The only thing I can promise is my adoration for you. I'll do what I can to keep us all safe."

Dario's expression dropped, and he pulled her into his chest. His heart thudded, and she knew he was terrified for her. "I love you, Dario. Go outside and wait for me. I'll be quick."

He released her, kissed her forehead, and walked out the door.

Malkia focused on the closed door for a moment, the weight of the whole moon pressing on her shoulders. She brushed off the negative feelings and sank to the ground, hopeful of discovering what she was missing.

If she could connect with Jasper, Damon, and Misty, maybe she could reach her parents. Her mind turned to them and her baby girl, Esta. Like a burst of wind, they sprang into her view, all of them sitting right before eyes as if they knew she would do this. Malkia gaped at them in shock. There she was, unmistakably Malkia's daughter, staring back at her with her inky irises. Just like Misty and the warlock, they knew she was there.

"Malkia!" her mother exclaimed, her tear-filled eyes dancing with joy. "We've been waiting for you to channel us. We have so much to tell you."

"Can you really see me?" Malkia asked, frozen in place.

"We can see and hear you," her father said, his tone sharp and biting into her heart, bringing back fearful memories she had long forgotten. "We have been watching you for some time now and waiting for you to contact us so we could finally speak about your tasks. Do you recognize your sweet little angel?" He tugged Esta forward, giving

Malkia a better view.

Her sobs came without restraint as she reached her hand forward, yearning to touch her child. She wept uncontrollably, her body rocking with a mixture of deep despair and complete and utter joy.

"Oh, my sweet child. You'll do splendid. Look at me," her mother said as she edged closer, near enough to touch.

Malkia reached her hand out but touched empty air, gulping back more tears.

"Listen. You have little time. Your daughter is waiting for you, and as soon as you want, you can return to us. But for now, you must stop Damon. He's a troubled man but can be saved." She paused, a smile twitching on the edges of her lips. It didn't match the sadness in her eyes. "He's one of us. You're the only one on that moon who can channel any of us, and your other abilities are far more extraordinary and make you exceptionally dominant. We need you to remember your capabilities." Her mother glanced back at her father, her lips setting in a straight line for a moment, as if she had more to say.

Her father's stern expression hardened even more.

Malkia remained quiet. She couldn't believe what her mother was telling her. The thought of her being as powerful as she was saying petrified her. She looked at Esta over her mother's shoulder, who was no longer a baby and a stranger to her, and she wished Father Time could take her back.

Malkia glanced at her father and then back at her mother, thinking of how she could make this all better. She wanted to fix it, including erasing the last eight years without her daughter. "Why did you not return for me? Why did you keep me from my baby?" Malkia asked, swallowing back a sob.

"Malkia, focus, *now*," her father bellowed, halting her sobs completely. Her mother jumped and shot her a pained look. Something wasn't right. "You have thousands of people depending on your actions right now. Our warlock has dismantled the spell placed on your abilities. Pull it together and remember who you are."

As soon as Malkia's father spoke those words, her mind calmed. She floated above her family, and in that moment, she remembered everything. Her abilities came flooding back to her mind, and the euphoria of the sensation created ripples of electricity through her body. She wiped her tears away and eased her body back to the ground, where she was now facing her parents and daughter again. "I remember, and I can do this. I love you, Esta, and as soon as this is over, I will be with you again."

Her daughter's smile was enough. It was all Malkia needed and seeing Esta next to her father made ending this even more urgent. His disdain for Malkia had never ended. It was etched in every one of his features as he stared at her. All her memories had returned, and she would not rest until her daughter was out of his reach. She blew a kiss to Esta, then dropped the channel.

The energy of her powers pulsated around her, enthralling and empowering her all at once. Fear no longer consumed her, as the intense energy within had always been there.

Malkia walked to the door, feeling a brightness flow through her body. She felt radiant and strangely uplifted. She pulled it open, and Bella and Dario took several steps backward when they saw her.

"You're glowing, Malkia." A smile spread across Jasper's face, his elation dancing into his eyes. "You must have remembered."

"I did," she answered, scanning over everyone. "I can stop Damon. It's important he's not hurt in this. They have given me instructions to bring him in unharmed."

"What?" Dario exclaimed. "That was not what we agreed upon. He needs to be punished." His eyes narrowed and a familiar look edged across his face. Hadn't she just seen that same expression on her father's face?

"No, he doesn't," Malkia and Jasper both said in unison.

Malkia's hands rested on her hips. "Dario, you and I will discuss this later."

The breath noticeably came up short in his throat, and he turned away, coughing into his elbow.

Malkia turned to Jasper. "The witches can stop blocking the spell put on me and focus on holding back the warlock. I'll return with Damon if I must execute his witch myself. Tell your people to hold down their positions and not let anyone in while I'm doing my work. I'll be back as soon as I'm finished." She could not face Dario after his absurd behavior that would have to be addressed later.

She strode away, but her steps were so quick, it was as if she were running. Not having to think about it anymore, she walked with such ease and grace, it even amazed her.

When she approached the front gates, she noticed the guards watching her, their jaws dropping as she floated by them. When she reached the front door, she didn't hesitate. She surrounded herself with her purple light and floated effortlessly through the door. Their gasps followed her to the other side.

Within a few seconds, she saw Damon and his witch. She deepened the purple light around her, making it larger, stronger, and impenetrable. The next second, an array of dark colors struck her purple light—the same magic the witch had flung at her before. It nearly knocked her over, but she righted herself quickly. Before she knew it, she was standing in front of Damon. His eyes widened when he realized who was inside the light.

"Hi, Damon," Malkia said. She held her arms open. "Please call off your witch. We need to talk."

Damon's face turned crimson with fury as his anger exploded. "What are you doing, Malkia? All you have to do is surrender, and you will save all these people. I only want you. I don't care about any of them." He waved his hand erratically at the castle behind her.

Malkia smirked and clapped her hands together. "We both know that is a lie. As soon as you have me, you are planning to slaughter all those people and keep me as your prisoner. Unfortunately for you, I cannot allow any of that."

Damon clenched his fists. She sensed his anger building. Twisting to see what was making a noise behind her, she noticed one mutt sprinting toward Damon, with Astrid in his grip. When they reached Damon, he grabbed Astrid by the roots of her hair and yanked her against him, his eyes narrowing toward Malkia.

"Last chance," he bellowed, pressing his sword against Astrid's throat.

"Don't do it, Damon." She took a step toward him.

He shrugged, sliding his sword across the tender skin and slicing Astrid's throat clean open.

"No!" she shrieked. Her jaw dropped with disbelief as Astrid sputtered, attempting to catch her breath. Her arms flailed in front of her, and she stared regretfully at Malkia as pain swept across her face.

Damon released his grip and Astrid tumbled to the ground, blood spilling from her mouth and the wound across her throat. Tears overran Malkia's eyes, watching the life go out of her friend's face. She jerked her gaze back up and glared at the hateful man in front of her.

Continuing to hold her defensive light, she focused on the disgusting mutt she knew she would have to terminate. The warlock was still working on invading her shield, but she was only infuriating Malkia more. She focused on the witch and the other people surrounding her, chuckling venomously. "Do you really think you have a chance against me?" she yelled at the crowd. "You have already lost this battle."

With a speed so quick no one saw her move; she reached the mutt and shot her hand through his chest. She yanked his beating heart out before he could even flinch, shredding bones and muscle. His surprised eyes went blank as he slumped to Malkia's feet.

The gasps from the crowd and Damon's curses did not phase her. She whirled around and did not hesitate as she wrapped her arms around Damon's waist and flew into the air, away from the crowd. Damon struggled against her, but she kept her grip. "Hold still, Damon. I don't want to drop you."

"How are you flying? Do you have a warlock helping you?" Damon asked angrily.

Malkia squeezed him tighter and pushed away the yearning she felt for him, even after she watched him murder her friend. The desire made her cringe. She could remember her moon, her parents, her life before this one, and all her powers, but she could not figure out why this savage made her heart skip a beat.

He wiggled against her tight grip.

"Simmer down," Malkia replied, ignoring his questions.

She landed in one tower of the castle toward the back, far away from Damon's warlock. She would need to restrain him there while she took care of the witch and ended his battle.

Malkia radiated her light out, surrounding Damon. As she walked away from him, it grew to encompass the entire room. He ran toward her but stopped short at the end of the light.

"Let's see how much you enjoy being held against your will." Malkia smirked. She patted the light, then flew off toward the warlock.

TWENTY-SEVEN

Her Father's Disdain

SHE SHOT TOWARD Damon's group and focused on the warlock waiting for her. Another dark light struck her, but it didn't stop her. Malkia aimed at the warlock and smashed into her with full force.

They both rolled and Malkia collided with a tree, nearly knocking the breath right out of her. She surrounded herself with the defensive light again, but it was weak. She rolled to her knees and jumped to her feet to face the warlock, along with Damon's army. The warlock sprinted toward her; her arms stretched out to send the next curse.

She crashed into Malkia with a strength that nearly took her completely down. Strengthening the light surrounding her, Malkia bounded toward the horrid woman. She gripped the witch by the neck and flew into the air, strangling her with her arm. Malkia soared into the sky before the woman became almost unbearable to hold. The warlock was preventing their ascension, and Malkia realized she would need some help to destroy this woman.

She shot toward the castle and Jasper's room. She knew at least one witch would be waiting there. Malkia burst through the doors and came face-to-face with Bella.

Bella screamed, jumping backward. "Malkia, you frightened me!"

Malkia edged the warlock in front of her, keeping a firm grip around her throat. The woman's strength was preventing Malkia from taking the advantage. A cramp in her legs and hips snaked toward her torso, increasing to a point of excruciating agony. She peeked down to look at the cause, but noticed nothing. Sweat beaded on her forehead as the pain built, becoming an overwhelming and radiating heat coursing uncontrollably throughout her body. She stared desperately at Bella and Kacey. Jasper's guards circled around her, pointing their swords at the warlock.

"I need your help," Malkia breathlessly cried, sweat running down her face. "Her life has to end, and she's too strong for me to do it on my own."

"No, she's not." Jasper's voice echoed behind Malkia. "You have it in you right now to end her life. Right now, right here. All you have to do is know you have that control."

Malkia spun around with a tight hold on the warlock and peered at Jasper, Dario, and Mataya. The look on her sister's face was almost enough to stop her, but she felt an intense urge to have this over and never worry about fighting this woman again.

The strain on her abilities and her own muscles was becoming unbearable, and tears tumbled from her eyes as she tried to control the pain slowly rolling through her body. Realization hit her like ice-cold water. The witch was tearing her apart from the inside, and the strain alone was going to finish her.

As her sweat dripped to the floor and pain tore up toward her throat, Malkia dug deep for the strength. Flashes of light coursed through her arms and the fire she had felt earlier pressed against her hands. She gripped the warlock's head, then yanked it to the side and cried out with relief when she heard the neck bones break. The warlock's body wrenched, then crumbled to dust at Malkia's feet.

Her pain dissipated, and relief spread through her body. She collapsed to the ground, weeping. Dario's arms wrapped around her, and he pulled her into his lap. She felt her sister's arms around her as well, her cries echoing in her ears.

The pain was horrifying. Blinking back tears, she shifted her gaze upward and took in the blurry faces of the three witches, Jasper and a few of his guards. Dario was staring at her, his face scrunched with concern.

Bella was the first to speak. "What happened? Your body was glowing. And the pain in your expression chilled me to the bone. I have never seen anything like it."

"We all saw it, Malkia," Dario said, his voice nearly a whisper. "What were you feeling?"

Malkia's face was wet from tears, and they kept falling. "She was—" She choked back a sob, the agonizing pain too fresh on her mind. It had started while they were flying, and it wouldn't surprise her if there was permanent damage inside her body.

She calmed her whimpers and took several deep breaths to ease her trembling body. Skye, Kolten, Alex, and Jayde walked inside the room, wearing the same concerned look on their faces.

"The witch was tearing me apart from the inside. It felt like I was going to explode." Malkia wiped her eyes with the sleeves of her shirt. "It felt like she had twisted all my organs and muscles into pretzels, and I was going to explode. I have never felt so much pain and agony in all my life."

Dario cradled her close again. She nuzzled her head against his chest and let her hair fall in her face. A heat of embarrassment prickled up her neck, and a desire to run overwhelmed her senses. She loved most of these people, and she knew she was going to break their hearts when she told them she had to leave. It was a pain she couldn't bear—far worse than the one she'd just experienced.

"Damon," Malkia muttered, abruptly sitting up straight.

"Where is he?" Jasper asked.

"I left him entrapped in one of your towers. He's going to be livid."

Bitterness overtook her emotions as she stared at the people watching over her, sensing they could see the animosity in her eyes. She was far more powerful than any person on this moon, but she felt smaller and more inferior to the rodents in the walls.

She despised her existence right now.

Malkia rose, glancing at Dario, then turned toward Mataya as she raked her hand through her hair. The agony in her heart rose abruptly, and without a word, Malkia ran from the room before any of them could stop her.

She had to see Damon. An intense urge to strangle him overcame her, but her heart yearned for him at the same time. She hated him and she loved him. The conflict tugged her heart in all kinds of directions, and she needed to end the torment.

She launched herself into the air like a hawk. When she landed on the top of the tower, vile words greeted her.

Her hatred for Damon flooded her mind and heart. He was the cause for so much of her agony, and he was the reason her life had been turned upside down. This spoiled grown man believed he deserved more in life than others. He was a menace to her life, and it would have been better if she could squish him like a bug.

Malkia walked inside the light, and he ran at her, but when he reached her, he stopped and tugged her into his arms. She already knew it was what he was going to do. They couldn't resist one another. He pressed his warm lips against hers, hungrily tasting her.

Time slipped away. Malkia wanted him more with each moment they held one another. It was several breaths before they broke apart.

Damon ran his fingers through Malkia's hair, gazing at her with a dark desire in his eyes. "What have you done to me? What have you done with my witch?"

Malkia put her hands on the sides of his face and softly kissed his chin. Then she kissed his nose and returned to his mouth. She softly pressed her lips against his and quietly whispered, "You don't have to worry about any of that."

She grabbed the sides of his head and leaped over his shoulder, all the while clutching onto his head, expecting to break his neck and be done with him. However, he slipped right out of her grasp, and when she landed on her feet on the other side, he was gone. She glanced around and saw him running behind her toward the door.

Malkia bounded into flight and landed in front of him, blocking his escape, but he ran full force into her and sent her tumbling to the side. He sprinted around her, but only made it a few steps before she enveloped him in her protective light and imprisoned him once again.

Damon whipped around and glared at her. "You were going to kill me!"

"You bet I was!" Malkia yelled back. "You're a monster, a demon who deserves to die. Pain and suffering follows you wherever you go. You are *disgusting*, and nothing else in this life would make me happier than to see you dead on the ground."

A wounded expression slid over his face, but he recovered quickly, raking his gaze over her with freezing contempt. Malkia returned the glare.

Jasper, Dario, Alex, and a few of Jasper's guards scurried up behind Damon. They stopped short when they caught sight of the two of them, their eyes burning with hatred for each other.

"Are we interrupting anything important?" Jasper demanded, his gaze darting between the two.

"Just his death," Malkia mumbled quietly.

"You're insane!" Damon screamed at her, squinting furtively. "I have done nothing to deserve this!"

Malkia clenched her jaw. Dario and Jasper circled around Damon, finding a better view of the situation. She wanted them to leave, realizing it would be simpler if there were no one here to witness his dismemberment.

She lunged toward Damon, just as a light flashed before her eyes. It blinded her. Falling to her knees, she shielded her eyes with her hands as the bright light burned around her.

"Malkia, stop this nonsense," her father said, his voice echoing loudly around her. "Take control of your emotions and bring Damon home."

Malkia curled up in a ball on the ground with her hands by her face, ready to cover her eyes if she needed to, but the light had dissipated, and her father was nowhere to be seen. Damon, Dario, and Jasper stared intently at her.

"Did you see that?" she asked, looking desperately from side to side, searching for her father.

"See what?" Dario replied, his voice thick with emotion.

"The light." Her voice quivered. She must have been the only one to witness and hear the encounter.

"Malkia, are you well?" Dario softly asked, reaching down to help her up.

She eyed the three of them, untrusting of her circumstances. Everything had seemed so clear earlier. The power had been intoxicating, and she had felt unstoppable, but now she wanted nothing more than to crawl into a hole. Damon looked like a caged animal, ready to run, and Jasper kept his gaze glued to her as if waiting for her to burst into flames. The pity in Dario's eyes threw her over the edge.

She placed her face in her hands, feeling the heat of embarrassment crawl up her neck. *How did I allow myself to lose control? This power is a burden, far above my capabilities.* Her head pulsated, a pain throbbing in her temples. "Can you please hold on to Damon? I have to breathe. I will deal with him when I return."

She turned to Jasper, who nodded and shifted out of the way to let her pass. Whisking by him, she pushed into a sprint once she was free of their stares. She had to escape and collect her thoughts. All these changes and responsibilities were afflicting her mind and soul.

She flew to the forest and landed in a large tree, where she was unseen and protected. She needed to be alone but had a feeling her parents were watching her. *Will I ever be alone again?* "Do the Light

Beings even exist, or have you always been the presence I have felt my entire life?" she cried to the heavens.

The birds chirped and insect wings filled the silence. The lack of response from her parents was frustrating, knowing they had to be close. She felt used and deceived.

A faint buzz grew louder, and she watched in wonderment as a bright white light appeared below her. She shifted to gain a better view and noticed a man standing where the light had been.

"Malkia, please descend," her father said sternly, tilting his head slightly to peer upward at her.

Her childlike emotions surfaced, and she was petrified by what she was about to face. He had always had that effect on her. Memories of his complete disregard of her existence swirled in her thoughts. Her mother had been a guardian between Malkia and the hatred her father had for her. But why?

The fire in her veins burned against her flesh, reminding her that the power within her exceeded any ability known to humankind. Her father no longer could force her to play small, and his control was nonexistent. She leaped from the tree and landed smoothly in front of him. His nostrils flared at the sight, and he eyed her with icy contempt.

"I am confused, Father," she hissed as she stepped forward, straightening her posture. "All this time, I have been here alone, wondering why I felt different, wondering what happened to my baby girl, and you had the ability to arrive at any time." She hesitated for a moment, drawing in a deep breath to keep her heart from beating out of her chest. "For being a father who supposedly loves his daughter, you sure have a funny way of showing it. If you're so dominant and all-knowing about my life, why didn't you take the time to remind me who I am long before now?"

Her father's jaw twitched, and he crossed his arms over his chest. "Malkia, your questions are unneeded. I'm your father and the one in charge of this mission. It needs to end exactly the way we intended."

She pursed her lips, her eyes narrowing to slits. "No, Father." The ice in her voice stung her throat, but she continued anyway. "My questions are important. You must have mistaken my empathy for compliance, but I am no longer a child you can bully into submission."

Her father stepped closer, using his height and power to intimidate her. She almost backed down, but a strength rose inside her, so she held her position, standing straighter to match his stance.

"Do not try to threaten me," she said with a steady tone, pinning him with a frosty look. She stood her ground. "What is your strategy? Your mission? I have just been a pawn in an undertaking of yours, and I want to know why."

Her father's expression relaxed, an arrogant smile twitching on the edges of his lips. "Malkia, you were created to do my bidding. We engineered you for a specific reason, and when we hid you here so many years ago, it was difficult to leave as I did not want you to fall into the wrong hands. However, your existence only meant one thing to me, and it wasn't to become attached to you."

She gulped back the twinge of pain his words had on her heart, refusing to let him see he could still hurt her.

He tilted his face slightly upward, a gleam of deviltry sweeping across his eyes. "It was so you could extinguish our enemies, ridding this universe of the filth it has been cursed with. Maybe you think you

are a pawn, but you are so much more than that. You're our weapon…
and the reason we will conquer this war. We placed you here to be
protected until you were strong enough to join us in the fight. *Now*, you
are ready. We can win this conflict, and you can have planets to name
as your own. You may possess this moon if it means so much to you."
He waved his arms around at the trees. "All we ask is for you to bring
Damon in and, together, you two finish this conflict."

Malkia stood in silence, wishing she could ignore the stab of grief
consuming her heart. Her parents never loved her, and there weren't
any Light Beings watching over her. Even after all she had seen, the
visions had been an illusion. There were only people hiding her away
as a weapon to be used when they saw fit. She wanted to cry and scream
at the sky. Her whole life was a lie.

A noise whispered in her mind; a sound like the one she had
encountered with the two-headed dragon. However, this time, she
recognized and understood it. They *were* the dragons. She could speak
with dragons telepathically, and the realization shone brightly within
as she faced off with her father.

"I don't need you, and I refuse to fight your war. You weren't
protecting me because you loved me." She stepped closer, a heated fury
spreading across her cheeks. "You were hiding me so no one else
would damage your precious weapon, but here's my truth," she hissed
in his face. "I will never be what you want me to be. Give me back my
daughter, *now*."

With a swish of its wings, a massive dragon swooped through the
vegetation and landed softly behind Malkia.

Tantiana. The dragon's name entered Malkia's mind. *I found you.*

The dragon nuzzled her nose in between Malkia's shoulder blades. Her father's jaw dropped with widened eyes. He took several steps backward and faded in and out of view. Malkia jumped closer to him, realizing he was not real, just as he disappeared from her sight.

"No!" she screamed at the spot he had stood, balling her hands into fists. Her heart ached. How would she find Esta now? She whipped around to face the dragon. "Tantiana, take me to the castle."

Tantiana bowed her head, and Malkia climbed onto her back. The dragon's scales were smooth, but the edges made it easy for her to hold on as Tantiana leaped into the sky and flew to the castle.

When they reached the walkway leading to the tower, Malkia hopped off the dragon's back and turned back to watch as Tantiana settled on the ground outside the castle. She blended into the forest with ease with her green and blue scales.

Jasper and Dario were leaning against the rock wall when she entered the room, with a few guards lining the entrances. They saw Malkia and jumped up from their resting stance. Damon had cowered away and was hiding in the shadows.

Killing Damon no longer consumed her mind. In fact, she pitied him because of his weakened state and obscured aura. He had been a pawn in her father's game as well, and she was going to remind him who he was. Then, her only agenda would be to rescue her daughter.

She breezed past the guards and made it to Damon before anyone reacted. She knelt before him and touched his cheek as he tried to scoot away from her.

"I will not hurt you. Give me a minute to explain what I have learned. You and I have more in common than either of us realized."

He shoved her arm away and avoided her eyes.

She moved closer to him. "Will you please look at me?"

Damon lifted his head slightly, glowering. Fear permeated his eyes, and seeing his ragged expression made her chuckle. She knew it was inappropriate to laugh, but she couldn't stop the onslaught as tears ran down her face, her laughs growing louder. The surrounding men stared with looks of disbelief and confusion. She must look insane, but she had never thought more clearly in her life.

The power pumping through her veins was a gift—a chance to right the wrongs of yesterday's battles.

She slowly quieted as she eased to the ground cross-legged in front of Damon. A team of heathens was about to form, and she was proudly going to lead it. A woman who never wanted the role of leader and she was finally embracing the position. Because retrieving her daughter and putting a stop to the people who had set out to ruin this moon was what mattered most.

Come closer. Malkia reached out to Tantiana.

"Let's make this simple for all of you."

Malkia heard Tantiana land on the wall outside the tower. The group of men jumped back, fumbling for their archery equipment. She waved her hand, encircling Tantiana within her protective light.

"I would like you to meet Tantiana. She's not to be touched by anyone but me. The dragons will do what I say and only what *I* say." She patted her chest, then rested her hand there. "The reason they retreated to the underground is because my father decided I didn't deserve to know about these powers I possess. Not until it was time for them to use me in the plot they had against every moon of Theia."

Jasper stepped closer, and Malkia noticed Dario behind him with a deadpan expression that sent chills down her spine. Her eyes narrowed as she stared hard at him. He noticed her gaze, and he forced a smile that did not sit right with Malkia. Drawing in a deep breath, she clasped her hands together and looked around the room. She would deal with his strange behavior when they had privacy. It could no longer wait.

"As a child, I remember my family and people of my moon were at war with some of the most powerful creatures in this system. I did not know it then, but now it is clear to me after my conversation with my father. They planned to use me and Damon to destroy these civilizations. They want to be gods, and desire to rule all of Theia's moons." She pointed at Damon and then at herself. "We are the keys to their victory. Damon was manipulated by using his own powers against him by the warlock I killed."

"She's dead?" Damon snapped, lunging at Malkia.

A burst of light slipped from Malkia's hands, holding Damon away from her. "You are better off without her. Just give it time. The hex will vanish soon."

"How do you know this?" Dario asked, circling around Jasper and kneeling a few feet from her.

"I can sense it. The colors swirl like green slime around his aura."

Dario hung his head.

"Why are you disappointed?" she asked, snapping her fingers at him. "We now know he had no control over his actions. It's a good thing. For him at least."

Dario met her gaze and brought his prayer hands to his lips. "Definitely not disappointed. Just trying to process all you have become in this short time."

"It's who I've always been. It was hidden, just like the dragons."

"Tell us more about the dragons," Jasper said, tucking his hands inside his pockets and sagging against the wall behind him. "Why are they important?"

"My father forced them to the undergrounds. Then he blocked their escape, determined to keep them concealed until I was well prepped and groomed for his mission. A few weeks ago, they broke out and began searching for me. They are important because they were brought to Esaki to protect her inhabitants and I am the only one who can communicate with them. I need them to keep everyone safe, because today, I begin my own war. I will free my daughter from the grips of my people." She glanced around the small group, a devilish smile dancing on the edges of her lips. "You are with me or against me."

She turned toward Damon. His expression had relaxed, and his terror dissipated. A guarded smile surfaced. "I'm with you. You and I, we are in this together, regardless of whether we like it. I will follow you to the end of the stars if that's what it takes for me to make amends for what I have done."

Malkia twisted from her waist to see everyone else. "How about the rest of you?"

Dario rose to his feet and then offered his hand to help her off the ground. "You know I'm always on your side. I'll also follow you to the end of the stars. My world is wherever you are."

She rolled her shoulders back and exhaled with a sigh. The past few days had been long, and Dario was right, so much had changed. She reached for Damon's hand and assisted him up.

"The next step would be to unite our people and formulate a strategy to end the wars above. There are no gods out in the universe protecting us. It has been a lie from the beginning. It is time to take our power back and end the control my family has had on us." A glow rose to her cheeks, and the warmth spread through her veins. "But first, I need to find Mataya."

Malkia signaled for Tantiana to move into the forest again. She continued toward her sister with the line of men behind her. Knowing what was ahead of her and that she had the powers of Esaki and Eris behind her, she relished in the thought of finally reuniting with Esta.

Her golden child—a miracle not even her tyrant father could resist loving.

The End.

Find out Malkia's fate in *Enyo's Warrior*. Available on Amazon.

I love to hear back from my readers!
If you enjoyed this book, please leave a brief review on Amazon.
Thank you for reading!

THEIA'S MOONS

Damon's Story

Who is this man? Never-before-published short story about the man who has the ability to steal her heart.

Damon

Twenty-Four years in the past

HE WATCHED HER from the shadows, tilting his head in amusement. With wide eyes, she stared at the group of strangers in her house, nibbling on her bottom lip as the heat stained her cheeks. A smile spread across his face as he leaned forward, flashing her one of his winning smiles. Catching her off guard, she skipped back a few steps, colliding with that insane woman with the ragged teeth.

She's a fright to see. Damon cringed in thought. He watched the confused girl look up at the squat woman and then back at her mother, racing into the safety of her arms.

He chuckled to himself and settled back into his chair, eyeing the frightened girl whenever he could. His mother had said she was the most powerful of the children, but that his abilities were a close second. She had beamed with pride when she informed him that her parents had agreed to an arranged marriage between the two of them. Whatever that meant.

Malkia glared at him from the safety of her mother's arms and his brows furrowed, watching her guarded look toward her father.

"Malkia, have you been listening?" her father snapped, slightly raising his voice.

"Yes, Father," the young girl said, a tear glistening in the side of her eye. She peered down at her trembling fingers, before continuing, "No,

Father. I'm too tired to understand all that you're saying."

Damon pursed his lips as he saw her father's eyes narrow before turning back to the adults. He tuned out what was being said, studying the girl they said would be his someday. Her green eyes shone like emeralds and her silky, golden hair hung around her face like an angel. He resisted the urge to reach out and touch it as it fell over her mother's shoulder.

Startling him from his thoughts, his parents rushed him out the door. He yanked his arm loose from his mother's grasp and stole one last glance at Malkia. She now stood in the room alone, her eyes shifting around in confusion. Who was this extraordinary mystery girl?

Three years in the past

TEARS STUNG HIS eyes and the rage whirling within twisted relentlessly at his heart. Two of his children laid at his feet, strangled and stabbed by the masked attackers. His throat thickened with sobs and he tilted his head to the darkened sky, turning his cries into a scream that shook the smoldering structures around him.

Sinking to his knees, he heaved them both into his lap, trembling from the fury shooting through his entire nervous system. He didn't notice when Genevieve arrived, but when his focus returned, her hands were running through Rory's hair while humming their bedtime song. His blood-shot eyes squinted over at her, scrutinizing her blank expression.

"Genevieve?" his voice was barely a whisper. "Where's Landon?"

Her hum grew louder, shaking her head to dismiss his words. An ice pick jammed into his heart as he twisted to face her, clutching onto her shoulders.

"Where is Landon?" he asked, raising his voice an octave as his blood froze within his veins and his vision blurred with rage.

She ignored him again, leaning over and kissing Rory's and Dawn's cheeks. Her humming was grating at his nerves, and it continued to rise in volume, crushing his heart and soul with the thought of his youngest child's safety.

"*Genevieve?*" he snapped, clutching her chin and forcing her to face him. "What has become of Landon? Where is he?" He could feel the heat of his skin blistering, while a storm of ice thundered through his insides.

Her eyes finally focused on his face, tears glistening in her now petrified irises. "They took him. I couldn't stop them." She paused, gasping at the realization. "*Oh, my dear Theia.*" She screamed, her eyes widening at the sight of her two dead children. "*What have you done?*" Her shrieks sent chills down his spine, while he watched her eyes shift wildly from him and back to the kids.

"What do you mean they took him?" Damon cried, rising from the ground.

"The sky people," her voice trembled, and the tears tumbled down her cheeks, wetting his daughter's hair as she inhaled her lingering scent. "How could this happen?" Another scream tore from her lips as she wrapped her arms around both her deceased children. "How could you let this happen?" Her eyes darted up to meet his, icy contempt spreading across her face.

"Genevieve, is Landon alive?" he asked, ignoring her questions.

"Did you see someone take him?"

"I-I don't know," she mumbled, burying her face into Dawn's neck. "He was with me, then a flying ship settled in the clearing and I blacked out from—something." Her hand drifted to the back of her head, running over the dried blood on her scalp. Her fingers quivered as the answer rose in her angry eyes. "When I woke, he was gone."

His heart beat hard against his chest as his eyes scanned the black sky. The clouds hung low and rain threatened to fall at any moment. There were no lights, and nothing to show a flying ship had invaded their moon again.

The townspeople emerged from the forest and their underground hideouts. Damon searched the crowd for his five-year-old boy, praying to the gods the people had swept him up in their rush and he had hidden with his neighbors.

Briefly glancing down at Genevieve and his two older children, a silent tear trailed down his ash covered cheek. *What happened? Why have the sky people returned to target my town?* He reached over his wife and scooped up Rory, nodding for her to pick up Dawn. "We need to take them to the center of town and prepare their bodies to return to the stars."

Genevieve didn't argue, thankfully. She nodded, wrapping her arms around Dawn and lugging her off the ground. As he walked, he scanned the crowd again, looking at all the children and their filthy faces. The dust from the attack and the ashes from the fires covered every single person, along with each home and building that was left standing. It was going to be difficult to find Landon in this chaos.

Damon peered over at his wife, clearing his throat of the smoke and dust. "I need to find Landon. You stay with the children's bodies and begin their preparation."

A few tears escaped her eyelids, cutting rivers through the soot on her face. She threw him a sideways look before nodding again. "The sky people took him," she muttered. "I heard them whispering. They were searching for you and needed leverage for some kind of plan."

Damon's heart stopped, along with his feet, as he turned to face her. "What?" he asked, a muscle in his jaw twitching.

Genevieve's darkened eyes turned upward, meeting his. "I told you this was your fault. They came here to hurt you. Our children perished by your hands."

Her words cut through him like searing knives, slicing his heart in two and heating his entire body with rage. Turning toward the center of the village, a fiery bubble rose from his stomach, inching its way toward his mind. When he reached the group of townspeople, all tending to the ascension of their deceased loved ones, he settled Rory onto the ground and brushed his thumb down his son's cheek. Without another word to Genevieve, he pivoted on his heel and ran for the forest.

THE MORNING SUN swept across Damon's face, and he pried open his eyes, adjusting to the view of the tall grass dancing with the wind above him. A rock pushed into his spine, and he grimaced from the ache of lying on it all night. He propped himself up on his elbows and scanned the landscape of the forest in front of him.

The night before, he had run for miles and had finally collapsed in a small clearing high above his village. There had been no signs of the sky people or Landon, and he was thinking Genevieve had made a fool out of him.

Rising from the terrain, he brushed off the dirt and weeds from his clothing, his broken thoughts returning to the death of his children and the destruction of his village. Raising his eyes, he nearly jumped out of his skin when he saw an older woman standing a few yards away from him, just outside the shelter of the trees. Her silver hair was pulled back into a bun on top of her head, while her dark eyes bored into his heart, as if she knew who he was. Stepping toward her, she didn't budge, but a smile twitched on her lips as he moved closer.

"Who are you, woman?" he asked, halting in his tracks when she was close enough to hear.

"I know of your abilities, Damon," she said, standing straight and allowing a wide smile to rise on her lips. "I sensed the arrival of the sky people and when I entered your town, the memories of who you are invaded my mind. They came to destroy you." She paused, searching his face for any recognition of what she was saying. "You know who you are, right?"

He stood frozen, remembering the words of his lunatic parents. *You're not from this moon. Your birth parents reside on Eris and sent you here to keep you safe from the wars of their moon and the creatures who want to control you.*

Shaking his head in disbelief, he swallowed the ball of fear rising in his throat and stared hard at the old woman. "You must have mistaken me for someone else. My name is Damon Ranix."

She stepped toward him, leaning against a staff as she walked. "Don't play coy with me," her voice was quiet, but held a strength that shook Damon's soul. "I've come here to save you from their dominance. They've slaughtered all three of your children and will return to finish the job by murdering you. Your blood line is a threat to their existence."

His blood boiled, hearing her speak of his children. "How do you know they're all dead?" he bellowed at her, his insides trembling from the fire raging through his body.

Her eyes fell to the ground, releasing a deep sigh. "I saw them take your small child." She peered up at him through her eyelashes. "They tore him to pieces and scattered his remains across the countryside." This time her tone was gentle, filled with a knowing anguish.

His entire body trembled, and his knees nearly gave out underneath him. "*No, it can't be true,*" he cried, his eyes darting every which way, as if he would catch sight of something that would discount her story. "*You are lying.*" His screams filled the surrounding air, quieting the chatter of the forest animals.

She shook her head as he stared wide-eyed at her. "I can help you, Damon. There's a reason our paths have crossed." Taking another guarded step forward, she raised her hand toward him. "I can remove the pain and then help avenge your children's deaths."

"How?" He whimpered, the palms of his hands pressing into his eyes, forcing the tears to subside.

"I'm a warlock," she said, a crimson light glowed within her palm. "I'll ease your grief and bring logic back to your mind. Together we will ensure justice for your family and townspeople." She tilted her head to the side, her brows furrowing in thought. "I can also assist you in remembering your true origins."

Eyeing her with untrusting disdain, his heart slowed to a more peaceful rate, and the fire cooled within his veins. He inhaled deeply, filling his lungs with much needed air, before nodding in response to all she had said. Defeat washed over him, wanting nothing more than to give up, but he became entranced with the cerise glow that swirled from her hand. It wrapped around his body and a calm consumed his mind as he closed his eyes and allowed her magic to eat away the pain clawing at his heart.

Four days in the past

DAMON RESTED HIS forehead against the bark of a tree, thinking of those emerald eyes. This woman was so familiar, but he couldn't place her face. Having her in his tent had been a struggle. His scrambled emotions made it difficult for him to be logical, and all he could think about were those mesmerizing eyes and golden hair.

Where have I seen her before? He thought, groaning in frustration as he pressed away from the tree.

His eyes wandered across his camp, landing on the caged tent where she slept. A craving was suffocating his heart and mind and he needed to find some relief.

His first thought was to run, like he had done so many times in the past, to ease his frustrations and rage. But he turned toward the old woman's tent. Oridian had kept him humble for several years now and she had returned his memories of his young life to him. Although he could manipulate most people with his mind, the green-eyed beauty had resisted him. His warlock usually possessed the answers to these mysteries.

As he approached her tent, she stepped outside, her brows furrowed in concentration. "I already know your question," she said, waving away his unspoken words. She closed her eyes, twirling a lock of her silver hair as she spoke. "I can sense the powers within that woman, but they remain dormant or possibly blocked." Oridian opened her eyes, narrowing them in disgust. "She will be the end of you if you don't break her. She must never remember—," her voice trailed off, blankly staring at the forest behind Damon.

Turning to look, he only saw darkness. "What is it?" he barked, frustrated by her vague answer. He twisted back to see the woman.

Oridian's eyes widened, a gasp sweeping across her lips. "She will lead you to the man who's responsible for the death of your children!" She met Damon's eyes as he took a surprised step back.

His body came to attention as a forgotten sorrow clenched at his heart. "What did you say?" he asked, his voice barely a whisper. He rubbed his temples, feeling one of his headaches surfacing.

"She's the key," Oridian said, nodding in excitement. "She has all your answers buried within her. You must take control of her and pry that information from her." A weary smile tugged at the corners of her mouth. "You'll finally have the revenge you so duly deserve."

Flames of anger thundered through him as the faces of his children flashed before his eyes. Glancing down at Oridian, he nodded, pressing his lips into thin lines as he allowed the rage to fuel him.

"Patience, Damon," Oridian whispered, clasping his forearm. "She's not the enemy, but with her mind, you will finally find the one who is. There's a connection between you and her. Use that. Feed off that and when you have broken her down, take what is yours."

He inhaled deeply, closing his eyes and finally giving in to the wrath poisoning his veins.

If you enjoyed this book, please leave a brief review on Amazon. Thank you!

Malkia's adventure has just begun!

Find out her fate in Enyo's Warrior!

Acknowledgements

THIS REWRITE HAS been a revelation into my past and the phases I flowed through while originally composing this novel. Malkia embodies a significant amount of my inner work from that time, and I noticed through her stress, anxiety, and panic attacks she experienced, I had been living through identical emotions. Journal writing can be a great tool for insight into ourselves, but rereading and rewriting a fictional story that portrays my past reactions has been absolutely mind-blowing.

How far I have come.

When I was diagnosed with anxiety and panic disorder, I had no clue how to manage my episodes, aside from medication. I spent years struggling and doing my best to fit into society's norm without revealing my inner turmoil to those who surrounded me. I worked on my darkness and in my spare time, I wrote *Eyes Wide Shut*, slowly and unknowingly weaving myself into the fantasy tale. It was my therapy.

By the time I finished this book, I had weaned myself off the little white pill and had successfully learned to be more mindful, aware, and present in my body, keeping my stress in check — for the most part. It remains a battle at times, but eight years later a much easier one to manage with meditation, breath work, and exercise.

Through it all, I appreciate each and every one of my family, friends, and readers who have cheered me on, especially when I did not believe in myself.

My mom passed away in 2009, but she will be forever my loudest cheerleader. She was dyslexic and disliked writing, leaning heavily toward scientific brilliance, but she LOVED that I was artistic and full of a vivid imagination, and read every single one of my stories when I was young. Her support was priceless and is greatly missed. Thank you, mom and dad. For always nudging me to work hard and to never give up, no matter how dark it seems.

And to my love, Steven. For believing in me from the beginning of our life together and always encouraging to be better than I was yesterday.

My new book covers are happiness! I appreciate the work Niki Ellis Designs put into my them. She put up with all my revisions and steered me in better directions for each design to follow the storyline. This one is such a beautiful cover and I enjoyed working with her on this project.

Thank you, Angie and team, for all the hard work you put into editing my debut novel. I know it was not easy and I appreciate your patience and encouragement. Being an indie author can feel lonesome at times, but I am reminded of the unwavering support I have when I work with Novel Nurse Editing.

For those who read this rewrite ahead of time and provided constructive criticism and feedback, I will forever be grateful. ARC teams who care about the success of authors are a rare gem and my appreciation for mine runs deep. I wanted this story to find a place in many hearts and I could not accomplish it without this amazing community.

A special thank you to Brandon Burgon, for my earlier book cover and creating a gorgeous illustration that I will use at a later time for special projects dealing with this series. To see more of his work, visit his website at: www.burgonartworks.com

More by the author

Theia's Moons Series

Eyes Wide Shut

Enyo's Warrior

Protectors of the Stars

Guardian

The Chaos Awakened Saga

Marked Chaos

Expanded Chaos

Transformed Chaos

Novels

Be My Leprechaun

Novellas

Wrong Side of the Mirror

Novelettes

A Web Through Time

Wicked Heart

Wicked Soul

Jolly Old Monster

Unable to Wake

About the Author

International Bestselling Author Niki Livingston writes tales of epic and dystopian fantasy worlds filled with magic, mysticism, and mystery.

When she's not busy writing enchanting stories of diverse women rising in their power and strength, she spends her time walking her rescue puppy, quieting her mind with meditation and yoga, diving into the newest books of Veronica Roth and Laurie Forest, and binge-watching The 100 and The Wheel of Time.

For all her latest releases and updates, subscribe to Niki Livingston's newsletter!

www.NikiLivingston.com